"Tell me  *"*
Beau mu *y.*

"This. You.

He chuckled. "You've got me, darlin'. I'm here for the duration."

But how long was that? Laurel wondered. As long as he got what he wanted? Until he found out that she carried another man's baby?

It didn't matter. Not right this very moment. All that mattered was that Beau was here now and he was kissing her, seducing her. All that mattered was that right now he wanted her. Right now he needed her. Right now he probably even loved her.

Right now, that was enough.

And later...

Later would be soon enough for regret.

Dear Reader,

This September, four of our beloved authors pen irresistible sagas about lonesome cowboys, hard-luck heroines and love on the range! We've flashed these "Western-themed" romances with a special arch treatment. And additional treasures are provided to our readers by Christine Rimmer—a new JONES GANG book with an excerpt from her wonderful upcoming single title, *The Taming of Billy Jones,* as well as Marilyn Pappano's first Special Edition novel.

In *Every Cowgirl's Dream* by Arlene James, our THAT SPECIAL WOMAN! Kara Detmeyer is one feisty cowgirl who can handle just about anything—except the hard-edged cowboy who escorts her through a dangerous cattle drive. Don't miss this high-spirited adventure.

THE JONES GANG returns to Special Edition! In *A Hero for Sophie Jones,* veteran author Christine Rimmer weaves a poignant story about a ruthless hero who is transformed by love. And wedding bells are chiming in *The Mail-Order Mix-Up* by Pamela Toth, but can this jilted city sophisticate find true love? Speaking of mismatched lovers, a pregnant widow discovers forbidden passion with her late husband's half brother in *The Cowboy Take a Wife* by Lois Faye Dyer.

Rounding out the month, *Stranded on the Ranch* by Pat Warren features a sheltered debutante who finds herself snowbound with an oh-so-sexy rancher. And Marilyn Pappano brings us a bittersweet reunion romance between a reformed temptress and the wary lover she left behind in *Older, Wiser...Pregnant.* I hope you enjoy each and every story to come!

Sincerely,

Karen Taylor Richman
Senior Editor

Please address questions and book requests to:
Silhouette Reader Service
U.S.: 3010 Walden Ave., P.O. Box 1325, Buffalo, NY 14269
Canadian: P.O. Box 609, Fort Erie, Ont. L2A 5X3

MARILYN PAPPANO

OLDER, WISER...PREGNANT

SPECIAL EDITION®

Published by Silhouette Books
America's Publisher of Contemporary Romance

SILHOUETTE BOOKS

ISBN 0-373-24200-X

OLDER, WISER...PREGNANT

Copyright © 1998 by Marilyn Pappano

All rights reserved. Except for use in any review, the reproduction or utilization of this work in whole or in part in any form by any electronic, mechanical or other means, now known or hereafter invented, including xerography, photocopying and recording, or in any information storage or retrieval system, is forbidden without the written permission of the editorial office, Silhouette Books, 300 East 42nd Street, New York, NY 10017 U.S.A.

All characters in this book have no existence outside the imagination of the author and have no relation whatsoever to anyone bearing the same name or names. They are not even distantly inspired by any individual known or unknown to the author, and all incidents are pure invention.

This edition published by arrangement with Harlequin Books S.A.

® and TM are trademarks of Harlequin Books S.A., used under license. Trademarks indicated with ® are registered in the United States Patent and Trademark Office, the Canadian Trade Marks Office and in other countries.

Printed in U.S.A.

Books by Marilyn Pappano

MARILYN PAPPANO

After following her career navy husband around the country for sixteen years, Marilyn Pappano now makes her home high on a hill overlooking her hometown. With acreage, an orchard and the best view in the state, she's not planning on pulling out the moving boxes ever again. When not writing, she makes apple butter from their own apples (when the thieves don't get to them first), putts around the pond in the boat and tends a yard that she thinks would look better as a wildflower field, if the darn things would just grow there. You can write to Marilyn via snail mail at P.O. Box 643, Sapulpa, OK 74067-0643.

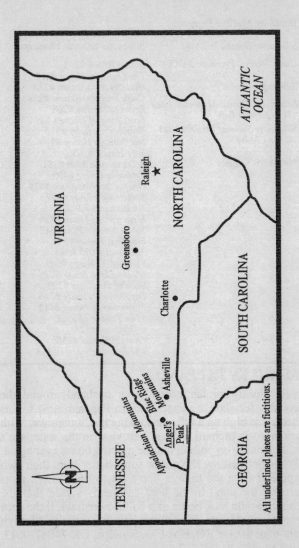

VIRGINIA

ATLANTIC OCEAN

Raleigh ★

NORTH CAROLINA

Greensboro ●

Charlotte ●

SOUTH CAROLINA

TENNESSEE

Appalachian Mountains

Blue Ridge Mountains

Asheville ●

Angel's Peak ●

GEORGIA

All underlined places are fictitious.

N

Chapter One

The bus came to a stop in the middle of town with the squealing of brakes and a whoosh of diesel fumes, and the driver opened the door. In the third seat back, Laurel Cameron made no move beyond tightening her fingers around the straps of her well-worn backpack.

"Miss?" The driver met her gaze in the mirror. "Angel's Peak. Isn't this your stop?"

She wanted to say no, to insist that she'd changed her mind, to dig into her small supply of cash and offer whatever it would cost to remain on the bus to its next destination. But she'd done enough running. It was time to go home.

Forcing a breath into her tight lungs, she stood up, gripped her two bags and exited the bus. She'd expected to feel some sort of jolt the moment her feet touched North Carolina soil, some recognition, some tremendous relief to be home. She felt nothing but fear. Guilt. Regret.

She moved to the distant edge of the sidewalk, right up

against the brick wall of the five-and-dime, and watched as the bus pulled away. Her best chance at escape was leaving her behind. If she wanted to go now, she would have to walk or hitch a ride—both means of transportation of which she'd taken advantage in the past, but not anymore. She had too much to risk now.

When she'd left town five years ago, riding on the back of Buddy's Harley, she'd taken hard, unblinking looks, trying to fix in her mind pictures for the inevitable homesickness that lay ahead. It had worked, too. In all those years, she'd never forgotten the slightest detail of her hometown. It all looked the same—so familiar, so dear.

And so distant. She felt the same way she had every time she and Buddy had ridden into a new town—like a stranger who didn't belong, who could never belong—and she had no one to blame but herself. Angel's Peak had always been home, had always welcomed her, until she'd rejected it, until she'd alienated everyone who mattered. Had they missed her while she was gone? Would they welcome her back? Could they forgive her?

Did they still love her?

She would soon find out.

Two women passed on the sidewalk, giving her a look that was partly curious but mostly dismissive. People had been looking at her that way for five years, as if she were nobody or, worse, as if she were someone to beware of. Considering the transient life they had lived—moving on every time Buddy took a notion, never having enough money and always looking disreputable—she couldn't even blame anyone for the suspicion and distrust.

But she hoped it would change now that she was home. Once she'd proved that *she* had changed.

Tugging her denim-and-khaki ball cap lower, she started walking in the general direction of home. Cameron Inn was four miles out of town, a three-story house with brick columns and acres of trees dressed in their spring best. It had been in her father's family for generations and had been her own home for twenty years. Now she wasn't sure she had the right to go back there.

She could call and find out if her mother wanted to see her, but what if the answer was no? If Leah was going to turn her away, wouldn't it be harder for her to do so face to face than over the phone? If she simply opened the door and found Laurel on the doorstep, wasn't she more likely to give her a chance to apologize?

Laurel hoped so. She was betting her future—*their* future—on it.

She walked out of the downtown area, past the library and the police department, the turn for the high school and the fast-food drive-in where she and her friends had hung out. She kept her head down to avoid meeting anyone's gaze and doggedly placed one foot in front of the other in spite of the scared little voice whispering warnings in her head. Buddy had planted the ideas before they'd ever left Angel's Peak, and her guilt had latched onto them tightly and convinced her of their truth. *They don't love you. They'll never forgive you. You're nothing but trouble. They're glad you're gone. They don't want you back.*

She'd had only a month on her own to undo the damage, only four weeks to convince herself that she and Buddy had both been wrong. The simple fact that her steps were slowing, that her muscles were tightening and her fear was growing, proved that she hadn't yet succeeded.

She *had* been nothing but trouble. In the last five years that she'd lived at home, she had made everyone's life miserable. How many times had the simplest of conversations with her mother degenerated into screaming and tears? How many times had her stepfather looked at her with such disappointment? How many times had her brothers and sister displayed such reluctance to be around her because they'd known that, whatever the occasion, she would ruin it for everybody? Even her grandmother, who had always doted on her, had come to dread her company. Even her grandfathers had found her unpleasant.

The sidewalk had given way to a dirt path when her halting steps came to a complete stop. For five years she'd wanted to come home, and for five years she'd been convinced that there was no home left for her. What if she'd been right? What if she walked into the inn and no one welcomed her? What would she do then? Where would she go? How would she survive?

A stream of traffic passed by, and she found herself looking for her mother's car, for one of the vans that belonged to the inn. When the cars were gone, her gaze drifted across the street. Right there on the edge of town was one of Angel's Peak's few other motels. MountainAire Lodge couldn't hold a candle to her family's place. The inn was elegant, beautiful, every room decorated with period furnishings. The lodge featured an office that looked like a shabby mountaintop chalet and rooms that were standard low-ceilinged, flat-roofed, cinder-block-and-ugly motel style.

MountainAire Lodge was also cheap, and it could give her one last night before facing the very real possibility of heartache. One last night to prepare her apologies, to find ways to make things right. One last night to muster some courage.

Grateful for the reprieve, she crossed the street and the potholed parking lot to the chalet office, used a made-up name and paid twenty-two dollars and change for a key to Room 10. The room was exactly what she expected—better than some places she'd lived, worse than others. For all the beautiful mountain views that surrounded the town, the sole window looked out on the parking lot, and in spite of the motel's name, inside were the usual cheap-motel smells of stale smoke and must.

Laurel stood in the middle of the shabby room, finished her look around and swallowed hard. "Welcome home, girl," she murmured. "You'd better pray that this isn't as good as it gets."

After setting her bags on the bed, she closed the drapes, switched on every light in the place and the television, then sat down. She couldn't begin to describe how desperate she was to go home and make things right, and yet she was almost as desperate to never go back. Staying away forever—living without her family forever—just might be better than finding out that they neither loved nor wanted her.

Much of her life she'd been torn apart by her own emotions. Her first fifteen years had been perfectly normal. Oh, her father had died, but it hadn't been a devastating loss. Terence Cameron had never been much of a family man. Life had gone on without many noticeable differences. To provide for the family, her mother had turned their home into an inn, and Laurel had made beds, waited tables and washed dishes, but she'd had plenty of time for herself, too.

She couldn't blame what had happened on her mother's eventual remarriage, either. Laurel loved her stepfather, and her step-grandfather. Bryce had made their family complete, and he had made Leah so incredibly happy. He'd been a father figure to the older kids—Laurel, Doug and Megan—and a real-life father to their younger brother, Matt. His coming into their lives had been good all around.

Something had simply happened, something she couldn't understand and certainly couldn't explain. One week she'd been a relatively sweet, happy child. The next she'd become the daughter from hell. Maybe, in its beginnings, it had been a natural enough process. Teenagers were moody, difficult and rebellious. All the experts said so.

But she'd gone beyond that. Every small defiance made the next one easier. Every minor disagreement grew into a major battle. Apologies became harder to make, grudges easier to hold. And her friends had certainly been no help. They'd been the source of the biggest arguments, had fed her deepest resentments and cultivated her most destructive insecurities.

But in the end, *she* was to blame. She had created the problems, encouraged the fights and fostered the unhappiness. Even when she'd wanted nothing more than to run crying to her mother, she had shouted hurtful words that made Leah cry instead. When she'd needed her parents and their love more than ever, she'd shoved them away harder than ever.

But she had changed. She *had*. They would see it, and they would forgive her and welcome her back. For five years that had been her only dream. Tomorrow it might become reality.

Or it might shatter into so many pieces that it could never be put back together again.

The sun had set by the time Laurel roused herself for dinner. A restaurant shared space with the MountainAire office, a place with food on a par with the motel. She wouldn't consider eating there if she wasn't more than a mile from the nearest alternative and low on cash, but she'd learned to make the best of limited choices.

Slipping the room key into her jeans pocket with her cash, she stepped outside. The parking lot was less than half full, and most of the rooms were dark. This was one of the few places in town where she didn't have to worry about meeting someone who would recognize her. Locals rarely ate at the restaurant, it wasn't likely she would know the staff, and all the guests were out-of-towners. Still, she was grateful for the ball cap that shadowed her face and the too-big jacket that swallowed her.

In the restaurant, she ordered a sandwich and chips to go. After adding a soda from the machine outside the front door, she headed back toward her room, turning the corner, then coming to an abrupt halt to avoid bumping into the man there.

He stopped suddenly, too, then stepped to one side. "Excuse me." The words were reflex, the tone impersonal. All she had to do was nod and go on by, end of incident, but her feet had taken root, and her head, if she nodded, would continue to bob like one of those tacky plastic dogs in a car window.

Five years had passed since she'd heard that voice—five years, a month and three days—and there'd been nothing impersonal about it then, but she knew it as surely as she knew her own voice. As surely as she knew her shame.

Beau Walker.

She dared only a glimpse at his face, enough to see dark hair, dark eyes, stubble on his jaw, then ducked her head even lower. Praying that he wouldn't recognize her, she clutched her dinner a little tighter and forced her feet into motion. With each step, she expected him to call out, to grab her arm for a closer look, to ask, "Hey, aren't you—?"

With each step that none of that happened, she breathed a little easier and walked a little faster. She would be safe in her room—safe from him, though not from her memories of him. As if obsessing over all the wrongs she'd done her family wasn't enough, now she could add all the wrongs she'd done Beau—the ways she'd used him, the ways she'd betrayed him, the ways she'd hurt him. Hurting him had been the last straw. That had put her beyond redemption.

She anxiously counted the doors—seven, eight, nine—before reaching her own. Her trembling made fitting the key into the lock difficult, but she managed, then took one last look to assure herself that he was gone, that she was safe.

She found no such assurance. At the end of the sidewalk, illuminated by the yellowish glow of a street lamp, he stood motionless, watching her. She imagined she could feel the weight of his gaze across the distance—had always imagined so. In the beginning it had been amusement in his eyes, then awareness, desire, satisfaction, affection.

In the end it had been derision. Scorn. Hatred.

She let herself into the room, closed and locked the door and sank onto the bed. Her breathing was irregular, her muscles cramped, her chest tight. While she was gone, she had never given herself many chances to think about Beau. He'd been one sorrow too many, one regret too great. It had been easier to push him out of her mind, to pretend that he had never existed.

But he did exist. In the flesh. Living, breathing, hot…

Laurel swallowed hard on bitter memories.

Did he work at the motel, or was he a guest simply passing through? If she'd given him any thought, she would have guessed that he'd moved far away. He'd had no family in Angel's Peak but a father who mistreated him. They'd lived in a shabby house a few miles outside town, and he'd worked a job he hated, fixing cars at the local garage. The good folks in town had looked down on him for being poor and scorned him for being wild. The parents had lived in fear that he would turn his considerable charms on their daughters, and the police had hassled him every chance they got for nothing more than who he was.

Oh, and he'd had one other thing—a girl who'd thought she was slumming by hanging out with him. Who had used him to upset her parents, who had flaunted him to prove how rebellious she was.

One of them had been slumming, all right, but it hadn't been her. By the time she'd thoroughly destroyed their relationship, just as she'd done with her family, she had sunk as low as she could go. She hadn't been fit for anyone better than Buddy, for any life better than the one she'd had with him. She had deserved everything that happened to her in the last five years.

Everything, she thought with a scared little smile, except the best thing. Her hope for the future, her reason for coming home, her purpose in living. Maybe Beau Walker did hate her. Maybe her family hated her. They were entitled. She had let them all down.

But her baby... She would never let her down.

Never.

Beau stood at the window of Room 16 and stared across the parking lot at the room the woman had disappeared into last night. For just one moment, when they'd almost bumped, he'd thought she was a stranger. Then some long-buried awareness had surfaced, and he had known. It was Laurel.

When she left five years ago, everyone had assumed she would be back in a few weeks or months. Buddy Jenkins didn't stick with the same woman for longer than that. He got what he wanted and walked away.

But two weeks had passed, then two months and two years. People had forgotten her. Her friends had stopped talking about her. Her family stopped searching for her. It was as if she had never existed.

Beau hadn't forgotten. He had loved her from the first time he'd laid a hand on her, when she was nineteen and he was twenty-two. He'd taught her a few lessons about sex, and she taught him a few about life. He'd learned that a man could survive anything, that love could turn to hate and that the ability to forgive required a better man than he could ever be.

Five years, and she was back. Why? And why was she staying here? Why hadn't she gone to the Cameron Inn last night? Why settle for this dump when the family mansion was only a few miles away?

His eyes burned, and he rubbed them wearily. He'd tried to sleep last night, but had wound up spending the better part of the night right here. Once he had picked up the phone to dial her room, then had hung up again. Once he had grabbed his jacket and started out the door to bang on her door, but he hadn't taken even one step outside.

What would he say to her? *I hate you, Laurel? Damn you to hell?* He'd said those things, and a whole lot more, a whole lot uglier, the last time they'd talked. He'd made her cry, and it had made him feel better, and that had made him feel like a bastard. She'd left him feeling guilty when he'd done nothing more than want her, love her, and he'd hated her for that, too.

What *could* he say? Nothing. And so he had remained here. Watching. Remembering.

From the brief glimpse he'd gotten of her face, he would say the past five years hadn't been kind. She looked older than twenty-five, wearier, more disillusioned. She was thinner, more vulnerable, and she'd cut off all the beautiful, long hair that had been her vanity—and his passion. He had loved the look of it, the smell, the feel. When they'd made love, he'd wrapped his hands in it, binding them together.

The bond had been an illusion. Everything about the two of them together had been an illusion. She had broken his heart and his spirit, and he had hated her ever since.

Across the room, the alarm on the night table started beeping. It was six o'clock, time for him to get ready for work. He wondered what time she would get up and what she would do, where she would go. Maybe visiting her family was on her agenda. He knew she hadn't seen them yet. His current job was at the Cameron place, and though he had little enough contact with the family, news like this would have gotten around.

Long after the clock stopped beeping, he turned away from the window, brushed his teeth and shaved. He didn't look so hot in the mirror—like he'd spent a restless night—but no one on his crew would notice. When there was nothing left to do but leave, he returned to the window and the watching.

He took a break after a while to call his assistant foreman and tell him he would be late. He answered one page and a call on his cellular, watched the skies darken and threaten rain and thought for a moment about getting some breakfast, when finally her door opened.

She wore the ball cap again and carried two bags. No one in town would look at her in her worn, ill-fitted clothes and cap, carrying two worn, tattered bags, and guess that she was a Cameron, certainly not Laurel Cameron. The Laurel Angel's Peak knew was immeasurably young and vain. She lived for herself, dressed in second-skin clothes to best show off what nature had given her and took enormous pride in being sexy, sultry and a flashy, brassy blonde. She loved to party, loved trouble and had little respect for authority.

Or herself. That had been her first and worst problem.

She followed the sidewalk to the corner, her head down, her shoulders hunched, as if she wanted to escape notice. She was good at it. Most people would pass by her and not be able to identify one thing about her fifty feet later. He wondered what her life with Jenkins had been like that she'd felt the need to become inconspicuous. Or was it only because she was back in Angel's Peak with the people she'd treated so badly?

He watched even after she was out of sight, then, refusing to consider his actions, he left the room and drove around front.

She had turned in her key, apparently, and was waiting to cross the highway. He pulled to a stop beside her and hit the power button for the passenger window. The tinted glass slid slowly down, revealing first that silly cap, pale skin and frowning brown eyes. When she recognized him, her eyes went blank and her mouth remained in a thin line, but a muscle in her jaw twitched.

"Want a ride? I'm headed that way."

She didn't ask why he assumed that she was going home. She simply tried to look tough, as if climbing into the truck with him wasn't the last thing in the world she wanted. No surprise there. "No, thanks." Her voice sounded rusty, as if she hadn't used it in too long—or as if she had cried too many tears. Over Jenkins?

"Are you sure? It's going to—"

Before he could finish the sentence, the sky opened up, not with a light rain that gradually increased, but with a deluge. It pooled on the bill of her cap before running off the sides, and it made her look utterly miserable. She closed her eyes for a moment, then opened the door, settled her bags on the floor and climbed into the seat. By the time he'd rolled the window up, she had fastened the seat belt and sat looking down at her hands in her lap.

For a time, Beau simply looked at her, but a honk from the car behind them made him shift his attention to the road. He waited for a truck to pass, then pulled into the eastbound lane. "When did you get into town?"

"Yesterday."

"Why stay at the MountainAire?" An unpleasant thought occurred to him. "Is Buddy with you?"

"No."

"Someone else your mom and dad wouldn't approve of?"

"No."

"Because you have always had this thing for guys your parents judge unsuitable." Like him. That had been his biggest attraction for her. He had known it from the beginning and hadn't cared. He had figured that they would use each other, have their fun and walk away.

But it hadn't been that simple. He hadn't counted on falling for her. He hadn't counted on being walked away from rather than doing the walking.

"Are you back for a visit or what?" Less than a mile had passed since his last remark. He didn't know why he couldn't just drive the few remaining miles to Cameron Inn in silence. That was obviously what she wanted, and he sure as hell didn't want to carry on a friendly little conversation.

But a little information never hurt. She *was* the person he'd hated most in his life—the person he'd loved most. Having some idea of her plans could help him avoid running into her again.

She was looking out the side window now. "I plan to stay if…"

If her family would have her. If they would forgive her. Of course they would. She was their daughter. They were her parents. While that had never counted for anything with his own parents, Leah and Bryce Cameron were different. They actually gave a damn whether their kids lived or died.

"Where's Buddy? Did you dump him as soon as you found someone better?"

Finally she looked at him. She looked fragile, as if one blast of the anger he was keeping inside could destroy her, and afraid. She was afraid to go home, afraid that they might turn her away.

"Where do you live?" she asked, but he knew she wasn't interested, not really. She just wanted the subject turned away from Jenkins. He wondered why.

"The same place."

She glanced around the truck, tried to surreptitiously glance at his clothes. She was remembering the house she'd visited only once five years ago and comparing it to his obviously improved status now. His jeans were faded, his T-shirt cheap, but his work boots carried the price tag top quality demanded. The truck was brand-new, loaded with all the options and had cost more than he was capable of dreaming about five years ago.

Of course, back then the only times he'd dreamed of money had been in conjunction with Laurel. He'd wanted to give her things, had thought that doing so would enable him to hold on to her a little longer, had thought he might buy her love. But he'd never had any money, and she had left him anyway.

For Buddy Jenkins.

And for the first time in his life, he had felt like the trash people had always accused him of being.

"If you live here, why were you staying at the motel?"

"I'm doing some work at the house." He didn't explain further, didn't volunteer that the shack she remembered was gone, that the "work" he was doing was building a new house. It was none of her business, and he no longer wanted to impress her. He no longer wanted her, period.

The wipers worked rhythmically to sweep the rain off the windshield, and he lapsed into silence, pretending that driving required his attention. Before more than a few minutes passed, the turnoff for Cameron Inn came into view. There had been a time when he'd wanted more than almost anything to turn into this wide lane, to drive right up to the big white house, walk in the front door and announce that he was there for Laurel.

He never had, though. They had always met in town. At the time he'd thought that refusing to bring her boyfriend home, the way a good girl should, was just one more part of her rebellion. Then he'd seen the way she looked at his house, and the way she'd looked at him, and he'd known the truth. She was ashamed of him. She might have been rebellious, defiant and wild, but she was still enough of a Cameron to be ashamed.

If his heart hadn't already been broken by then, that knowledge would have done it.

Now he drove up the drive five days a week. Her parents were accustomed to seeing him about. They even shared meals with him in the inn's dining room on occasion, and they were paying him a hell of a lot of money for his services. How times had changed.

Before they'd covered half the distance to the inn, Laurel roused herself to speak. "You can let me out here."

He slowed but didn't stop. "Why? Afraid Mom and Dad will think less of you for accepting a ride from me?"

The muscles in her jaw tightened again, but she made no effort to reply.

Maybe she simply wanted to approach the house on her own, or maybe she wanted to turn and run the other way. Either way, he didn't give her a choice. When he reached the small gravel lot on the north side of the house, he pulled to the side, right where the walkway started, and stopped.

When she didn't move right away, he shifted his gaze from the house—imposing, impressive, beautiful as hell—to Laurel. She looked as if she were trying to disappear into the seat. Her face was pale, and her hands were trembling.

She really was afraid. Where was the confidence and arrogance bred into generation after generation of Camerons? Hell, lacking that, where was her common sense? This was her family. She belonged to them, and all the teenage rebellion in the world couldn't change that.

It wasn't his intent to be sympathetic. He just wanted her out of his truck so he could get to work. He'd already lost half a morning because of her. That was why—the only reason why—he spoke. "They've missed you a lot."

Her gaze darted his way, her expression frightened, vulnerable and eager to believe. "You think so?"

He nodded once.

With a deep breath, she gathered her bags and climbed out. At the last moment before the door closed, as an afterthought, no more, she murmured, "Thanks."

He watched her hurry through the rain, climb the steps to the broad veranda and wrap her fingers around the doorknob. For a long moment she stood there, then, squaring her shoulders, she went inside.

Feeling angry, edgy and unsettled, Beau pulled away and followed the drive around back to the work site. There was no reason for the feelings, no reason for dredging up bitter memories. Nothing had changed. His life was the same to-day as it had been yesterday and a thousand yesterdays before.

Laurel was home. He'd seen her. They had talked.

End of story.

Nothing had changed.

Laurel stood in the front hallway that served as reception for the inn and took a long, slow look around. The heart of pine flooring looked the same as it had for two hundred years. The check-in desk of antique mahogany still gleamed a deep, rich red under the chandelier. The stairs still curved gracefully to the second floor, where all the guest rooms were located, and the grand ballroom—now the dining room—was still the most gracious room she'd ever seen with its teal and peach walls, starched linens, marble fireplace and Queen Anne chairs. It still smelled exactly the way she remembered—of polish and wax, flowers and pot-pourri, old wood and new life. She closed her eyes, breathed deeply, gathered the combined scents close to her.

Footsteps sounded on the stairs, muffled by the antique runner, soft and light, like a child's. She opened her eyes and found herself facing a young girl dressed in jeans and a hand-painted T-shirt. The child had stopped a half dozen steps from the bottom and now sank down to sit close to the railing, twining one arm around the baluster beside her. She didn't speak but studied Laurel with solemn brown eyes—familiar brown eyes.

Laurel had spent a lifetime looking into those eyes—every time she looked at her brothers and sister, at her father, stepfather and grandfathers, every time she looked at herself. Eyes of that particular color and shape were a dominant Cameron trait, one she hoped to pass on to her own child, as someone in the family had apparently done with this one.

"Hi," she said, barely able to breathe for the tightness in her chest. "What's your name?"

"Annie Cameron."

"Do you live here, Annie?"

She nodded, her dark curls bouncing.

"Who's your mother, Annie?"

"Leah. My daddy's name is Bryce, an' I have two grandpas— Grandpa Frank and Grandpa Peter—an' a grandma Martha an' brothers an' sisters, too." Her voice was baby-soft and insubstantial. It was one of the sweetest sounds Laurel had ever heard, and it made her want to curl up into a ball and cry her heart out for the years she'd wasted, the miracles she'd missed and the sister she'd never known.

She didn't give in to the urge, though. Not yet. "Is your mother here?"

The girl nodded, but didn't rise from the step. "I'm not s'posed to go upstairs."

"I won't tell that you did. Do you know where she is?"

This time the nod was accompanied by Annie's rising. She hopped down the remaining steps, her tennis shoes squeaking on the wood at the bottom, then started down the hall toward the back of the house. At the closed door of the inn's office, she pointed, then shoved her hands into her jeans pockets. "I'm hungry. I'm going to the kitchen."

Laurel watched her go, then swallowed over the lump in her throat. It wasn't too late to turn around and walk out. Life had obviously gone on—and gone on well—for her family. Her parents had gotten the baby they'd tried for so long, had replaced their troublesome runaway daughter with one as sweet and lovable as they deserved. They didn't need the troublemaker back again.

But *she* needed them. More importantly, her baby needed them. Her baby deserved every chance that Laurel didn't.

She took one step forward, hesitated, then moved once more. Her hand trembled when she rapped on the door. Her entire being trembled when her mother called an invitation to enter.

Her brain was trying to convince her fingers grasp the doorknob when abruptly the door was opened from the other side, allowing her mother's voice to filter out. "That timid little knock... I swear, Annie, no one has knocked on my door like that since your sister Laurel—"

The words dried up as Leah's gaze, settled somewhere around Laurel's knees, slowly moved up. Her face paled, and she raised one shaky hand to her mouth, still staring.

Awkwardly Laurel reached up and pulled off the ball cap, twisting it in nervous hands. Her hair was shorter than it had ever been and, for the first time in ten years, was the same rich brown she'd been born with.

Her action just made her mother stare harder.

Tears seeped into Laurel's eyes and clogged her throat. She wanted to plead with her mother to say something, anything, but she couldn't find the words, couldn't force out more than the slightest breath.

"Oh my God," Leah whispered at last, her voice broken, her own eyes watering. "Laurel? Is that—?" She brushed her fingers across Laurel's hair, touched her cheek, then burst into tears. "It is you. Oh my God, it *is!* Laurel, baby, I've hoped and prayed..." The rest of her words were lost in a sob as she gathered Laurel into her embrace.

Closing her eyes on her own tears, Laurel let the heaviest of her burdens seep away. Her mother was happy to see her—had wanted to see her, had *prayed* to see her. Even if the rest of the family turned her away, her mother was happy, and that might be enough.

After a satisfyingly long hug, Leah held her at arm's length. "You've grown up so much... Your hair... Oh, honey, you're so thin...and so pretty. Where...? What...?" For one moment, her expression turned guarded and cautious. "Are you home to stay?"

"If I'm welcome."

Leah hugged her again. "Of course you're welcome. This is your *home*. We're your *family*. Tell me where you've been and what you've done. Oh, honey, you've missed so much. You have a new sister, Annie, who's four, and Meg's getting married next month, and Matthew graduated from high school this year, and Douglas is a lawyer, and—and—" She caught her breath and, for a time, simply looked at Laurel. "We missed you so much," she said quietly. "We tried to find you. We wanted to bring you back home, but…"

She wouldn't have come, Laurel admitted regretfully. She *couldn't* have come, not until she'd done some growing up. Not until she'd played out all that anger and rebellion that had made them all so miserable.

"I wish the rest of the family was here, but Matthew's out with friends, and Meg's gone shopping. She prefers Meg over Megan now. She's all grown up," Leah said, her voice unsteady once again. "Bryce is picking up guests in Asheville, and Douglas is at his office. He's got a place of his own in town now, of course, but we still see a lot of him. But come into the kitchen and say hello to Colleen, and I'll introduce you to Annie. She's usually around there begging treats from the staff."

"I met her," Laurel said abruptly. "She's a doll. You and—" She'd called her stepfather by his first name when they'd met, but soon after the wedding, all the kids had followed Matthew's lead and called him Dad. He'd been the sort of loving, attentive father they'd never had, generous with his time and himself in a way that their father had never been. Now, though, she wasn't sure that she still had the right to call him Dad. He had Megan, the good daughter, and Annie, a beautiful daughter all his own. What did he need with her?

Letting her mother pull her out of the office and toward the kitchen, she forced herself to finish the thought. "You and Bryce must have been thrilled. I know how long you tried.''

"We'd given up hope," her mother acknowledged. "And then it happened."

"'Good things come to those who wait.'" Wasn't she living proof? She'd been through ten years of disruption, disappointment and sorrow, and now she was being rewarded. She was home, her mother had welcomed her back, and in seven months she would be welcoming her own baby into the world.

At the door to the kitchen, Leah stopped and grasped both of Laurel's hands in hers. "We never gave up hope for you. Not a day went by that we didn't worry and wonder and pray. Not a day that we didn't miss you and want you back. Not a day that we didn't love you."

After pressing a kiss to Laurel's cheek, Leah released her and pushed the door open. As Laurel whispered a prayer of thanks, her mother went through the door and called, "Annie, Colleen, look who's here. Look who's come home."

Home. Laurel savored the word for an instant before following her mother into the kitchen. Yes, thank God, she was home.

By bedtime, Laurel was more than ready for a few hours alone. It had been an exciting day, an overly emotional one, and she would treasure it forever, but now she was tired. She needed privacy and quiet to take in all that had happened.

Not everyone had been as happy to see her as her mother and young Annie. Her grandparents had welcomed her without reservation, but they knew from firsthand experience the futility of holding grudges. Peter and Frank had lost twenty-six years to a family feud. They'd missed holidays, weddings, funerals and births, had lost out on memories that could never be replaced. The experience made them more forgiving, less judgmental.

Bryce's welcome had been both warm and reserved. He wanted to give her the benefit of the doubt, she knew, because of his father's experience, but he remembered too well the pain and heartache she'd caused her mother. He was wary, and she couldn't blame him.

Douglas, twenty-three and just finishing his first year of law school the last time she saw him, was a full-fledged attorney, working in the D.A.'s office. Known as a tough prosecutor, he had little tolerance for criminals and, if the looks he'd given her through dinner tonight were anything to judge by, even less for wayward sisters. Of course, he knew about that last night, the night she'd brought Buddy here to the inn before they'd headed his Harley out of town. He probably saw little difference between her and a criminal.

Little Miss Goody Two-shoes Megan had grown up into Ms. Goody Two-shoes Meg. She had graduated at the top of her high-school class, had finished at the top of her college class, too. She was more beautiful, more capable, more perfect, than ever, and just looking at her reminded Laurel of how badly she failed to measure up.

Then there was Matthew. Only twelve years old when she left, he was a high-school graduate now, over six feet tall, as handsome as all the Cameron men who had preceded him. He was smart and funny and mature for his age, and he loved her as completely and unquestioningly as he always had. Along with their mother, he and sweet little Annie were the bright spots in her world tonight.

A tap at the door interrupted her thoughts. Leah had put her in her old room, on the second floor at the back of the house. Meg's room was across the hall, Douglas's old room—now Annie's—on one side and the communal bathroom on the other. She stood up from the twin bed where she'd dreamed so many dreams and cried so many tears and opened the door to find Meg standing there.

Her sister was dressed for bed in a white gown and matching robe, with her long brown hair brushed until it gleamed. Even in nightclothes, with her face scrubbed free of makeup, she was beautiful. She made Laurel feel inadequate. "May I come in?"

Laurel stepped back, then closed the door behind her. Meg sat in the only chair, so Laurel returned to the bed. She'd barely settled in when her sister spoke. "You have the most incredible sense of timing."

"What do you mean?"

"How did you manage to stage this remarkable homecoming only weeks before my wedding? Have you been keeping track of us, waiting for something important to happen so you could come home and ruin it, the way you ruin everything?"

Laurel drew her knees to her chest and clasped her hands around her ankles, as if the position could protect her from the anger in her sister's voice. "I don't—I didn't want to ruin anything, Meg. I just wanted to come home."

"Why? You stayed away for five years. Why couldn't you have stayed away another three weeks? What was so important that you had to come back now? Why did you have to come back at all?"

Laurel hadn't told anyone about the baby, not yet. She couldn't just waltz in and say, "Hey, folks, I'm home—and, oh, by the way, I'm pregnant, penniless and alone." She had thought her presence was surprise enough for one day. Telling them about the baby could wait for another. "I didn't know about the wedding, Meg. I just wanted to come home."

"And so you did, just like always. You never gave a thought to anyone else. You always just did what you wanted. Obviously, you still do." Meg made a gesture of disgust. "You haven't changed at all."

Her sister's anger bewildered Laurel. She and Meg had always been close, right up until the time she'd turned her back on the whole family. They had rarely argued, had rarely even disagreed, over anything. So where was all this hostility coming from? Did Meg really believe she hadn't changed at all? Did she expect Laurel to pull the same old stunts and ruin the most important day of her life?

"You don't have to invite me to your wedding, Meg," she said quietly, though being left out of such a big celebration would break her heart. "If you don't want me there, just say so, and I won't come."

"Oh, yeah, right." Meg's sarcasm was scathing. "As if Mama would let me get away with that."

"Mom doesn't have to know anything about it." Of course Leah *would* know, and she would want an explanation. How much of a setback would it be to Laurel if she let the family think that she was selfish enough to skip out on her sister's wedding?

Meg rose from the chair, her quiet elegance turned jerky and graceless with emotion. "You know, we were perfectly happy without you. You didn't have to come back at all."

"Megan—"

Her sister walked out the door, closing it gently behind her.

Laurel stared after her for a long time, then switched off the lamp and slid under the covers. She hadn't expected her homecoming to be easy, she reminded herself. Five years ago she had wanted easy. That was why she'd ended up with Buddy instead of Beau, why she'd run away instead of dealing with her troubles, why she'd stayed with Buddy instead of following her heart back home to North Carolina.

She didn't care about easy now. She wanted worthwhile. She wanted her family, both for her and for her baby. She would show them that she had changed, would prove to them that she was, finally, deserving of them, no matter how hard it was. But, please, God, she whispered silently, don't make it *too* hard. *Don't set me up to fail.*

Because this time around was too important. The odds were too high. This time around, for her baby's sake, for her own sake, she couldn't afford to fail.

Chapter Two

After yesterday's rain, Wednesday morning dawned dry, warm and clear—or, at least, it would be clear, once the sun burned off the blue haze that gave the mountains their name. Laurel watched the sky lighten from the padded window seat in her room, watched the trees emerge from the retreating darkness and the grass glisten with morning dew. From this side of the house, she saw manicured lawn, woods and distant mountains, with only an occasional roof or chimney peeking through the trees to remind her that others shared the mountain with them.

It was a beautiful, peaceful scene, the one she had dreamed of most often while traveling with Buddy. The Kansas plains, the Texas Gulf Coast, the Arizona desert— none could compete with this single sight. Sometimes she had feared that she would never see it again. Now she knew that she would never leave it again.

She had taken an early shower and was dressed for the day in jeans, T-shirt and her most comfortable shoes. High on her list of priorities was earning her keep. She'd had chores from the moment the inn had opened its doors, everything from yard work to making beds to waiting tables and washing dishes. Those last years home, she'd thought she was the most mistreated young woman in all of America, used as unwilling labor in a venture that she didn't give a damn about. So what if the inn bought her clothes, provided her a home and kept her in food? She'd been above menial labor, had complained long and loud about her burdens, done shoddy work and eventually stopped working at all.

She knew now that there were worse ways to earn a living than making beds or waiting tables. She had been ill-prepared for working in the real world, where Mom wasn't the boss and family peace and harmony didn't count for a thing. She had learned to work, and work hard, for minimum wage or less. No one deserved to benefit from her lessons more than her family.

The house was quiet as she made her way down the back stairs, but the kitchen was alive with activity. Colleen, chief cook at the inn since its opening fourteen years ago, was supervising breakfast preparations, but she took a moment to muss Laurel's hair. "I like it short," the older woman pronounced.

"Me, too."

"And brown."

"Me, too," she admitted sheepishly. She'd gone the bleached-blonde route for the shock value, initially, then stuck with it to please Buddy. Once he'd walked out of her life for good, the first thing she'd done—her declaration of independence—was have it all cut off, then spend a substantial amount of her precious horde of cash to get it back to its natural color.

"You need some meat on your bones," Colleen decided after a long look. "Sit over there. I'll get you some breakfast."

"I'm here to help, not get waited on."

"Sit over there," the cook repeated, gesturing toward the booth at the end of the room. "Around here, the help eats, too, you know."

Laurel obediently went to the booth and found Annie, still wearing her nightgown, already settled in with breakfast and milk in front of her. "Morning, Annie. You're up early."

"Before the chickens," the girl said proudly with a mouth full of food. "I'm having blueberry pancakes. See?" She stuck out her tongue with a chewed-up bite of pancake in which Laurel could, indeed, see blueberries.

"Get that tongue back in your mouth, Miss Annie Leah Cameron, and don't talk until you swallow." Colleen set another serving of pancakes and milk in front of Laurel, then fixed her hands on her hips. "You have to watch this one, Laurel. She's in danger of being spoiled rotten."

Though her tone was scolding, Laurel suspected that Colleen was one of those happily doing the spoiling, and Annie's sunny grin at the cook confirmed it. "There's nothing wrong with a little spoiling now and then, Colleen, is there?"

"Wait until it's your young one that's being spoiled, and we'll see if you still feel the same way."

With her smile faltering, Laurel turned her attention to her pancakes, pouring syrup over them with great care, cutting the first bite in a perfect wedge. She sincerely hoped that the family was willing to spoil her baby, that they accepted her child with the same unconditional love they offered Annie. She hoped they wouldn't think less of her for having a baby without a husband, for having a baby with a no-good loser like Buddy Jenkins for the father. She hoped they wouldn't suspect that she'd come home not because she'd loved and missed them, but because she needed something from them.

Colleen returned to work, and Annie announced that it

was time to wake her parents before taking off at a run across the room. After watching her go, Laurel turned to gaze out the window.

There was a small back yard, bisected by the driveway, then the two guest houses where her father and her stepfather had grown up. The driveway continued back into the woods, finally reaching the small cemetery where Camerons all the way back to old Abe, who built the house in 1787, were buried. The driveway was in pretty sad shape—muddy from yesterday's rain, rutted and with hardly a piece of gravel anywhere in sight. It looked as if it had handled some pretty heavy traffic recently. She wondered why.

The question disappeared almost immediately and was replaced by another of much greater interest as a familiar pickup truck came around the corner. She doubted there were many—if any—other brand-new trucks of that particular shade of deep purple in Angel's Peak.

So what was Beau Walker doing here?

He drove past the second guest house, the one that served as Leah's workshop for her crafts, then pulled off into the grass and climbed out. He was dressed the same as yesterday—faded jeans, snug T-shirt, boots—and he looked...

Handsome enough to make her mouth go dry.

Sexy enough to make her mind go blank.

Familiar enough to make her heart ache.

And he was coming this way.

Her first impulse was to follow Annie's lead and jump and run. Her second was to scrunch down in the booth as far as she could and hope to go unnoticed. But she didn't run, and she didn't shrink down. She remained where she was—though she did put her fork down. Easier to hide her hand's trembling when she wasn't holding anything.

He came up the steps and let himself in the back door as if he did it every day. Only family and employees used the back entrance routinely. Surely her mother would have told her if he worked here. Surely someone would have warned her.

"Morning, Beau."

Peeking over the top of the booth, Laurel saw Colleen greet him with one of her rare smiles.

"We're running a little late this morning. Want some orange juice while you wait?"

He stopped her with a hand. "I'll get it myself." His back was to them when Colleen spoke again.

"Have you heard the news? Laurel's come home. She's having breakfast right over there."

This was the perfect time for becoming unnoticeable, Laurel told herself, but she didn't try. She couldn't even drop her gaze as he turned to look in her direction.

The set of his features was hard and gave no clue what he was thinking or feeling. It was just as well, because it was too early in the morning to deal with overt hostility or outright hatred. She would get enough of that as soon as Meg came downstairs, and she could deal with it on only one front at a time.

The hall door swung open, and her mother, followed by Annie, came into the room. Leah saw Beau first, then Laurel, and stopped short. Annie pushed past her and skipped across the floor to stop right in front of him. She tilted her head back until her gaze met his and said, "Morning."

"Morning."

"I got a new sister. See?"

Beau's glance was so fleeting that Laurel hardly felt it. "She doesn't look new to me."

Annie giggled. "Not new like that, silly. New like…you know. Her name's Laurel. Isn't she pretty?"

"I think *you're* pretty."

He had neatly sidestepped Annie's question, Laurel thought, finally lowering her gaze, then ducking her head for good measure. She didn't know if he'd ever thought she was pretty—she couldn't remember him saying so—

but she had no doubt what he thought now. Pretty is as pretty does, her grandmother was fond of saying, and in that context, there'd been nothing pretty about Laurel since she was younger than Matthew.

Of course, whether Beau thought she was pretty didn't matter. What mattered was what he was doing here. How he happened to be friendly enough with her baby sister for Annie to call him silly. Why no one had thought to mention to her that she would be running into him on the premises.

As Laurel looked up again, Leah moved, finally freed from the dismay that had stopped her, and greeted him with a troubled undertone to her voice. "Good morning, Beau. How is the work going?"

"Everything's fine."

"I told Annie I'd bring her over..." Clearly uncomfortable, she glanced at Laurel. "Sometime."

"Yeah. Sometime." He blew his breath out noisily. "Listen, I can send someone over for—"

"Here you go." Colleen set a box on the island in front of him. He set his juice down, picked up the box and murmured something Laurel couldn't make out on his way out.

After a moment's silence, Leah slid onto the bench opposite Laurel. "That was awkward."

"Why is he here?"

"He's doing some work for us."

"What kind of work?"

"Business has been so good that we decided to expand. We didn't want to make any changes on the house itself, so when the opportunity to buy two old houses arose, we took it." Leah gestured toward the stand of trees just the other side of the purple truck. "We moved the houses here, back in those trees, and Beau is supervising their restoration. That's what he does—period restorations. He's very good. Very respected. We were lucky to get him."

Laurel cut her pancakes into pieces, but she knew she couldn't swallow even one single blueberry right now. She wasn't sure which part of what she'd just learned was the most unexpected. That Beau was good at what he did? He'd always been conscientious, even when he hated the work.

That her parents had hired him? The same parents who had warned her too many times to stay away from that Walker boy, who had nudged her into making reality of their worst fear?

Or that he'd taken their job? Feeling as he did about her, she figured he would have wanted to stay hell and gone from anything and anyone associated with her. But to take a job from her parents at her family home…

A home from which she'd been absent for five years. If he'd had any clue that she would return before the job was over, he probably would have refused it. But he wouldn't quit now. Beau never quit.

"Why…" She cleared her throat, pushed her plate away and looked out the window in time to see him disappear into the trees. "Why didn't someone tell me?"

Leah covered Laurel's hand with hers, squeezing it gently. "Oh, gee, I don't know. My firstborn daughter came back home after five years away, and I was so relieved to find out that she was alive and so thankful to learn that she didn't hate us that I just didn't think to discuss with her the business expansion and the crew who's handling it."

Laurel couldn't resist smiling at her mother's feigned innocence. "I never hated any of you."

"You did a good imitation of it, honey."

"I was just so…" She sought the right word and found too many to choose from. Angry. Afraid. Insecure. Needy. Rebellious. Out of control.

"It doesn't matter. No explanations are necessary. What matters is that you're here."

"No. I owe you and Bryce and everyone so many apologies. I caused so much hurt, so much trouble. I don't have a clue how to begin to make everything right."

"You're here, sweetheart. That's enough."

"No, Mom, it's not enough. I need—"

The rest of the family descended on the kitchen at the same time—Bryce and Frank from the hallway, Matthew and Meg from the stairs, and Peter and Martha from the back door. Laurel swallowed her protest and got to her feet. "Sit here, Grandma. I'll help Colleen with breakfast."

"You don't need to wait on us, dear," Martha replied as she sat down.

"I know, but it'll be good practice."

"For what?"

That question came from Meg, looking incredibly perfect this morning. Her T-shirt was silk, her slacks pleated and pressed. Her makeup was as expertly done as any cover model, and her thick dark hair gleamed. Looking at her, Laurel was painfully, even enviously, aware of the contrasts between them. Good, bad. Success, loser. Perfect, flawed.

Swallowing hard, Laurel answered her sister's question. "I thought I would help out in the dining room."

"That's my job," Meg said stiffly.

"Maybe you'd like a few days off."

"No, I wouldn't."

"Well, if we both work, it'll cut the load in half."

Meg's hostility was thinly veiled in her dark eyes, though her voice—for the benefit of the family—was polite enough. "That's not necessary. I'm used to the work. Why don't you take a few days to settle in? You look as if you could use the rest."

For just one instant, the old Laurel surfaced, the one quick to take offense, the one who found criticism in the most innocuous of remarks. She disappeared just as quickly, though. She wasn't going to argue with Meg on her second day back. That wasn't why she was here. Showing how she had changed, that she was responsible and mature, the way a soon-to-be mother should be—that was why she was here. Making right old wrongs, finding a place in the family for herself and her baby—those were the important things. Not Meg's resentment.

With that in mind, she managed a smile that was breezy and sincere. "Thanks for your concern, Meg, but I'm fine. Don't worry about it. I'll find something to do, I'm sure."

After making one last adjustment on the template in front of him, Beau secured a three-foot slab of wood in the lathe, put his safety glasses on and flipped the switch that set the wood spinning and the bit in motion. For the first few passes along the length of the pine, the bit removed everything, then the guiding bit that followed the template began shaving off here, skipping the wood there, slowly giving shape to the wood block.

Only three of the intricately turned balusters that supported the veranda railing and the stair railing on one house remained intact, with a half dozen that were usable in the other house. He'd made plywood templates for each of the four styles. Now he needed…oh, only ninety or so to complete that part of the project.

Fortunately, it was pretty mindless work—or maybe that was unfortunate, because he surely did need something that demanded his total attention. He was tired of thinking about Laurel, tired of old memories. And it wasn't just her. Thinking about her reminded him of other people, incidents, feelings—things better left in the past.

Growing up in Angel's Peak hadn't been the most pleasant upbringing a kid could ask for—at least, not for him. He'd been born into the wrong family to have any value to the town. Why, everyone knew those Walkers weren't good for anything but bad luck and trouble. His mother had had the good sense to get out when Beau was too young to remember her. His father hadn't had good sense, period. Jim Walker had started drinking at fifteen and had been an alcoholic by sixteen. He'd been a mean son of a bitch sober, and a meaner one drunk. There'd been no love lost between him and Beau.

No love. Just a shared history and a natural attraction for bad luck and trouble. Jim's biggest weakness had been booze. Beau's had been Laurel. She was the only thing he'd ever wanted with the same kind of raw, uncontrollable hunger that his father had felt for the whiskey. She had been the best, the prettiest, the sweetest part of his life.

Losing her had hurt more than any beating his old man had ever dished out. It still hurt.

He was ashamed to admit that.

The room brightened as the door swung open. He looked up automatically, expecting to see one of his men or maybe Leah. Even though he'd claimed the larger part of the space, this was still her workshop.

He didn't expect to see Laurel.

Switching off the lathe, he removed his glasses and watched her. She looked surprised, uneasy, as if he were the last person in the world she wanted to see.

He probably was.

And the sentiment went double for him.

"I—I didn't mean—" She rubbed the toe of her sneaker back and forth on the edge of the rug, clasped her hands together, then slid them in her hip pockets. "I just came back from a walk and heard the equipment and thought—" Another wary shift, a shrug. "I thought Mom had finally gotten those power tools she'd wanted. I didn't know—"

He didn't need the explanation. She wouldn't have walked through the door if she'd known he was in here. He didn't care if she turned around and walked right out again. He would be happier if she did. In fact, he would be happiest of all if he never laid eyes on her again.

Like he'd been happy the last five years? the skeptic inside him wondered.

Refusing to consider the question, instead he waited for her to mumble something and run away. It didn't happen, though. After a long, unpleasant moment, she moved one step closer. "What are you making?"

"A baluster."

"Can't you just buy them?"

"Not like this." He picked up the original from the table beside the lathe and ran his fingers admiringly over its sweet curves. He had stripped a dozen layers of paint from the old wood, had sanded until it was smooth as glass. It was hand-turned, over a hundred years old and an impressive piece of work.

She took one more step. "Mom says you're very good at what you do, that you're widely respected."

"And which part surprises you? That I could be good at anything or that I could earn respect from anyone?"

"Neither." Though her voice was even, her face flushed pink, and her movements were still nervous. She reminded him of a wild creature about to take flight.

This was definitely not the Laurel he used to know. That girl had been bold, aggressive, greedy. Needing reassurance that she was pretty, she had demanded—and gotten—it from every boy she knew. Needing proof that she was desirable, she had teased and tormented every male who crossed her path. And needing...

What was it she'd needed from *him?* Why had she set her sights on him? Because he was the only one whose knees didn't visibly buckle when she walked past? Because he was the best at pretending indifference when she was at her sultriest? He had hidden how incredibly much he wanted her, had laughed at her games instead. He had called her little girl, patted her on the head and sent her off to play with the boys, with a warning to leave the men alone. Of course she had come back, again and again, until he'd had her exactly where he wanted her: naked and underneath him.

And then she'd had *him* exactly where she wanted him:

on his knees. Head-over-heels in love with her. Hers for the taking—or the tormenting.

Over the next few months, she'd done plenty of both.

And then she'd left. He'd told her he hated her, told her that he wished he'd never met her. He'd cursed her and called her names, and watched each ugly, hurtful word find its target, until she'd run away in tears.

He had meant every word he'd said that day, and they still held true today.

She was moving again, sideways this time, paying extraordinary attention to things around the perimeter of the room. When her wandering brought her within a half dozen feet, she glanced at him. "Mom says you restore old houses. How did you get into that?"

"You think because I grew up where I did that I can't appreciate fine old houses?"

She flushed again. "No. I just think restoring fine old houses is a big change from repairing neglected automobiles."

"I lost my job at the garage five years ago. I got into a little trouble with an old girlfriend's new boyfriend, and I wasn't able to work for a week or two, so my boss fired me. I had to find some other way to eat."

For a moment she looked surprised, then guilt became the dominant emotion. She came toward him, one hand extended. "Beau, I'm so—"

"I don't want to hear it."

"Please, just let me say—"

He turned his back on her, flipped the switch and set the wood block spinning again. After slipping his glasses on, he fixed his gaze on the pine and refused to acknowledge anything else in the room, refused to see anything but the narrow segment of pine the bit was shaping.

But he knew when she left the room. He didn't see the change in the light, didn't hear her footsteps or the closing of the door. He felt the difference in the air, felt it in his nerves that quivered, in his muscles that tightened, then relaxed. She was gone, and he was alone. Exactly the way he'd always been. Exactly the way he wanted to be.

Alone and lonely.

The lonely part was always there—always had been, except for a few short months—but the alone part didn't last long. He was removing the finished baluster from the lathe when his privacy was once more disturbed, this time by Laurel's mother.

Leah came to stand on the other side of the lathe, watching as he stood the baluster on end next to the original. If he'd made even the slightest mistake in measurements on the template, the new spindle wouldn't match the old, but as far as he could see, they were as close to identical as two totally different pieces could be.

"Looks good." Leah touched the rough-cut wood, then rubbed the original in comparison. "One down, how many to go?"

He checked the notes he'd made. "Ninety-three."

"Only ninety-three." Her voice was warm with humor. "Well, you should have that done in no time." She watched him fit another blank into the lathe, then stepped back so he could work.

She watched silently, as if she found the process fascinating. In the beginning, her scrutiny had made him nervous, considering who she was, who he was. It hadn't lasted long, though. Work was the one area in his life where he felt a hundred percent confident. He'd studied hard and worked harder to make a name for himself in the restoration field. He knew his business.

Unfortunately, as of yesterday, business wasn't the only thing between them.

When he removed the second baluster, she confirmed that with her first words. "Are you okay?"

In all the months he'd worked here, she had asked that question only once, when she'd bumped the ladder he was using and he'd fallen to the ground, landing at her feet. He'd been fine, and she had promised to keep her distance on her visits to the site.

Now he felt the distance disappearing. "Why wouldn't I be?" His expression was intended to be as blank as the wood behind him, but it felt more like a scowl.

"We never talked about—" She gestured uncomfortably. "About what happened before."

That was true. From the time Bryce had first approached him about taking on this job, through countless meetings and discussions, there had never been any indication on either side that they shared any sort of past. They had treated each other as perfect strangers—which, technically, they'd been. All those times they'd warned Laurel away from the big, bad Walker punk, all those times he'd encouraged her to flaunt their authority with him, they had never met face to face. All the Camerons had known of him was his reputation, and all he'd known of them was theirs, as seen through the eyes of their defiant teenage daughter.

"There's nothing to talk about," he said with a shrug as he set up the lathe once more.

"Beau—"

"Look, trust me—you *don't* want to get into this." And he sure as hell didn't.

She looked as if she wanted to argue but thought better of it. She was a smart woman. Any discussion of the past would eventually have to include his side of it, and he knew without a doubt that she didn't want to hear the sort of things he would say about her daughter, not when she was still basking in the glow of having that daughter home again.

"So...are you okay?" she asked again.

"I'd be fine if I could be left alone long enough to make a dent in that stack of wood behind me."

"All right. I'm leaving." She backed away toward the

door. "I'll post a Do Not Disturb sign on the door. I'll stand at the bottom of the steps and warn everyone away. We'll give you complete and utter privacy."

"Right," he said dryly, but the effect was minimized by his grin.

She stared at him, her own smile faltering. "You don't smile very often, do you? And we—my daughter, my family and I—are part of the reason why."

He scowled again. "Laurel wasn't the worst time in my life," he said scornfully, as if there were some truth to the lie. "My old man wasn't exactly Father of the Year material, and my mother left me long before Laurel did."

"Your father was a poor excuse for a man, and your mother owed you far better than you got. She was a fool, Beau, to go away and leave you behind. And we…" She looked as if she wanted to say much more, but settled for a simple apology before walking out and closing the door behind her. "We're very sorry."

The words—and the sincerity behind them—made him swallow hard. If life had been fairer, he would have had a mother, maybe one like Leah, and maybe he wouldn't have been so vulnerable to Laurel when she'd come along. Maybe he wouldn't have needed all the womanly things about her so much.

But he hadn't had a mother, and the best mother in the world might not have saved him from Laurel. After all, Leah hadn't been able to save Laurel from herself.

Besides, he was a Walker, and Walkers didn't expect fair. Wasn't that one of the lessons his father had drilled into him with his anger, his neglect and his fists? *Life isn't fair.*

Not for kids born into the wrong families.

Not for losers like him.

Not ever.

Dinner was served every night at six-thirty in the grand ballroom-turned-dining-room, with starched linens, candles

in gleaming sterling or rustic pewter holders, winter fires
or summer flowers. When the inn was full, so was the dining room. Even when the inn wasn't full, the family tables
that stretched across the back of the dining room were.

Though she'd offered to help serve the family and the
ten guests scattered throughout the room, Laurel was seated
with a napkin in her lap. She didn't need any help, Meg
had proclaimed—especially from Laurel, the icy look in her
eyes had silently added. Why, her younger sister was a
regular little Wonder Woman. She had a dozen jobs around
the inn, in addition to preparing for her very large and very
formal wedding in less than a month, and she did everything perfectly.

While Laurel searched anxiously—and, so far, futilely—
for some way to show that she could contribute, too.

Meg served salads to Laurel, to Douglas on her right and
Matthew on her left. In her waitressing days, if Laurel had
waited on someone who angered her as much as she apparently angered her sister, she would have been tempted
to let the dish slip and dump its contents in the offender's
lap. But not Meg. No, she set the plate down with the same
unhurried ease she applied to everything. She was incredible. Laurel's respect and confusion increased by the hour.

In all those years that she'd tormented herself with fears
of coming home only to be met by resentment and bitterness, she had never imagined it coming from her sister.
Meg had been just a kid. Other than the general disruption
to the family in general, Laurel had never done anything to
make her so angry. She had never hurt Meg, had never
caused her heartache or pain. So where was all this hostility
coming from?

Maybe Douglas could tell her, if he would. To say he
was underwhelmed with joy at her homecoming was a
slight understatement. Knowing that she wasn't dead or in
prison somewhere was the extent of his joy. To be fair,

though, waiting for her to disappoint their parents and run away again seemed to be the extent of his hostility.

"So…" Her brother's voice was low, meant for her ears only. "Been in any jails while you were gone?"

"You mean you haven't checked?"

His smile was like Bryce's—like their father Terence's, too, according to Martha. If she had a son, would he bear the same family resemblance, or would he have Buddy's stamp on his features? Whether a boy or a girl, she hoped for the hair and eyes of Cameron brown, for the strong jaw, trademark nose and easy smile. She hoped there was nothing in her baby's face, and certainly nothing in his behavior, that would mark him as Buddy's.

"As a matter of fact, I did," Douglas said. "Considering your last act of defiance before leaving here, I have to admit, I was surprised to hear the answer was no."

She closed her eyes for a moment on the shame that welled inside her. *Her last act of defiance.* That wasn't what it had been at all. She hadn't known that Buddy would follow her into the inn that night, hadn't realized how he would occupy himself while she packed her bags to leave. She hadn't figured out what was going on when she slipped out the back door and through the shadows to his Harley only to find him gone.

In fact, being the idiot she was, she hadn't figured it out until he came running through the dark, carrying one of her mother's canvas shopping bags. He'd shoved the bag into her hands, and she had looked inside and seen the light— figuratively and literally, because just then, Douglas had come driving up the road, his headlights blinding them both.

She had wanted to leave the bag behind—leave behind the cash and credit cards Buddy had taken from Leah's desk, the antique silver he'd taken from the china cabinet, the diamond stud earrings he'd lifted from a table in the family's private living room. But Douglas had been giving her his scornful what-a-loser look, and she'd known that if she insisted on leaving the bag behind, Buddy would leave her behind, too, and she'd wanted desperately—*needed* desperately—to get out.

"Where is ol' Buddy?" Douglas asked.

"I don't know."

"Where was the last place you saw him?"

"Arizona."

"When?"

"About a month ago."

"Oh. I see."

She looked at him. "What do you see?"

"Your boyfriend dumps you, and suddenly, after more than five years away without so much as a phone call, you want to come home."

"It seems a hotshot prosecutor like you should know better than to jump to conclusions."

"I was simply stating two facts. I'll reserve judgment until later."

How much later? she wondered. How many years would she have to be a good, trustworthy daughter, sister and mother before the skeptics among them ruled in her favor?

It didn't matter. She was back home to stay. She would spend the rest of her life proving it, if that was what it took.

But even a lifetime wouldn't be enough to convince Beau, she thought regretfully. No matter how many apologies she made, no matter how much penance she paid, he was never going to forgive her.

The entree followed the salad, then one of Colleen's sinfully rich desserts. After serving the last of the family, Meg slid into the empty seat across from Laurel with her own dessert. "Did anyone remember to tell you that Beau Walker is working here?" she asked too sweetly.

"I've seen him," Laurel replied cautiously. "I've talked to him."

"He actually talked to you? I'm surprised. You know,

considering his background, it's really remarkable what he's done with himself. He's a changed man. He doesn't have anything at all to do with that trash—'' Meg broke off, smiled and corrected herself. ''That bunch that he used to hang around with.''

No surprise that he didn't want anything at all to do with *her,* because she was part of that trash, Laurel acknowledged.

''He has quite a reputation. Of course, he always did, as you well know, but now people don't shudder with horror when they hear his name.''

''No one ever did,'' Douglas said, his dry tone a counterpoint to Meg's vivacious-Southern-belle delivery.

''Mama and Daddy did—though not as much as they shuddered over Buddy Jenkins. *Buddy Jenkins!* Now there's the bottom the barrel for you. By the way, Laurel—'' Meg batted her pretty eyes ''—when are you going back to him?''

''I'm not.''

''Did you two have a little lovers' quarrel? You should have learned by now that running away doesn't solve anything. I'm sure if you go back and make a proper apology and expend a little effort, he might be persuaded to take you back.''

Losing her appetite, Laurel laid her fork down and clasped her hands tightly in her lap. So Buddy, who was bottom of the barrel in Meg's estimation, *might* be persuaded to take Laurel back. What did that make her? The slug in the dirt underneath the barrel?

''I'd be happy to advance you the money to pay your way back. I'll even throw in some new clothes, so you don't look quite so tacky. Heavens, the way you've let yourself go, it's no surprise that the man no longer wanted you.''

''Knock it off, Meg,'' Matthew said with a scowl. ''Laurel's not going back. She's home to stay.''

"So she says." Meg's artificially sweet voice took on a brittle tone. "So it's a red-letter month for the Cameron children. Douglas gets a promotion. Matthew graduates from high school and has a few months free before starting college on a full scholarship. I graduate with honors from college, and I'm getting married. And Laurel comes home, apparently broke, apparently used up and thrown away and with no place else on earth to go. Our parents must be *so* proud of us all."

Blinking back the tears that welled, Laurel laid her napkin aside and stood up. Ignoring her mother's "Leave those alone," she gathered a tray of dirty dishes and escaped into the quiet of the empty kitchen, where for a long time, she bent over the sink and concentrated on not crying, on not giving in to the queasiness that rocked her.

When the door swung open, she quickly straightened, not wanting to give her mother reason to worry or Meg the satisfaction of knowing she'd brought her to tears. It was Douglas, though, carrying a plastic basin filled with dishes. He set them on the counter beside her, and they worked together in silence, scraping, rinsing, loading the dishwasher. The familiar routine soothed her nerves, calmed her emotions and, finally, allowed her to ask quietly, "Why is she so angry?"

For a time Douglas didn't answer, but gave all his attention to the task at hand. When the last dish was loaded, though, he dried his hands, leaned back against the counter and shrugged. "Maybe because you disappointed her."

That was no surprise. She'd disappointed everyone in her life. But not everyone reacted the way Meg did.

"She looked up to you, Laurel. You were her big sister. You guys were close. Then suddenly, you not only turned your back on her and the rest of the family, but you became a totally different person—and not a nice one. She couldn't look up to you anymore."

So now Meg looked down on her. It was a plausible

theory, but there was more to it than that. She could see it in Douglas's face. "What's the rest?"

He was quiet again for a time, then he turned to look out beside her. "You know how they say that when one child in a family is stricken by a devastating illness, sometimes the other children grow resentful because the sick kid gets all their parents' attention? That's how Meg felt about you. Did you know she had straight As all through high school?"

Laurel nodded. Meg had been class valedictorian, an honor that had been an all-too-vivid reminder of Laurel's own barely passing grades. She had also been class president, prom queen and head of a championship cheerleading team. She'd done volunteer work at a local nursing home, taken part in story hour at the library and tutored kids from the state home on the north side of town. She had been remarkable even then.

"Do you remember her graduation?"

"Only vaguely." She'd been under orders from Leah to attend, but she'd had no intention of showing up, until Beau insisted. Wild, reckless, no-good-for-her Beau had turned responsible and forced her to go, and, in retaliation against both him and her mother, she had created a scene. The details were mercifully sketchy, but the incident had involved too much booze and the shortest, skimpiest, tightest dress she could squeeze into.

"Do you remember her prom? She was queen, and she was beautiful. How about the play she starred in? She had half the audience in tears from the first scene on. What about her first date? Any of the awards she won? Her sixteenth birthday?" He gave a shake of his head. "Do you remember anything at all about her from those five years?"

She was ashamed to give a truthful answer: very little. Those years had been so difficult. Everything in her had been focused on herself, on her anger, desperation and fear.

"Well, unfortunately, Mom and Dad don't remember

some of that stuff, either, because they were so busy trying to save you, worrying about you, crying over you. You did everything wrong and got all their attention. The rest of us did everything right and got pretty much ignored. Matthew was just a kid. I don't think he noticed so much. I was away at college most of the time and didn't need their approval so much. But Meg did. She was the perfect daughter, but nothing she did really mattered. Only you mattered. You were the most important thing in Mom and Dad's lives. Even after you left, you were still making our lives miserable."

There was a lump in Laurel's throat and a smothering pain in her chest. "I'm sorry."

"I know," he replied, and he sounded as if he meant it. "But the words aren't enough. They're too easy to say, too easy to not mean at all. It's going to take time and a lot of effort on your part to make amends. Mom and Matthew are thrilled to have you here. So are Grandma, Peter and Frank." He paused, and his voice grew husky. "I'm glad you're home, too. But I work every day with people who lie as easily as they breathe. It's made me a skeptic. I've got to see proof."

"I expected as much."

"This is a really important time for Meg. You've upstaged or tarnished a lot of her important times. Just keep your distance and let her have the wedding she's dreamed of without fearing that you'll ruin it for her. Once that's over, she'll come around. You *are* her big sister, after all."

Laurel nodded solemnly, then was surprised when he suddenly hugged her before starting across the room.

"I'll see you later," he called over his shoulder. "By the way, I like your hair short."

She absently stroked one hand over her hair as she wandered to the booth across the room. The lights over the sink didn't banish the darkness in this corner. She felt alone and protected in the high-backed booth.

*This is a really important time for Meg. You've upstaged
or tarnished a lot of her important times.* It hurt her to
admit that Douglas was right. He was also right that the
best thing she could do was fade into the background until
Meg's wedding was over. She would keep a low profile,
would do nothing to diminish her sister's pleasure in the
big day. Unfortunately, that meant keeping the baby a secret awhile longer. One homecoming wouldn't overshadow
a wedding. One homecoming, combined with Leah and
Bryce's first grandchild, Martha, Peter and Frank's first
great-grandchild, very well might.

She laid her hand protectively over her stomach. Okay,
so no one would know. Not until the happy bride and
groom were back from their fabulous honeymoon and had
basked in the glow of newlywed life for a week or two.
She'd waited a month already. Another month wasn't so
long.

Chapter Three

After settling his bags in the truck floorboard, Beau checked out of MountainAire Lodge and turned toward downtown. He'd been staying at the motel for two weeks, had lived in an inexpensive apartment for the five months before that while work progressed on the house. Today, though the place was far from finished, he was moving in. The living room, kitchen and bath were livable, and that was all he needed.

That, some groceries and some breakfast.

He pulled into the parking lot of one of Angel's Peak's two fast-food restaurants, parking near the back. The place was busy, as it always was on Saturdays. He waited patiently in line, then, once he had his food, went looking for a table. He chose one near the back of the non-smoking section, taking the seat facing the wall.

He didn't realize until he was sliding the straw into his soda that he knew the woman at the table in front of him. Her head was bent over the local paper, so all he saw was sleek brown hair, but he recognized her immediately. Hell, he would have known her if she'd been completely hidden by the paper, just from the queasy feeling that suddenly appeared in his gut.

While he stared, Laurel looked up, glanced around the room, then abruptly met his gaze. Her face flushed, and she looked away, then back again. She looked as skittish as he used to feel as she folded the paper and got up. "Don't worry. I'm leaving, so you won't have to—"

He interrupted, gesturing toward the cup she picked up. "Orange juice? That's breakfast?"

She seemed taken aback by the fact that he'd made a halfway cordial remark. So was he, frankly, because he *wasn't* feeling friendly. He didn't intend to ever feel friendly toward her again. Maybe he was just relieved to be moving out of the motel and into his house. Maybe that small accomplishment made this morning special enough to be decent with anyone.

"Are you here alone?"

She nodded.

"Looking for a job?"

Blankly she looked at the paper, folded open to the classifieds. Once more she nodded.

"So you're really planning to stay. Why?"

"Because it's home."

"Five years ago all you wanted was to get away from home."

"Five years ago all *you* wanted was *me*." Her expression turned dark, closed in. "Things change. People change."

He studied her while removing the wrapper from his biscuit sandwich. "You're right. People change. *I've* changed. I've grown up, learned a lot about myself. I found out that I can survive anything—anyone. But one thing hasn't changed. I still wish I'd never met you."

For a moment she closed her eyes. She looked so miserable that he felt like a bastard, like he'd kicked an innocent kitten for nothing more than inadvertently coming too close. *She* had been in the restaurant first. If he wasn't able to deal with that, he should have moved to another table or taken his breakfast home.

Disgustedly he pushed the food aside. "That was out of line. I shouldn't have said..."

When she opened her eyes, they were damp with tears, but she smiled anyway—the saddest, sorriest smile he'd ever seen. "Considering what I did before I left, you're entitled."

The tears pricked at his conscience. The smile made him remember vividly those sexy, sultry, damnably arrogant smiles she used to such good effect in the past. The words annoyed him. "How does that work? You hurt me five years ago, so that justifies me acting like a bastard now?" He shook his head. "That's stupid."

"It's human nature. It's fair." She shrugged. "I know you're not thrilled that I'm back. You're not the only one. But I'll stay out of your way. You won't have to see me. You won't have to talk to me. You can forget I'm here."

Yeah, like that was going to happen, he thought, still annoyed. She'd been in town four and a half days, and he hadn't forgotten about her for a moment. Every morning and evening when he drove past the inn, he thought of her. There was no job too demanding, no sleep too heavy, to escape her. It could drive a man crazy.

But wasn't crazy how he'd always been with her? Crazy with wanting, with not having, with losing.

Crazy with loving.

"Sit down." Disturbed by that last thought, he spoke the words more harshly than he'd intended. She looked as if she'd rather run away, but hesitantly she slid into the hard plastic chair. "My job at your family's place is good for another six or eight months. I'm not quitting. You say you're not leaving, so it looks like we're stuck with running into each other from time to time. We can make it hard, or we can make it—'' Abruptly, he stopped, blew out his breath noisily. "Hell, there is no 'easy' with you. There never has been.''

"I'm sorry," she murmured in a voice that made him think she'd been saying it a lot lately. God knows, she had a lot to apologize for, but the words weren't going to cut it. The kind of hurt she'd caused couldn't be eased with words, except probably with Leah. But Leah was her mother, and mothers—good mothers, at least—were supposed to forgive their children everything.

Not that he knew much about mothers, good or bad. They were foreign creatures to him.

This Laurel was more than a little foreign to him.

She met his gaze, looking a little stronger, a little more in control. "I know the words don't mean much, but I *am* sorry for everything. I didn't come back here to cause trouble for anyone. I just didn't have anyplace else to go. But I'll do my best to stay out of your way, to stay out of your life." She managed another of those sad smiles. "I've got to go. I didn't tell anyone where I'd gone."

"I didn't see your parents' car in the parking lot."

"I didn't take their car. I walked."

"That's over four miles."

"I needed the exercise. Now I need to get back."

"I'll give you a ride."

"That's not necessary."

"No, it's not," he agreed. Especially when she'd just promised to stay out of his life. Especially when he *needed* her out of his life and out of his mind, before he was out of his mind.

"You haven't finished your breakfast."

He looked at the food, cold and unappetizing now, and shrugged. "I'll get something later." He swept everything but his soda onto the tray, then dumped it in the nearest receptacle on their way outside.

Once they reached the truck, he moved his bags to the

back, then watched her balance the juice while fastening her seat belt. "You used to insist on coffee or booze, even in the morning."

"I never developed a taste for either. I just thought they made me look grown up." She hesitated, then gestured toward his soda. "You never did drink coffee or much booze."

"My father was an alcoholic. You think I wanted to end up like him?"

"Does he still live here?"

He backed out, then pulled onto the street before answering. "He's in the nursing home a few blocks over. I see your sister when I'm there sometimes."

"You visit him?" She sounded surprised. Everyone who knew their history did.

"Yeah. He's nearly seventy years old, and he's senile. He's sober because they won't let him have any whiskey in the home, and he doesn't have the strength to punch anyone. He doesn't have a clue who I am. Hell, most of the time, he doesn't have a clue who *he* is." He paused. "This is the best our relationship has ever been."

"Why do you visit him?"

"Because he's my father."

"But that never meant anything to him."

"I don't care what it meant to him or to anyone else. I have to live with myself. You may think it's stupid—"

"I don't," she interrupted. "I just never figured you for a forgiving man."

He eased to a stop at the red light, then looked her way, waiting for her to look back. When she did, he said quietly, "You figured right. I'm not the forgiving type. If that's what you're looking for, you'll have to look someplace else."

His warning darkened her eyes and made her withdraw emotionally, even physically. That was exactly what he wanted, wasn't it? To keep her at a distance? To keep himself safe?

So why did he regret the distance before they'd gone a mile? Why did he wish he could recall the words, rewind the clock to those few minutes of relatively normal conversation?

Because he was crazy. Certifiable.

He cleared his throat as they passed the turnoff to the Wells place and awkwardly asked, "How did Darla take the news about the wedding?"

When Laurel looked at him, her face was utterly blank. "Darla? What news?"

"Darla Wells. Meg's best friend. Her maid of honor. At least until you came back."

For a moment, she looked puzzled, then her expression turned to cynical amusement. "You think Meg would replace her best friend as maid of honor with *me?* She doesn't even want me to come to the wedding. She's afraid I'll spoil it for everyone."

Again he wished he'd said nothing, because clearly audible underneath the cynicism was hurt. Impossible-to-camouflage, soul-deep hurt.

"Are you going to the wedding?" she asked, trying to sound a little more normal.

"I've been invited."

"By the bride or the groom?"

"The groom. I've done some work at his family's house."

"So are you going?"

He waited for a car to pass, then turned into the drive. "I don't know." He had planned to attend. He liked Kevin O'Donnell, and Meg was friendly enough. But that was before Laurel had come home. Now...

As if she'd read his mind, she said flatly, "Don't stay away on my account. I'll be the quiet little mouse hiding at the back so no one—especially the bride—will know I'm there."

He knew from that morning at the motel that she could make herself pretty unnoticeable, but at a wedding? In a pretty dress? Looking her best? Every man there—including the groom—would zero in on her. Including Beau. Considering some of the stupid, impossible fantasies he had once built around her, it would probably be best if he stayed far, far away.

Considering his failure in the last four and a half days to do what was best for him, he doubted that he would be any wiser or stronger in three weeks. He would probably show up at the wedding, watch Laurel the whole time and regret the future they'd never had. Then the rest of his month—probably the rest of his year—would be shot to hell while he tried once again to fit his life back into the narrow little space in which he allowed himself to live.

Maybe she would leave before then. All her talk about staying could be just that. Maybe she would decide that being good was too hard. Maybe being the Laurel Cameron she was supposed to be would lose its appeal, and she would go back to wherever she came from.

Back to Buddy?

His fingers tightened around the steering wheel as he stopped at the end of the sidewalk. Laurel hesitated a moment, then glanced at him. "You can get some breakfast here."

"No, thanks."

"It's no trouble."

He shook his head and waited for her to get out, willed her to walk away without a look back. He concentrated on sending her into the house and up the stairs to her room. Without closing his eyes, he could see her packing those two ratty bags and heading down the drive for the highway that would take her away. He wished she would do it, hoped she would, but didn't expect it. That would be the easy way out, and, as he'd remarked earlier, nothing was ever easy with her.

"Thanks for the ride."

Even as he nodded in acknowledgment, she opened the door and slid out. Tuesday he'd watched her walk to the door. This morning as soon as she was safely away from the truck, he spun the wheel in a tight circle and headed away from the inn and toward home.

His house was six miles from town at the end of a winding potholed road. There might not have been a Walker born yet who was worth the cost of the air he breathed, but somehow they'd managed for four generations to hang on to one of the prettiest pieces of property in the county.

Had Laurel noticed the view the one time she'd come here? He doubted it. She'd been too frightened by the results of her childish game and too appalled by the conditions in which he lived to notice the wildflowers that spread across the meadow, the rhododendrons that bloomed in scarlet or the view of distant mountains stretching for miles in three directions.

For a time after her visit, he'd been so ashamed that he'd considered moving into town. But there'd been no one to take care of his father, and no way he'd wanted to live in town with Jim. And so he had stayed, fixing the place where he could, saving the rest of his money for a better place someday.

Someday had come six months ago. He'd demolished the old house himself and had taken great pleasure in doing so. He'd torn down shingled exterior walls and ripped out patched and repatched interior walls. He'd taken off the rusted tin roof, cut apart jerry-rigged plumbing, pried up floorboards covered with layers of worn old linoleum and hauled away the cinder-block foundation. It had been quite a job, but he'd refused offers of help. From the moment he'd seen the way Laurel looked at his home, he'd hated every shabby, ragged part of it and had found the demolition satisfying on a gut level.

His new house was built on exactly the same location, to take advantage of the best views. It was a log house—well suited to its site, with lots of big windows, nothing fancy. It certainly didn't compare to the grandeur of the Cameron house, but it was all he needed. Hell, with three bedrooms, it was more than he needed.

After parking off to one side, he climbed out and, for a time, simply looked at the house. He never saw it that he wasn't filled with pride and amazement that it was *his*. It was a good house, the kind that could survive for ages, like those he worked in every day. With a little care, it would still be standing in a hundred years for the latest generation of Walkers to visit.

If there *was* another generation. He couldn't say beyond a doubt that there would be. He hadn't had a date in too many months, hadn't had anything more in much, much longer. He'd told himself that he was too busy with work to spare any time for romance, but that wasn't exactly true.

In the beginning, he'd been too torn up over Laurel to even look at another woman. Once the loneliness had become more than he could bear, he'd started seeing other women—women who were blond, who were reckless, who were too good for him, women whose sole attraction for him was their resemblance in one way or another to Laurel.

After another self-imposed exile from the dating life, he'd given it another try, this time choosing women who reminded him of no one but themselves, whom he liked for their own personalities, their senses of humor, their intelligence, wit and warmth.

But no matter how hard he tried, none of those relationships had gone anywhere. It was as if they reached a certain level of intimacy and he was unable to go any further. He hadn't tried to analyze why, because he'd already identified the one defining factor in all of his relationships—Laurel.

He'd chosen the first group of women specifically because they reminded him of her and the second group specifically because they hadn't. Maybe he had also rejected the second group for the same reason. Maybe consciously he wasn't looking for someone just like her, but subconsciously he was.

And so, for the time being, he'd given up dating, women and sex.

And now Laurel was back.

She had damn near destroyed him last time, but she wouldn't get a chance this time. She'd promised to keep her distance.

All he had to do was let her.

Laurel was up early Tuesday morning. By the time Colleen arrived to open up the kitchen, she'd done two loads of the inn's laundry and turned her considerable energy to weeding the flower beds that edged the gravel parking lot. It was the one chore she knew Meg wouldn't take away from her. Between allergies and a lifelong dislike for yard work, her sister was happy to stay inside and out of Laurel's way.

"You know, we pay a yard service to do that. You don't need to."

She glanced over her shoulder to see her stepfather watching her from the sidewalk. "With three kids at home, you shouldn't be paying a yard service to do anything," she remarked mildly. "Besides, the service isn't earning its pay. The weeds are about to overtake these beds."

Bryce looked, then agreed with her assessment. "They don't mind the mowing, edging or weed-whacking, but they do seem to think that weeding is a little too much to ask."

"If it doesn't involve a gas-powered machine, they're not interested. Typical men." She sat back on her heels, enjoying the feel of dew-damp grass against her bare legs. "I like gardening. I like seeing something I'm responsible for grow and flourish.'' After causing so much trouble, after watching every important relationship in her life wither and die under her care, there was something very satisfying about seeing a plant take root and thrive. It gave her hope that she could help her baby do the same.

Bryce studied her for a moment, then commented, ''You never did care much for housework, did you?''

Her smile was as rueful as the shake of her head. Some of her most spectacular fights with Leah had involved such simple chores as making beds or folding linens. She'd hated picking up after herself and had especially hated picking up after strangers.

No, that wasn't quite true. What she had really hated was authority—anyone's authority. Running away hadn't freed her from it, though. She'd had to submit to Buddy's authority, or risk being left alone and penniless hundreds of miles from home. She'd worked countless menial jobs where every other employee in the place was senior to her and entitled to give her orders. It hadn't been long before her foolish rebellion had been beaten out of her—not literally, not by fists and blows, but by life, despair, hopelessness and regret.

''Since you're willing to help out, why don't you take over the yard work? If we're going to pay someone, we might as well pay someone who will do it—all of it—and do it right.''

''I couldn't accept money for it. After all, I'm living in your house.''

He brushed away her objection. ''Years ago your mother told you that when the inn was earning enough, she would pay for your help. Remember? Well, the inn's earning enough. It's been Matthew's and Meg's summer jobs all through school.''

Laurel remembered Leah's promise. It had been made only one day before Cameron Inn had opened its doors. She had been a kid—eleven years old—but she had understood the importance of the inn. If the venture succeeded, Leah would be able to support the family. If it failed...

They had shuddered to think of the consequences if the inn failed, and so they had all worked hard those first years. Everyone had pitched in without complaint, and everything had run smoothly.

Until Laurel's life had fallen apart.

"Besides," Bryce was continuing, "don't complain about the pay until you hear how much it is—or how little, as Matt says. Fortunately, room and board are included."

What about babysitting services? Medical care? The costs of delivering, feeding and clothing a newborn child?

The thoughts sent a panic through Laurel that could easily be mistaken for morning sickness—which, thank God, she experienced only on rare occasions. It wasn't fair of her to keep the baby secret from her parents. They had a right to know what they were getting into by offering her a job and a place to live.

As soon as Meg's wedding was over, she would tell Leah and Bryce everything. She owed her sister that much of a reprieve.

Bryce named a figure, then asked, "So what do you say? You want the job?"

The money wasn't a lot, as he'd warned, but it would buy her a few maternity outfits. Saved up over the next seven months, it would help pay down the doctor and hospital bills, and it could buy some diapers and infant formula. "I'd love it."

"Good. Now let me show you what you've gotten yourself into." He offered his hand and pulled her to her feet.

They walked around back, where Bryce stopped in the center of the small yard. "The two new houses are on the other side of those trees. We want to open up that area—remove most, if not all, of the trees—and put in some type of garden, something suitable for both this house and the two new ones. Leah doesn't want the guests who stay in those houses to feel cut off from the main house. What do you think?''

''I think removing eighty-foot pines is way outside my gardening experience,'' she teased, but already the possibilities were crowding into her mind. Formal gardens, boxwood hedges and symmetrical beds. Informal sprawl, native plants, lots of vibrant, fragrant color. Lush emerald grass with free-form beds and a reflecting pool, or a natural woodland with a fish pond. So many options, so many combinations.

''You give us a budget, and we'll cover whatever outside help you need, including a landscape architect.''

''I'd really like to draw up the initial plans myself,'' she said hesitantly. ''Then you and Mom can take them to a professional for approval.''

''You don't need a professional's approval, Laurel. Just ours.''

In more ways than he could imagine.

Bryce gestured toward the trees. ''Want to go back and take a look at the other houses you'll be working with?''

Her gaze shifted to the patch of scrubby grass the construction crew used as a parking lot. It was empty, but not for long. Beau would be along any moment now, and she had promised to stay out of his way. ''I'll do it later.'' Probably in the evening, after he'd left for the day, when she wouldn't feel as if she were trespassing.

''Then let's get some breakfast. Colleen was right last week. You do need to put on some weight. You're too thin.''

''What's the old saying? 'You can never be too rich or too thin.''' She had already gained a few pounds, enough so that her shorts weren't quite as baggy as before. Over the next seven months, she intended to gain quite a bit more.

''Well, the old saying is wrong. With what you've got ahead of you, you need to be strong and healthy.''

She opened her mouth to insist that she *was* strong and healthy, but the sound of a motor wiped her mind clean and left her staring at the driveway where it cleared the back corner of the house.

It was Beau, as she'd expected. Feared. Hoped. He acknowledged Bryce's wave with one of his own, but he looked grim, as if he didn't want to be here. Who could blame him?

The urge to turn and look until he was out of sight was almost irresistible, but she managed. Once inside the house she managed not to look out the back windows at all. When it was time for him to collect the coffee and pastries Colleen made for the crew each morning, Laurel managed to be in Leah's office collecting materials for garden sketches.

And she still managed to take a risk, still managed to get in his way.

After spending much of the morning planning and debating, she had decided that she had to see the two new additions to the inn property. How could she know what kind of garden was suitable for all three houses when she didn't have a single clue what two of the houses were like? It couldn't hurt to make her way through the woods, to stay out of sight in the trees and simply get a few quick glances at what she had to work with, could it?

That was how she found herself sitting on the ground, her back against a pine, her notebook braced on both knees, sketching the important details of the two houses—the windows, each house's position in reference to the other and to the main house, the verandas that crossed the fronts and wrapped around the sides.

And *that* was how she didn't notice that she was no longer alone until something, some poorly functioning internal system, warned her.

When she looked up from her sketch, the first thing she saw was a pair of work boots, then jeans, a T-shirt and, finally, a face too handsome for her own good. With his dark hair and dark eyes, classic good looks and equally classic bad-boy reputation, it was no wonder that she'd fallen for Beau all those years ago. The only surprise was that she'd been stupid enough to leave him.

His expression was carefully blank, no doubt to hide his annoyance at finding her invading his workspace. She was about to close up her notebook, offer an apology and run away home, when he spoke.

"What are you doing?"

She searched his words for some hint of hostility, some accusation that she was, once again, where she didn't belong. She found only a simple question, requiring nothing more than a simple answer. "My father asked for my help in planning a garden between the three houses."

"You know something about gardens?"

"Probably a little more than you knew about restoring old houses when you started."

Showing no response to the defensive tone underlying her words, he crouched a few safe feet away and pulled the notebook from her hands to study it. "I didn't know you could draw."

While thinking about the project, she'd doodled in the empty corners of the paper—a curlicued Victorian bracket here, a nonexistent baluster there, an elaborate five-globed street lamp at the bottom. They were reasonably good likenesses, but nothing to merit attention.

After a moment, he handed the notebook back. "That's where you're supposed to say, 'There's a lot you didn't know about me.'"

Gazing past him to the nearest house, she shook her head. "You knew everything you wanted to know."

He mimicked the shake of her head. "I didn't know anything that mattered. I didn't know you were a virgin. I didn't know you were seeing Skip McCandless. I sure as hell didn't know that you would run away with Buddy Jenkins."

An inconvenience and two shameful names from her past. The inconvenience hadn't mattered, though it would have been disposed of with more finesse if he'd had prior warning. She had learned that in all their subsequent times together. The last two, though...

"I wasn't 'seeing' Skip." She'd had only three dates with Douglas's insufferable friend, the arrogant young man whom her family had found so much more suitable than Beau. They hadn't known, not even Douglas, exactly what kind of young man Skip McCandless was.

No one had known until the night she'd stood up Beau for dinner with Skip.

The memory was as vivid as if it had happened only last night. The dress she wore, the scent of her perfume and Skip's cologne. The music in the restaurant, the food, the friends of Skip's who had joined them.

And the look on Beau's face when he'd come in looking for her and seen them together.

That was the night she had truly understood for the first time that she meant something to Beau.

It was also the night that whatever he felt for her had been destroyed, beaten out of him by four privileged young men who'd felt not even a moment's remorse for what they'd done.

No, the remorse was all hers, for bringing someone like Skip into Beau's world. For nearly destroying the only person outside her family who gave a damn about her. For being a sorry excuse for a human being.

"If you weren't 'seeing' him, then what were you doing with him?"

She looked at him, comparing him in her mind's eye to the way he'd looked after her last date with Skip. He hadn't been handsome then, not with one black eye, a busted lip, his face bruised, cut and swollen. He'd had a couple of cracked ribs, more bruises where he'd been kicked and a broken finger from one of the few punches he'd been able to land. Lying down had been out of the question for him, sitting up just barely tolerable.

But he'd been able to talk. In spite of the shallow breaths necessitated by his injured ribs, in spite of the cuts that had split his lip and distorted his words, he'd had no trouble at all telling her exactly what he thought of her. She had never been on the receiving end of such hatred, had never felt self-loathing in such equal measure.

Why had she been with Skip that night?

"I was using him," she said quietly. "To protect myself from you."

Her answer surprised him. Whatever he'd expected, whatever he'd believed over the years, that wasn't it. "To protect yourself," he repeated blankly. "From me." Then, with emotion, "*Why?* I'd never done anything. I had never hurt you, and I never would have. You *knew* that! Why the hell did you need protection from me?"

"Because you scared me. After we... After that first night, everything got so intense. You were possessive. You acted as if you owned me. You wanted to tell me what to do, who to see, where to go. You wanted my life to revolve around you, and it scared me."

Unable to remain where he was, Beau stood up and walked a few feet away, keeping his back to her. He wanted to deny what she'd just said, wanted to insist that all he'd wanted back then was to make her happy.

But it wouldn't be true. He hadn't just wanted her to be happy. He'd wanted her to be happy with him. He had wanted her time, her attention, all of her affection.

He *had* been possessive. He *had* wanted her world to revolve around him. She was the best thing to ever come into his life, and he'd wanted to hold on to her. He had loved her with a great passion, and he'd been afraid of losing her.

Through his need to keep her, had he helped accomplish the very thing he'd feared?

It wasn't a question he wanted to answer. He wasn't ready to accept responsibility. He was still angry with her, still bitter. He still had a scar or two from her betrayal, physical as well as emotional. He still lived with the emptiness she'd created, still regretted what might have been.

He stared at the two houses before him, tangible evidence of what was good in his life right now: his work. Ironically, he owed that to Laurel. If he hadn't confronted her with her boyfriend, McCandless and his pals never would have jumped him. If he hadn't been unable to work, he wouldn't have been fired from the garage and the job he hated. And if he hadn't been desperate for something to fill the hours he'd once spent with her, for something to fill his mind and keep out thoughts of her, he never would have thrown himself into the new job with such determination. With such intensity.

...everything got so intense.

His smile was thin and bitter. "My old man taught me one lesson well—good things don't come along very often, not for people like him. Like me. When something good does come along, you grab it, hold on tight and never let it go." At least, not until you'd choked the life out of it and there was nothing left to hold on to. His father had done it with his mother. Audra Walker had been the best thing to ever happen to Jim, but his drinking, his temper and his jealousy drove her away.

Just as *he* had helped drive Laurel away.

He heard movement behind him and knew she was standing there, close but still so far away. "It wasn't your fault," she said softly. "None of it was. I was just so..."

Rebellious. Defiant. Angry and afraid. Insecure, unsure, desperate to belong somewhere, to belong to someone. Fearful that she was too bad, too troublesome, to love. He had recognized all that back then, because he had lived with it himself, and he had used it to his advantage. He had given her the place to belong, the person to belong to. But his own insecurities and desperation had made him take it too far, and in the end, he had lost her.

She could lay claim to all the blame, and he could let her, but it didn't change the fact that some of it was his.

She spoke again in that soft, sad voice. "If I could go back and change things, I would. I would undo it all. I would make everything right—"

"I wouldn't." He turned and saw that she was, indeed, too close—and too far away. "If you undid it all, you would have been Little Miss Perfect like your sister. You never would have given me the time of day."

"It would have been better for you if I never had."

He had loved her, hated her, needed her, obsessed over her, resented her and damned her. But not once had he ever truly wished he hadn't known her. Oh, he'd told her that, but it had been a lie. Deep inside, past the bitterness and hurt, past the emptiness of lost hope and broken dreams, he was grateful to have known her. At least for a time, he had loved someone. He had been wanted by someone. At least for a time he had been important to someone.

And that, he knew too well from his limited experience, was worth all the hurt and despair in the world.

"If you undid it all, you would be a different person."

She smiled uneasily. "I've spent most of my life trying to become a different person. I think I might almost be there."

"Is this person someone you like?" Because she'd never liked herself before. She had been her own worst critic, her own least-forgiving enemy.

She considered his question a moment, then nodded. "I think so. I know I'll never be perfect like Meg or my mother, but I think I can live with a flaw—or five or six."

Unable to think of a response to that, he looked at the houses again. "Want a tour?"

"I don't think so. Not right now."

When he looked back, she was closing her notebook,

capping her pen, preparing to leave. He was glad to see her go, glad to be left alone again with the work that consumed him.

Wasn't he?

For a moment her gaze met his. Her manner was wary and awkward, and she seemed at a loss for words. No more apologies, he hoped, when she did finally speak.

"With this garden project, I can't promise I'll be able to stay out of your way, but I'll do my best." She walked a few feet, then turned back. "For what it's worth, you weren't a part of the past that I would undo." Her negligible shrug indicated just how much she thought it was worth.

Beau watched until she disappeared into the woods, then slowly returned to the house and the second-floor window he'd abandoned when he saw her. He had already removed the wooden stop that held the window in place, along with the bottom half—the lower sash—of the double-hung window. Now he needed to remove the upper sash, replace the cords that allowed the windows to open and close, then reassemble the window. It was a fairly straightforward job, especially since this was the eighth time he'd done it today.

As he worked, he let his thoughts wander back outside, but not too far. Just to the wooded area below that would become a garden and tie these two houses to the main house. If the choice were his, he'd go for a natural effect—lots of trees and shrubs, winding paths carpeted with pine needles, benches in the shade to escape the heat of the Carolina summers. It would be peaceful, cool and would require very little maintenance and no gardener.

However, considering that the inn already sat in the middle of acres of manicured lawn, he expected something along that line back here. The Camerons would probably yank down all those old pines, doze away everything else and start over from scratch with large expanses of grass broken only by neatly ordered, symmetrical beds. The effect would be that of a ritzy resort—or golf course—but it would set off these two houses like the jewels they were. The possessive part of him couldn't help but appreciate that.

Possessive. It wasn't a word he would choose to describe himself, but it fitted. He had so few things in his life worth holding on to that when he found something to claim, he did so fiercely. Like these houses. From the very moment he'd accepted the Camerons' job, he had involved himself in the smallest details. It went beyond dedication, was more than perfectionism. He felt as responsible and protective of these houses as he was of his own.

Like Laurel. There had been a time, all those years ago, when he'd thought he would resist her. He had taken one look at her—provocative clothes, silky, bottled-blond hair, all posturing and attitude—and he'd known that she could break a man's heart without even trying. She was innocent girl and worldly woman, bad luck and trouble, and he'd decided to let her mess up some other sucker's life.

But she had decided that she wanted him. She had set her sights on him, and he had surrendered. It was the worst decision he'd ever made.

And the best.

He removed the old sash cords, measured lengths of new cord and fixed them in place. He was careful with the sashes. The wavy old glass was original to the house and would be costly to replace if the idiot handling it was too lost in the past to pay attention to his job.

Once the window was reassembled and operating smoothly, he stared out. The glass distorted everything, putting curves in places where they didn't belong, softening and diffusing hard lines. He liked it for its historical accuracy, but looking through it for long made his head ache.

Thinking about the past also gave him a headache.

Living in the past—that was him. Stuck somewhere between five years ago and a hundred and five years ago. He needed a present. A life. A woman. And, no, damn it, not the woman who immediately came to mind. So what if he'd finally acknowledged that he bore some responsibility for what had happened. It didn't mean Laurel was blameless. It sure as hell didn't mean he was free to get involved with her again, because he wasn't. He wouldn't. He couldn't.

Not even if she had changed. Not even if she made him remember better times along with the worse. Not even if she was all he could think of.

He was all kinds of idiots, but not *that* kind. No one got a second chance to destroy him. There were other women around, other women who could distract him.

Right, the obnoxious inner voice whispered smugly. Just like he'd been distracted the last five years. Hell, he'd been so distracted that, at some point, he'd given up on both women and sex and had settled for work instead.

Nothing had ever distracted him from Laurel. It was quite possible that nothing ever would. Possible as hell— and depressing as hell, too. While he didn't have to actively hate her, he didn't trust her, wouldn't want her, couldn't have her. He just had to learn how to live with having her around but not in his life. He could do it. He had to.

She'd left him no choice.

Chapter Four

"Whatcha doin'?"

Laurel looked up from a book on landscape design. It was Wednesday afternoon, the house was quiet, and her younger sister was standing in the doorway, with her hands behind her back, hair falling out of a ponytail and a smudge of dirt darkening her nose. "I'm reading. What are you doing?"

Annie gave a great sigh. "Nothing. Mama's working, an' Daddy's working, an' Meg's shopping—an' she wouldn't take me." The last was spoken with a dose of disbelief, as if she couldn't comprehend any situation in which she might not be welcome.

"She didn't? Is she shopping for wedding stuff?"

Nodding her head enough to make her hair bounce, Annie ventured a few feet closer. "I'm gonna be in her wedding. I'm gonna be a flower girl, an' I'll have a pretty dress an' flowers an' new shoes, an' it's gonna be fun. Are you gonna be in her wedding, too?"

The innocent question made Laurel's smile fade a bit. In the last day or two, Meg had given up the verbal attacks. Instead, she pretended that Laurel was invisible. She didn't look at her, didn't speak to her, didn't acknowledge her existence in any way. Laurel wasn't sure which was preferable—scathing words or no words at all.

"No, sweetie," she replied, closing the book and making room for Annie on her bed. "I'm just going to be a guest." A fact for which she could blame no one but herself, but it was still going to break her heart.

"What's that?"

"A sketch."

"Of what?"

"A garden. I'm going to put one in behind the house."

"Why?"

"Because it'll be prettier to look at than an empty yard, and it'll be nicer for the people who stay in the new houses to walk though a garden than through the woods."

Annie edged onto the mattress, then rolled onto her stomach, like Laurel, and scooted closer. "What are you gonna put in it?"

"I haven't decided." All she'd done so far was check out a half dozen books on her mother's library card, a dozen sketches and a lot of dreaming. She was no closer to making major decisions than when she'd started. She loved the idea of a formal garden as much as she loved the idea of an informal layout. She imagined acres of roses all neatly tended. Or wildflowers growing wild. Or rhododendrons sprawling across the ground. Or a carpet of the richest, lushest, greenest grass imaginable.

"Is your garden gonna have flowers?" Annie asked. "I like flowers."

Okay, so scratch the carpet of grass. "What kind of garden would be it be without them?"

Heaving another sigh that vibrated through her entire body, Annie changed the subject with the ease of the young. "Mama said she would take me to see the houses a long, long time ago, but she hasn't. I like seeing the houses." She gave Laurel a too-innocent look. "Would *you* take me?"

Laurel thought of Beau and immediately shook her head. "I think you'd better wait for Mom."

"Oh, please..." Annie rolled onto her back and smiled the sweet, practiced smile of a child used to getting her way. "Please, let's go. I'll be good."

This time it was her own child who appeared in her mind, sure to have the same big brown eyes, the same winning smile, and Laurel's heart melted. She wished the next seven months were already past, wished the baby was here and in her arms. Contrary to Buddy's reaction, the baby was the one thing she'd done right in her life—that, and coming home to her family.

She brushed her hand over Annie's soft curls, studied her sweet features and felt a surge of love and longing. Giving in to it, she rose from the bed, lifted her sister to the floor and turned her toward the door. "Let's take a walk, Annie. Maybe we can find something to do outside."

After leaving word with Colleen, Laurel followed Annie out the back door and into the yard. As always, her gaze automatically strayed to the parking area. The purple pickup was gone from its customary space. For the moment, it was safe to go anywhere on the property, and they wouldn't risk running into Beau. She knew the idea should cheer her. For some reason, it didn't.

For some reason... She knew all the reasons, starting with the fact that he was still incredibly handsome and incredibly sexy. Everything about him that had left her breathless five years ago was still there, only stronger. As he'd aged and matured, so had his appeal. He hadn't changed other than to get better.

She also knew the reasons none of that could matter. There was their past relationship, how badly it had ended and how deeply she had hurt him. There was her uncertain future—no real home of her own, no real job and so many changes to come. And there was her baby. Buddy's baby. Men were rarely happy to take on the responsibility for other men's children. Beau Walker having anything at all to do with Buddy Jenkins's child was outside the realm of her imagination.

There had been a brief time, when she'd first suspected that she was pregnant, that she'd had a few problems with the idea herself. Her first thought had been a prayer—*Please, God, don't let it be true*—and her second had been a regret. Buddy Jenkins was *not* the man she would have chosen to be the father of her children. Their relationship had never been a healthy one. They'd brought out the worst in each other. He had systematically destroyed her confidence and self-esteem—what little had survived her own actions here in Angel's Peak—but she had been unable to break away from him. She had been dependent on him in every way.

Until the day she'd told him about the baby. Five years of fighting, breaking up, getting back together, of can't-live-with-him-can't-live-without-him, five long years of miserable co-dependent hell, and all it had taken to free her was one statement, one order.

Of course you'll have an abortion.

Six words that had given her the courage she'd lacked all those years. Six words that had made watching him walk away one of the easier things she'd ever done.

Of course you'll have an abortion.

His assumption had sent an icy chill through her and, at the same time, brought a sudden clarity to her thoughts, her feelings. Things were never going to change between them. They would always fight. He would always treat her with contempt, and she would always be spineless and afraid and let him. No, Buddy Jenkins wasn't the man she would have chosen to father her children, and he wasn't the man she would choose for herself. She deserved better—and even being alone with a baby was better.

Being with her family was certainly better. Someday being with a man who accepted her baby would be best of all, but Beau wouldn't be that man. He'd disliked Buddy long before she had run off with him. Probably no man around here who had ever known Buddy would want to play father to his child.

So no dreams about Beau, about picking up where they left off, rekindling old flames or attractions that still remained. Her only dreams in the immediate future were reserved for the baby, as they should be.

"Please, can we see the houses?" Annie asked, tugging on Laurel's hand as they followed the rutted driveway around a curve. "Please?"

The first house came into sight through the trees, a dusky Wedgwood blue with ivory trim, elegant lines and a gracious air. Because she liked old houses and could use a look at the prospective garden from their viewpoint, and because Beau wasn't on-site, she gave in to Annie's request. "All right. We'll see the houses."

Annie pulled free and skipped ahead, skirting piles of lumber and debris, racing up the steps of the second house and ducking between workmen through the open door. Laurel increased her pace to catch up with her, but by the time she reached the foyer of the soft, crimson-hued house, there was no sign of her sister. "Annie?"

A carpenter who was carefully prying casing from around a door gave her a less-than-friendly look. "She's upstairs."

One of Beau's employees. Also one of Beau's friends? Perhaps one she should recognize from their time together? If so, she was sorry because she didn't remember him. Her primary interest back then had been Beau himself, not the people around him.

With a murmured thanks, she climbed the stairs to the

second floor. The railing she trailed her fingers along was beautiful—rounded, curving, stained a deep cherry and solid to the touch. The balusters that supported it, painted white, looked familiar—or was she mistaking one elegantly carved shape for another?

At the top of the stairs, she stopped and listened. Hammering came from downstairs, along with the sound of a power saw and deep, masculine voices. Up here it was quieter, the voices softer, more distant.

She followed the hall to its end, admiring the high ceiling, the elaborate moldings that encased each door and formed a chair rail along both walls, the ornate medallions that circled the base of each chandelier. It was a beautiful house, handsomely preserved and restored, and would delight the inn's guests. Her parents could be proud of themselves.

So could Beau.

The hallway ended at the door to a suite. The first room she entered was cozy, about twelve feet square, with a marble fireplace and a bow window that curved gently out to offer a breathtaking view of the same mountains she saw from her bedroom. The next, larger room featured the same view and a matching fireplace. The voices she'd followed came from the third room, a large bathroom with a clawfoot tub, in which Annie was lounging while visiting.

With Beau.

She stopped outside the door, unable to see him and unnoticed by her sister, and listened to the voice she'd once known as well as her own. "Does your mama know you've wandered off?"

"Nope. Mama's working. Everyone's working."

"Including me. And now you. See that wrench with the black handle? Hand it to me, will you?"

There was the sound of rubber soles on highly polished cast iron, followed by a question from Annie. "What're you doing?"

"Tightening these pipes."

"Why?"

"So they don't leak water onto the floor. When I finish, I'll take you back to the inn."

"Laurel won't like that."

"Why not?" There was no hostility in his voice, no anger, no emotion at all.

"'Cause she bringed me."

"Then where is she?"

Tiring of crouching, Annie sat back on the floor and spied Laurel in the bedroom. "Right there. Come'ere, Laurel, an' see what we did."

Laurel took a deep breath, then walked through the door. She allowed herself a brief glance at her sister, a briefer glance at Beau on his knees beside her, then swept her gaze around the room. "Nice bathroom."

"We aim to please," he replied, but the flatness in his voice denied the assertion.

"Sorry if she got in your way."

Annie gave her an indignant look from the floor. "I wasn't in his way. I was helping, wasn't I?"

He gave the pipe wrench one last turn, then laid it aside and got to his feet. A simple action to make the room shrink by half. "You're a good plumber's helper." He lifted one arm to wipe his T-shirt sleeve across his forehead, then asked, "What do you think of the place?"

Laurel watched Annie go into the bedroom, heading for the marble fireplace. "Stay right there, Annie," she said, then drew a small breath at being alone, more or less, with Beau. "It's lovely. You've done a really good job."

He started to respond to that—*You thought I wouldn't do a good job?* perhaps—then closed his mouth again and instead bent to pick up his tools. Laurel took advantage of the moment to look around the room again.

"The tub is gorgeous. Is it original to the house?"

He shook his head. "The original had been replaced with

a one-piece tub/shower unit. We got this one from a place in Massachusetts.''

"What about the paint job?'' She drew her fingers over the ivy pattern that twined its way around the top third of the tub's interior and was repeated more lushly on the exterior.

"An artist up there did it. She painted some tiles for us, too.'' He gestured behind her to tiles spread across a stack of boxes—dark green, bright white, ivy on white. "The sink's from a salvage place in Georgia. The window came from New York. The wallpaper—'' he gestured toward another corner "—is from a reproduction place in Pennsylvania, and we found the fixtures in Virginia.''

"Do you pick all these things out yourself?''

"Usually.''

"So you travel quite a bit on these jobs.''

He shrugged.

"That must be neat.''

"You've done some traveling yourself,'' he pointed out.

She tried to smile, but the reminder of Buddy made it a poor effort. "That was different, though. I didn't want to travel, and you always got to come home again.''

"You could have come home at any time in the last five years.''

She shook her head. She had wanted to come home, but she couldn't handle the shame or the guilt. She couldn't break the unhealthy attachment she'd formed to Buddy. She couldn't deal with all the consequences of her out-of-control behavior.

"Your parents would have welcomed you,'' he insisted.

"My parents weren't what kept me away.'' Her own failings had. Her own feelings. Not wanting to discuss either with the man who'd suffered most because of those failings and feelings, she deliberately changed the subject. "There can't be that many restoration jobs around Angel's Peak. Do you work elsewhere, too?''

"I've worked as a consultant on jobs all over the South, but I try to keep the long-term jobs within three or four hundred miles of here."

"Because you're seeing someone?" Though the thought had never occurred to her before, the instant the words were out, she realized how much she wanted to know the answer. Was there someone special in his life, someone who kept him close to home? Surely there was. Men as handsome and decent as Beau came along few and far between. The female population of Angel's Peak would have to be blind or stupid to let him go unsnagged.

He gave her a look that she could feel even if she *was* finding the stained glass window of tremendous interest. She knew that look—steady, intense and, more often than not, mildly amused. She didn't turn to face him, though. She didn't want to see that she amused him, didn't want to see that she didn't.

"No," he answered at last. "I'm not seeing anyone."

"Why not?"

This time he was still so long that she turned to make sure he hadn't left her talking to herself. He was wearing that look, and he wasn't amused. "Do you want me to say it's because you broke my heart when you left? Because no other woman could take your place? Because I've been pining away for you?" He paused the space of a heartbeat. "Because it's not true. There have been other women. There's just not anyone in particular right now."

She started toward the door, stopping for a moment beside him. "I know you haven't pined away," she said quietly. "I know that whatever you felt ended that night. I remember the next day."

After she left the room, Beau swallowed hard. He remembered the next day, too, with neither pleasure nor pride. Channeling his anger, pain—both physical and emotional—and sense of betrayal into vicious words directed at her had made him feel both better and worse, vindicated and ashamed. He'd told her lies, sharp-edged and meant to wound.

He was still telling lies. She *did* break his heart. No other woman *could* take her place. And, as much as he disliked the image, he *had* been pining away for her. He had been mourning her—or, at least, what he'd thought he had with her—since the day she'd walked out of his house five years ago.

He followed her into the bedroom. Annie was stretched on her toes, driving a block of scrap wood along the marble veins of the fireplace surround. Laurel stood at the bow window, arms folded across her middle, staring out. He went to stand nearby. "How long did you stay with Buddy?"

"Until five weeks ago."

"He usually didn't keep a woman longer than a few weeks. You must have been special." The words left a bad taste in his mouth, one that not even the strongest liquor, if he'd been partial to it, could wash away. She *had* been special—special to *him*. She should have spent those five years with him.

"It wasn't an easy relationship."

"Was it a happy one?"

She looked at him, her eyes dark, her expression bitter. "I wasn't looking for 'happy.' I didn't deserve to be happy."

He was surprised to discover that he regretted her answer. She had almost destroyed him and left him behind for another man. The least she could have done was be happy about it. "Why not? Because you messed up when you were a kid? Because you went a little wild and caused a little trouble?"

"A little wild?" she echoed. "A little trouble?"

He leaned against the window casing. "You *are* the standard against which every wild child in town measures her progress," he admitted mildly. "Though it's hard to believe, looking at you now."

She shyly glanced at him, looked away, then back again. "What do I look like now?"

Beautiful. Sexy. Wholesome. Perfectly normal. Respectable.

Every bad boy's dream.

Maybe even this one's.

"Reformed. Without the tight clothes, the bleached hair, the cigarettes, the booze and the attitude, you look like... Hell, I don't know. A kindergarten teacher. Like somebody's wife. Like a Cameron."

The teenage Laurel would have reacted with derision. The all-grown-up-and-womanly Laurel was flattered. She reacted with a blush and a smile that could go a long way toward making a man forget.

Even if he didn't *want* to forget.

"So..." He cleared his throat and fixed his gaze on Annie. "Why did you leave Buddy after five years?"

"He left me."

"Why?" he asked, though he already knew the answer. Jenkins was a crazy bastard. Any man who willingly walked away from a woman like Laurel was certifiable.

Any man, he amended, whom she hadn't already kicked when he was down.

She took a long time to answer. When she did finally speak, her voice was flat. "It was time—past time. I wasn't getting what I wanted. He certainly wasn't getting what he wanted. He decided to look elsewhere."

Definitely a crazy bastard.

And so was Beau, for indulging in this conversation. He knew from past experience that he was susceptible to her, knew how easily she could turn away. He was supposed to be keeping his distance, supposed to be figuring out how to live his life with her around but not in it.

He wasn't supposed to be softening toward her. He

wasn't supposed to be envying Buddy Jenkins for the five years he'd had with her. He sure as hell wasn't supposed to be thinking about how pretty she was, or how sexy, or how much he'd loved her.

"What was it you wanted? To come home?"

She shrugged.

"What if he decides he wants you, after all? What if he comes back to stay? Will you go back to him?"

She looked startled by his question. "No. Oh, no. Not ever."

"You sound pretty sure of yourself."

Her expression took on a hint of grimness. "I am sure. There's nothing between us. *Nothing.*"

Some part of him wanted to believe her, but some other part remembered how easily she could change. One day five years ago she'd spent the afternoon with him, making love on a quilt under the hot June sun. The next night she stood him up to play her seductive games with Skip McCandless.

"So what are your plans?" he asked.

She shifted, gave an uneasy shrug. "Right now I'm the inn's official gardener. Beyond that, I don't have any."

It must be nice, he thought as he watched Annie, to be able to run home to Mom and Dad and know they'll take you in, feed you, support you and ask nothing of you in return. He'd never had that luxury. He'd worked at one job or another since he was fourteen.

But in the long run, the discipline had paid off. He had his own business, a brand-new house of his own and money in the bank. He didn't need anyone to take care of him. He never would.

But it would be nice to know the family was there. Nice to know that someone cared, to not be so damn alone.

Annie maneuvered her pseudo-truck off the marble and onto the wall. "Not on the Sheetrock, Annie," he said absently, and the block of wood made an immediate U-turn back onto the stone.

"I never imagined you as the kid type," Laurel commented.

"I'm not." He'd never had the least desire to bring a child into the world or his life, and he knew too well what life was like for an unwanted kid. How many times had his father cursed him? Blamed all the problems of his life on him? Told him what an unwelcome burden he was?

Beau had grown up believing that Jim Walker's life would have been a hundred eighty degrees different if only *he* hadn't been in it. Jim wouldn't have been a drunk, wouldn't have been a mean bastard, wouldn't have been abandoned by the wife he loved obsessively if only Beau had never existed.

Of course, Jim had been a drunk more than twenty years before Beau had been born, and he'd been mean all his life. *He* had brought all the sorrow on himself, had chased away his wife all by himself. She had sneaked off in the middle of the night, leaving her husband passed out on the sofa and her son asleep in his bed.

For years Beau had tormented himself, wondering why she hadn't taken him with her. Had she feared that any delay would increase Jim's chances of stopping her? Had she considered a small child too big a burden to take on the run? Had she planned to send for him later, when she'd found a place to settle?

Or had she simply not wanted any reminder of Jim and their marriage to taint her new life?

Now, for the most part, he didn't care. He'd been left by someone much more important than the mother he couldn't remember, and he had survived. Losing Audra had become unimportant, except on the occasional holiday or birthday.

"You could have fooled Annie," Laurel said.

He looked at her blankly, then remembered her last words—*I never imagined you as the kid type*—and his response—*I'm not.* "Annie thinks everyone in the world adores her."

"Every child should believe that. So you just put up with her because she's the bosses' daughter."

"Something like that," he agreed, but it wasn't true, and one look at Laurel showed she didn't believe it for a second. "Annie's not like most kids. She's smart and funny."

"And spoiled, self-centered, cute, adorable, temperamental and nonjudgmental. She's exactly like most kids."

"If you say so. She's the only kid I know—the only kid I *want* to know." With a shrug, he changed the subject. "Want to see the rest of the house?"

The look in her eyes seemed to grow a little dimmer, a little grimmer, then she half smiled. "Sure."

With Annie alternately running ahead or tagging along behind, he gave Laurel a tour of the bedrooms on the second floor, then a walk-through of the first-floor rooms.

"I'm not exactly sure what Mom's plan is," she remarked as they walked from the parlor into the formal dining room and, from there, into the kitchen. "Aren't all the guests going to take their meals in the main house?"

"For the most part. Leah's planning to keep this kitchen stocked with convenience food—cereal, bread, drinks, snacks. She's also planning to make the entire house available to families or large groups, who will have the option of cooking their own meals and being completely separate from the other guests."

"Nice idea." She ran her hand over the butcher block that topped the central island. She'd been doing that a lot—touching this piece of wood, that chunk of stone—as if much of her pleasure in the house came from the texture. Just watching her was enough to make his throat go dry. It was enough to remind him of the ways she had once touched *him*. With pleasure. With seductive intent. With contentment.

"I love big kitchens," she murmured, turning in a circle

with her arms outstretched. "Most of my kitchens—when I even had one—have been dinky little places where you can't do anything. If I ever have one all my own, it's going to be huge."

"Then you'd like mine," he said without thinking.

She faced him, a speculative look shadowing her features, and he knew she was remembering the ramshackle house she visited five years ago. She hadn't gone farther than ten feet inside the door, but she'd seen the living room, the dining room, the kitchen—all one big dumpy room—plus the bathroom and his father's bedroom, the first visible through an open door, the second visible because there was no door. In a drunken rage one night, Jim had kicked it into splinters for Beau to clean up.

"Would you like to see it?" he asked, deliberately ignoring the warning voice screaming inside his head. He didn't need Laurel in his house, didn't need the image of her in his rooms imprinted in his brain, didn't need the scent of her perfuming his air or the essence of her becoming a part of the structure. He was crazy for offering the invitation in the first place, a fool for not rescinding it the instant it was out.

It wasn't as if she didn't give him a chance. For a long time she didn't say a word but simply looked at him—wary, unsure but interested. It was plenty of time to say, Never mind. Bad idea. Forget it. But he didn't, and suddenly she was saying, "Yes. Sure. If it's not too much trouble."

Trouble. That was all she was, he reminded himself, but still he didn't withdraw the invitation. Maybe he was more like his father than he realized. Jim had always had a self-destructive streak a mile wide. Apparently Beau had one, too.

And its name was Laurel.

After the dinner dishes were loaded in the dishwasher and the kitchen was officially closed for the night, Laurel went to her room and, for ten minutes, stood in front of her closet, looking for something to wear. The rods were filled with all the clothes she'd left behind when she'd fled with Buddy—the right size but outdated—and the sad bunch she'd brought home with her, but nothing grabbed her attention. Nothing was particularly flattering.

Finally she pulled a dress from the back of the closet. Her mother had bought it for her years ago, hoping that its sheer prettiness would overcome Laurel's bad-girl aversion to anything liked by an adult and decent. She had taken one look at it, deemed it suitable for Little Miss Perfect across the hall and never touched it again.

She stripped off her shorts and T-shirt and pulled the dress over her head. The airy, floral print fabric smelled of the rose-scented sachets that hung from the closet rods. It fitted over her bust, then fell to midcalf, floating around her, swaying with every move she made. It was the most blatantly feminine garment she owned, and it made her feel pretty.

She wanted to feel pretty tonight.

She added a pair of flats, brushed her hair and dug in her backpack for her skimpy supply of cosmetics. When she was finished, she looked in the full-length mirror that hung inside her closet door and smiled. She looked like a kindergarten teacher, Beau had said, and he was right now more than ever. She looked *innocent*. Trustworthy. Responsible and demure.

Oh, how far she had traveled that she relished looking demure.

She had offered to borrow her mother's car for the drive to his house. He had insisted he would pick her up. She wondered if, just once after all those times he'd never been allowed to, he wanted to pick her up at the inn door. She thought perhaps he didn't trust her to show up on her own.

Back downstairs, she went in search of her mother to tell her that she was going out. She found Leah and Bryce on the front porch, rocking in quiet harmony while Annie chased fireflies in the yard.

"You look lovely," Leah remarked, taking Laurel's hand without slowing her rocking. "Are you going somewhere?"

"Yes, if you don't mind."

"Need the car?" Bryce was half out of his chair, reaching for the keys in his pocket, when she stopped him.

"No. No, thanks." She hesitated. "Beau's picking me up."

Her parents exchanged a look, then Leah cautiously repeated, "Beau? You're going out with him?"

"Only for a little while. Mom, he's not like he used to be. Neither am I. For heaven's sake, he works for you. Surely you know that his reputation always far exceeded his deeds."

"I do know that, now that I know him." Leah's smile was faint in the dusk. "We like Beau. We like him a lot. We wouldn't want to see him..." She glanced at Bryce again, then amended that. "Either of you hurt."

Pulling her hand free, Laurel walked to the top of the steps and faced out. The lawn she would soon be mowing stretched almost all the way to the highway, with only a thick stand of trees at the far end to separate them from the road.

But the grass, and the hours of hard work it would require from her, distracted her for only a moment from what she'd just heard. Her parents were concerned that she might somehow hurt the man whom they had so adamantly warned her away from five years ago. They weren't convinced they could trust her to treat him fairly, and they were worried. About *him.*

That was a big switch.

As a pair of headlights swung off the road and into the inn driveway, she turned back to her parents with a ready smile to hide her injured feelings. She had no reason to be hurt, and they had every reason to be distrustful. Undoing all the damage she'd done would take time. Earning their trust would take tons of it.

"You don't have to worry," she said with more confidence than she felt. "Beau can take care of himself. So can I. I'm not looking to cause trouble for anyone, especially myself. I just want to be home." And to make a home for her baby. To give him—or her—a family, a future and a place to belong. "This thing tonight is nothing. Just…"

Just what? Making amends? Testing the waters for friendship? Maybe Beau's way of proving that things *had* changed? That he could come to the house and pick her up, just as Skip McCandless had always been welcome to do? That he could spend the evening with her and not feel a thing? That she really was as unimportant to him as he wanted her to believe?

Instead of choosing some way to complete the sentence, she turned to watch him as he climbed out of his truck. He wore jeans and a white T-shirt—the warm-weather uniform of bad boys everywhere and undeniably the sexiest attire a man could choose. Drop the temperature thirty degrees, and add a jean jacket—or, better, a black leather jacket—and she would melt right where she stood.

Suddenly, she knew exactly what *this thing tonight* was—her way of living dangerously. Of taking risks. Of tempting fate and flirting with a broken heart.

He hesitated at the bottom of the steps for just an instant, barely noticeable, then came to the top, standing opposite Laurel.

"Good evening, Beau," Leah greeted. Bryce added his own hello.

He responded with a nod.

"Hey, Beau, look what I got!" Annie came racing up the steps, her hands cupped together. "It's a lightnin' bug, an' I'm gonna put him in a jar an' keep him. He can be my night light."

"Only for tonight," he said, crouching beside her. "Lightnin' bugs aren't made to live in jars. If you leave him in one, he'll die."

"I don't want him to die." Annie pursed her lips, then brightened. "I know! He can just fly around my room."

"They're not made to live in your room, either. But if you let him go, you can watch him from your window and let him and all his friends light up the night out here."

She gave one of her classic sighs, opened her hands and let the bug fly free. "You're no fun."

"That's because grown-ups aren't allowed to be fun," Bryce said, lifting her into his lap. "You have a key, Laurel?"

She moved a tentative step away from the railing. "The one I've always had."

"It won't work. We changed the locks. I'll get you one." Leah went inside, then returned only a few minutes later. "Have fun. Don't stay out too late. See you tomorrow, Beau."

The key bit into her fingers as Laurel walked down the steps and to the truck with Beau. She would bet what little cash she had left that she knew exactly when they had changed the locks—the day after their daughter and her larcenous boyfriend had left town with several thousand dollars of *their* property. When the damage was already done, the threat already gone.

"It would have been more fun when I was younger and not quite so respectable," Beau remarked as he started the engine, then backed out.

Laurel glanced his way in the dim light. So she'd been right. Coming here to pick her up *was* part of what this evening was about. She tried to not notice the little twinge of disappointment she felt. "A lot of things are more fun when you're young and not respectable."

"Though being grown up and responsible has it benefits."

"Really? I'm looking forward to finding that out for my-self."

He slowed to turn onto the highway, then picked up speed before glancing at her. "It's really not fair. You spend a lot of time and energy building a reputation, then you grow up and realize it's the wrong reputation. Then you have to spend even more time and energy correcting it."

She thought about his turnabout from disreputable punk to accomplished craftsman—for the kind of painstaking, detail-oriented work he did was, indeed, a well-honed craft. "How did you do it?"

"You've got to find someone to believe in you. When I got fired from the garage and went looking for a job, only one person was even willing to talk to me. He was a car-penter, and he specialized in making impossible-to-find moldings for restoration projects. He taught me everything I know, introduced me to people who could help, helped me get my foot in the door."

"I would have to find a total stranger," she said softly as she gazed out the window at the empty road curving ahead. "No one who knows me is going to believe in me, not like that."

"Your mother does."

"My mother wasn't happy to hear that I was going out with you tonight."

His fingers tightened on the steering wheel, and his voice was underlaid with tension. "There's no surprise in that. She was never happy about it."

"She was never happy about it in the past because she was afraid of what you might do." She swallowed hard. "Now she's worried what *I* might do."

He was silent for a long—time long enough to reach Angel's Peak, then take the road north out of town that would eventually lead to his house. Finally, he made a sim-

ple statement meant, she suspected, to reassure. "Life is
never easy for anyone."

"It is for Meg. Always has been."

"You're kidding, right? You think being perfect twenty-
four hours a day is easy?"

"She was *born* perfect. It's the way she is. Douglas is
smart, Matthew is sweet, Annie is adorable, Meg is perfect,
and I—" She cut herself off, but naturally he wasn't willing
to let her stop there.

"And you?"

"I'm difficult." It was the least cutting and most accu-
rate description she could think of.

"You certainly are," he agreed without rancor or bitterness. "And being difficult is a hell of a lot easier than being
perfect. Ask Meg. She'll tell you."

He turned off the highway onto a county road. It was
paved, but maintenance was a low priority. He dodged the
potholes where possible, eased over them where it wasn't.

"Why do you live out here?" she asked, wrapping her
fingers around the door handle as they bounced over one
particularly deep rut. "Wouldn't a place in town be easier?"

"Why do you think easier is always better?"

Because *she* was difficult, and so the opposite had to be
better. But she didn't offer the answer. Instead, she re-
phrased her question. "Wouldn't a place in town be more
convenient?"

"Some things in life are worth the effort. This place is
one of them."

They passed a few houses, set close to the road, and a
few more at the end of narrow lanes. She had made this
drive only once before. All the way out, she'd been terribly
afraid of the trouble she had caused. All the way back in,
she had cried—for Beau, for herself, for the horrible person
she had become. It was then that she'd decided to leave
town. It was her only choice, her only way to live with

herself, and the best thing she could do for the people unfortunate enough to be in her life. She had never felt so lost and alone, not before, not since.

That was when she'd turned to Buddy.

The road dipped into a valley, crossed a rickety bridge, then began climbing again. It wasn't far to the fence posts that marked the beginning of Walker property, not far beyond that to the house.

Only it wasn't the house at all, not the shabby little place she remembered. Instead, this well-lit residence was new, with graceful lines, a solid air about it and a simple, straightforward beauty.

As Beau parked at the end of the graveled drive, she turned to face him. "When I asked you where you lived, you said, 'The same place.'" There was a faintly accusing tone to her voice that she didn't try to temper.

"The place *is* the same. The house is different."

"But you implied—"

"You assumed—"

She opened the door and slid out, then circled around to face the house squarely. He joined her a moment later. The house suited its site so perfectly that it looked as if it might have been there since the first settlers had moved into western Carolina. It was beautiful—and another reason, she suspected, that Beau had suggested this visit. He'd wanted her to see that he no longer lived in the shabby house where she'd shamed herself. He'd wanted her to see how successful he was, how his life had changed.

She was happy that it had, happy that his life was easier.

She was also saddened by the contrast. They'd had the same five years, the same education, the same disadvantages. He had a beautiful house, a new truck, a thriving business. And she had a temporary place to live at her parents', a temporary job given by her parents, no prospects for a better future and a baby on the way whom she couldn't support without help from her parents.

A baby to love, to cherish. A reason to be the very best person she could be. What more could she ask for?

"Want to go in?"

She nodded, and they followed a sidewalk of stone pavers to the steps that led to the door. He unlocked and opened the door, then waited for her to enter first.

The foyer was an elongated stair landing. About five feet across and twenty feet long, it led into a bedroom at the far right, up the stairs also on the right or down four broad steps into the main living area. Laurel slowly moved down the steps, impressed and delighted by the structure.

There was wood everywhere—floors the color of honeyed gold, exposed beams, gently rounded window and door casings, built-in cabinets. The fireplace wall was fieldstone and reached a peak some twenty feet up. Along with a set of French doors, tall windows made up the back wall, double-hung to take advantage of the mountain breezes as well as the view. The walls were heavily textured and painted a dark country green that extended into the kitchen, where white tile made a pleasing contrast.

"You just moved in." She made the statement as she opened cabinet doors, admiring all the nice little touches—the pop-up tray for a mixer, the appliance garage, the roll-out shelves—and envying all the space.

"Saturday. The second floor's not finished yet, but I was tired of living in town. I'll work on it nights and weekends."

"You lived in the motel the whole time it was being built?"

"Nah. I had an apartment. We expected to finish the downstairs at the beginning of the month, so I gave notice on it. By the time I realized the house wouldn't be ready after all, the apartment had already been rented to someone else. That's why I was at the motel."

"It's a great house. The sunsets must be spectacular."

"They are. The sunrises are better."

She circled the tiled island and returned to the living room. "No time to choose furniture yet?"

"Only in the bedroom."

She could easily envision filling the bare space with an overstuffed sofa and love seat in vivid prints, a big comfortable chair and chunky, massive tables. For the natural, rustic look, she would add nubby woven throws, reed and willow baskets, rusted iron candlesticks, maybe a piece of barbed-wire wall art.

Not that it was her space to fill.

With Beau trailing behind, she returned to the landing, opening one door that was a coat closet, another that led to a small bathroom. The third door was already open, leading into his bedroom. It was a large room, too, filled with windows, dominated by its own stone fireplace. A corner cabinet held a television, and situated in front of it were a chair and ottoman of the sort made for lounging. The only other furniture was the bed, carelessly made with a paisley comforter in navy and red, king size, with headboard and footboard of graceful wood arches.

The bed brought her a faint, sad smile. All the times they'd made love in the past, not once had they ever shared the luxury of a bed. They had put to good use the back seat of his old car, and they had often taken a quilt into the woods to some isolated spot, but a bed had been beyond their reach. He had refused to take her to his house, and she'd been unable to take him to hers.

She wondered, with a hint of envy, about the women who *had* shared beds with him, who would share this bed with him.

Chasing away the thought, she faced him where he leaned against the doorjamb. "This is beautiful."

"I'm pleased with it."

"You should be. You worked on it yourself?"

"I acted as contractor, and I worked when I could. I did all the trim myself, and I'll finish the second floor myself."

"Can we go up there?"

He shrugged and stepped away from the door.

There was less to see upstairs—two bedrooms and a bath with bare Sheetrock walls and plywood sheathing on the floors. Still, it was going to be—already *was*—a wonderful house.

Back in the living room, she opened the French doors and stepped onto the deck. It ran the length of the house and would be a perfect place for kicking back and watching those sunsets. Tonight it was a perfect place to catch the breeze, faintly perfumed with wildflowers and pine. "Great kitchen. Great house." She rested her hands on the railing, warm and prickly. "I'm impressed."

A few yards away, in the shadows, Beau smiled cynically. The whole time he'd known her, he'd been trying to impress her. Now he'd finally succeeded, and how? With material things. With a beautiful house and a great kitchen.

Would he have been happier if she *hadn't* been impressed? Of course not. He'd wanted her to like the house. It was just that, for so long, he'd wanted her to like *him*.

But not anymore. At least, not the way he'd wanted it before. Now he just wanted...

He didn't finish the sentence because he didn't know exactly what he wanted, and he didn't want to hear whatever answers his subconscious mind might supply.

For a long time she stared out over the shades and shadows that were mountains by day. Light from the living room spilled out, turning her skin pale gold, showing too clearly her pensive expression. When she finally broke her silence, her voice matched her look. "When I still lived in Angel's Peak, there were times I thought I would go crazy if I didn't get away. I had this desperate need to be someplace else. To be someone else. I thought that the Laurel I would be someplace new would surely be better than the one I was here."

He remembered the times she had talked longingly of

leaving. She had thought she could head for a new town in a different state and leave all her problems behind. He'd known that wasn't possible, had known that the only way to get rid of the problems was to deal with them, but she hadn't wanted to deal with them. She'd wanted the easy way out and had convinced herself that running away was it.

She had been wrong.

"I did change while I was away, but it wasn't because I was in Louisiana or New Mexico or California. I changed because I grew up. Because Buddy was so irresponsible that I had no choice but to become more responsible. Because it was a natural process of life." Her smile was self-deprecating. "None of which was my original point. I wanted so desperately to get away, but once I did, I wanted even more desperately to come back. There were times I was afraid that I would die in the desert or a city or a bayou and never see this sight again. I used to dream about the mountains, the wildflowers, the autumn leaves. About the people."

Had he been one of those people?

He didn't want to know.

Turning to face him, she smiled again. She was beautiful in the thin yellow light. The whole image—the long, loose, flowery dress, the ballet slippers, the short, sleek hair—was as un-Laurel as he could imagine, but it suited the woman she'd become far better than the bleached hair, booze and tough talk ever could. The old Laurel was someone to have good times with. The new Laurel was someone to fall in love with.

The thought startled him and made him take an involuntary step back. He wasn't looking to fall in love, especially not with someone he'd already fallen for once before. He was just—just...

Just taking his life in his hands. Just jeopardizing everything—the peace, the acceptance, the satisfaction—he'd worked so hard for. Just stepping in front of a speeding train.

Anxious for something to break the silence, he grasped at one of her earlier comments. "So you lived in Louisiana, New Mexico and California. What did you do?"

"Whatever jobs a person like me—new in town, not staying long and sorely lacking in skills—could get. I waited tables, worked in a lot of bars. I made change in a Laundromat, worked the night shift in a convenience store, was an aide in a nursing home and a maid in cheap motels across the country. I did a lot of hard jobs—dirty jobs— and if I was lucky, I got minimum wage and sometimes even tips." She smiled that smile again, belittling her experiences, herself. "It wasn't quite the life I had expected when I left."

"What did Buddy do?"

"Sometimes he worked."

And what did he do the rest of the time? Beau wondered. Gamble? Cheat? Steal? Sit back and enjoy himself while she paid the bills and put food on the table? Any of that would have been par for Buddy's course. He'd never been known for his willingness to work, for honesty or decency.

"Do you regret leaving with him?" He knew she did, knew she considered it one of those wrongs she needed to set right, knew she would undo it all if she could, but he wanted to hear her say it, wanted to hear an admission that Buddy had been wrong for her.

"I regret a lot of things."

"Is he one of them?"

Her expression uncomfortable, she looked away.

Maybe he was wrong. Maybe she didn't consider Buddy one of her major failings. Maybe only he and Skip McCandless fell into that category.

Finally she met his gaze again. "Yes," she said flatly. "Buddy is one of my regrets. Skip is another. What happened with you is another."

"Which part of what happened with me?" He sounded hoarse. Tense. "The ending? The beginning? Everything in between?"

Though the night was comfortably warm, suddenly she shivered. She crossed the few feet to the door, opened it, then hesitated long enough to answer. "The ending, Beau. Only the ending."

He remained alone on the deck, staring at the place where she had stood. It shouldn't matter. After all these years, all the hurt and anger, it shouldn't matter a damn that she regretted the way things had ended with *him*. It wasn't important at all because the fact was, it *had* ended, and ended badly. There was nothing left between them but sorrow and regret on her part, anger and bitterness on his. No love. No friendship. No desire. No affection. No lust.

Well, maybe a little lust. She was a beautiful woman, and he was a healthy man and already well acquainted with the pleasures of her body.

But lust was easily satisfied. It required nothing more than a willing woman—any woman—and he knew several. Lust could be eased for the price of dinner and an evening of his time.

Frankly, though, the idea of calling a woman—any woman—and trading two hours in a nice restaurant for two hours in his bed made him feel uncomfortable. It was so juvenile. So disrespectful. What kind of man used one woman to satisfy the desire stirred by another?

The kind he'd been ever since Laurel had run away.

Scowling at what that said about him, he went inside, locked the door behind him and headed for the kitchen. She was there, leaning against the counter, looking pretty and womanly, as if she belonged.

"It's a great kitchen," she said yet again when he stopped at the far end of the island. "Do you cook?"

"Some. Usually, I'm too tired when I get home, so I have a sandwich or get something on the way."

"It's a sin to have this kitchen and not cook in it daily."

"Do you cook?" He knew she'd had little opportunity growing up. When the house had been just their home and not an inn, Leah had been a stay-at-home mother who did most things herself. After the inn opened its doors, Colleen had claimed the kitchen for her own, feeding the family three meals a day alongside the guests.

"I do some wicked stir-frys, and I make a sinful salsa. I'm fair with the old standbys—roast, meat loaf, spaghetti, fried chicken—and I like to bake."

"I like stir-frys."

"Invite me over sometime and I'll fix one—" Abruptly she stopped. Her expression closed a little, and her voice stiffened. "Or it would be easier if I just gave you the recipe."

He suspected it was something in his own face that had caused her withdrawal—something like dismay that he'd all but asked her to offer to cook for him. If he needed a cook's services, he could afford to hire one. What he certainly couldn't afford was doing the homey stuff with Laurel—fixing meals together, sharing cleanup afterward, acting as if they belonged in the same house, in the same space. Acting as if they belonged together.

They didn't. He'd learned that lesson before, and it had damn near destroyed him. He couldn't do it again.

"I think I'd better go." Her voice was soft, a little confused, a lot apologetic.

He turned off a few lights, left the others burning and followed her outside to his truck. He knew he should apologize, but he couldn't. Wouldn't.

They made the return trip to the inn in awkward silence. When he stopped at the end of the walkway, she climbed out, her skirt swirling around her, then faced him. She looked very composed, very distant. "You have a lovely home."

"Thanks."

She started to turn away, then swung back once more. "Whatever I said wrong in the kitchen, I'm sorry. I didn't mean—" She finished with a shrug.

She hadn't said anything wrong, and they both knew it. He simply didn't have the courage to take the blame.

When he didn't say anything, she murmured a goodbye, closed the door and walked away. And, feeling much as he had five years ago, he watched her go.

Chapter Five

After breakfast Saturday morning, with the keys to Bryce's truck in her pocket, Laurel left the inn by the back door. She didn't have to work weekends, he'd insisted, but she refused to listen. Work was good for her. It made her strong—and heaven knows, in a few months, she would need strength—and it kept her from thinking too much, too hard, about Beau and their less than satisfactory visit a few nights ago.

Things had started to get a little sticky when he asked her if she regretted leaving with Buddy. Clearly, he'd wanted her to say yes, and she'd wanted to. She did regret everything about Buddy—except the baby. The baby was worth it all—the fights, the anger, the guilt, the insults, the shame. She would go through it all again and again if the end result was the same.

Then, in the kitchen... She hadn't realized how forward her comment—*Invite me over sometime*—was until she saw the distaste that darkened his face. Somehow she had forgotten that she wasn't there because she meant anything to him, because they might build a new friendship. He had wanted to show her how his life had improved. Period. His apparent fear that she had read something else into his invitation—something like interest or a second chance—had reminded her all too quickly.

She had seen him since then—coming to the inn to pick up the coffee and pastries, driving past, talking to his crew—but she had kept her distance. It was safer that way. Right now she needed to be safe.

"Where are you going?"

The sound of Meg's voice made a mockery of her last thought and drew her up short less than ten feet from the truck. Turning, she saw her sister in a silk blouse, linen skirt and heels, tapping one foot impatiently. "I'm going to Redfern's to get some plants for the beds on the south side of the house."

"*I* was going to use Daddy's truck today," Meg said petulantly. "He said Kevin and I could use it to move some of my things."

"He must have forgotten. No problem. I'll be back in an hour."

"I was going to use it *now.*"

Laurel gave her another look. Her sister always liked to look *just so,* but even she wouldn't wear silk, linen and heels to move items bulky enough to require a pickup. Still, preferring to avoid a scene, Laurel took a deep breath and fished the keys from her pocket. "Okay. Fine. I'll go to the nursery later. Here, go ahead and take the truck."

Meg folded her arms across her chest and refused to accept them. "Oh, right, so you can tell Mama and Daddy that I wouldn't let you go, and then *I* look like the troublemaker here. Huh-uh. Run your stupid errand."

After hesitating a moment to count to ten, Laurel started toward the truck. Just before she reached it, though, she turned back. "Your wedding is a week from today, right?"

Immediately her sister looked suspicious. "Yes, it is. What of it?"

"And then you and Kevin are going on a honeymoon? And when you get back, you're moving out of the inn and into his house?"

"Yes. Why?"

Laurel smiled sweetly. "Good." She'd turned her back when Meg retaliated with one icy word.

"Bitch."

"That's right. I'm the bitch. The troublemaker. The bad daughter. And you're—"

"You're the thief."

Slowly Laurel turned to face her, feeling a tightness in her chest. Meg's smile was just as artificially sweet as her own had been a moment ago. "I never stole anything."

"Tell that to Mama and Daddy. They think *you* stole the money and the credit cards and the silver. They think *you* took the diamond earrings he gave her on their anniversary."

"But it wasn't me. It was Buddy."

"You know that, and I know it. But no one else does. You can deny it now, but they'll always wonder, always suspect... They'll always believe you stole from your own family and lied to cover it up."

The subject hadn't yet come up, except with Douglas. He had barely touched on it, and she hadn't denied it. If she brought it up now and volunteered the fact that she'd been totally in the dark about Buddy's planned theft... Meg was right. Her parents would act as if they believed her, as if everything was all right, but privately they would wonder. They would always wonder.

"And how do you know it was Buddy?" she asked stiffly.

"I was watching out my window. I saw you come out with your bags and go to his motorcycle. You acted surprised that he wasn't there. And then he came out a few moments later with the bag.''

''But you have no intention of telling this to Mom and Dad.''

''Oh, I'll tell them.''

''If I do what in return?''

''Leave. I want you to go away and stay away until after my wedding.''

Laurel considered it for a moment, but her answer was already carved in stone. ''No.''

Meg's expression grew a dozen times tighter. ''If you ruin my wedding, I'll destroy you.''

''I'm not going to ruin anything.''

''Your just being here ruins it for me.''

Her sister's malice caused a lump in Laurel's throat and tears in her eyes. ''Meg, I'm not here to cause any trouble. I'm here because I have no place else to go.''

''Trouble. Bad luck and trouble. That's what people call you.'' Meg's smile was spiteful. ''That's what Beau calls you.''

Numbly Laurel turned away, fumbled open the door and climbed in. Once the engine was running, she rolled down the windows to dispel the collected heat, but before she could back out, Meg had walked up to her door.

''A little friendly advice, sis. Things have changed in the last five years where Beau's concerned. He was always handsome and likable. Now he's respectable, too. He's considered quite a catch around here—too good a catch for someone like you. The man can have any woman in the county. If I were you—'' her tone all but screamed *Thank God I'm not* ''—I would have to wonder why a man like that would be interested in a woman like me. I'd have to wonder about things like getting used. Getting even. Getting revenge.''

Biting her lip, Laurel shifted into Reverse and eased past her sister and out of the spot. She resisted the urge to peel out and spray gravel in Meg's direction. Instead she drove slowly and with great control into town, reaching the nursery parking lot without relaxing—without feeling—one bit. As soon as she shut the engine off, though, despair washed over her.

Bad luck and trouble. She'd been exactly that for most people in her life. No matter how much she changed, she might never escape that description, might never convince anyone that she *had* changed.

But the truth of the insult wasn't what upset her most, she acknowledged. It was the source. It was one thing for Meg to call her names, another entirely for Beau to. While her sister's insults stung, his hurt. It hurt a lot.

With a weary sigh, she pocketed the keys and went inside the open nursery gate. The air inside was warm, damp and smelled of rich earth and sweet perfume. Low tables spread in every direction, filled with flowers in full bloom and shrubs in one- and five-gallon containers. Larger shrubs and trees circled the perimeter of the space, along with fertilizers, insecticides and other gardening supplies. She claimed a cart and headed for a display of marigolds that spilled over two tables and onto the floor.

She was crouched, inspecting a six-pack of bright orange-red flowers, when an internal alarm went off, prompting her to raise her head and give the surrounding area a sweeping look. Her gaze locked in on two figures at the end of the row, engaged in what was apparently a lighthearted conversation. He said something that made her laugh. She laid her hand on his arm—innocent gesture or proprietary?—and he laughed, too.

Feeling a lump grow in her throat, Laurel shifted so that her back was to them. She hadn't seen Beau laugh so easily in longer than she could remember. She hadn't imagined him *ever* laughing with Darla Wells. Darla was one of those who had looked down her nose at them five years ago, who had treated them both as if they were beneath her notice.

Obviously, Beau was more than deserving of her attention now.

He's considered quite a catch around here... The man can have any woman in the county. Apparently, even Darla Wells, whose family was even more prominent in Angel's Peak's social structure than the Camerons were.

Was that what he wanted? A Meg clone? Perfect hair, perfect face, perfect body, perfect woman? Was that why he'd been so quick to defend Meg Wednesday night? Because he liked her type? Because he liked her best friend?

Well, if that *was* what he wanted, *she* didn't stand a chance in hell. Being imperfect and fatally flawed was the best she could manage.

Not that she was putting herself in the running for the position of Beau's latest girlfriend. Whatever he was looking for, it wasn't the bad-luck-and-trouble girl from his past. It *certainly* wasn't the pregnant woman she had become.

All she was looking for was peace. Acceptance. Forgiveness. And a place for her baby. Not a man. Not Beau. Not certain heartache.

Not even if that knowledge caused a little twinge all its own.

While debating the merits of dogwoods over Chinese maples, Beau listened with half an ear to Darla's conversation. She was an intelligent woman, often entertaining, but, he had discovered over the course of a half dozen dates last year, her primary interests were limited to herself, her life and her future. Somewhere down the list came her family and friends. He—his life, his future—mattered only in relation to her.

Suddenly her voice lowered, catching his full attention, and she moved a few inches closer. "Look over there. Isn't that Laurel Cameron?"

He followed the direction of her pointing finger until his

gaze settled on Laurel. She wore khaki shorts and a white T-shirt and was surrounded where she knelt by bright yellow, orange and red flowers. Her back was to them, and her head was bent, but he didn't need to see more to recognize her. He only had to heed the queasy feeling in his stomach.

"I'd heard she was back, of course, but this is the first time I've seen her," Darla went on. "Meg was right. She looks *awful.* She's so thin, almost like a drug addict or some poor person."

Laurel *was* thin, Beau acknowledged, though she was slowly gaining a few pounds. Colleen's cooking would add to that. But she didn't look emaciated or malnourished. She still had curves where she was supposed to, unlike straight-as-a-rail Darla.

"Poor Meg. I just can't believe her bad luck. I mean, really, would it have hurt Laurel to wait until after the wedding to come back? Did she have to come now and ruin everything?"

"What has she ruined?" Beau asked as he lifted the maple into his cart. Once it was secured, he settled his gaze on Darla, whose company had somehow grown less appealing in the last three minutes. Because she was being catty? Because she'd insulted Laurel? Or because he was unable to avoid comparing her to Laurel—and finding her lacking?

"Just her presence here is a burden on the family. She's never given them anything but heartache, and here she is back, ready to do it again." With a well-manicured hand, Darla tucked back a strand of blond hair that had somehow gone astray. For the first three or four of their six dates, he had been fascinated by her meticulous appearance. Her clothing didn't wrinkle, her makeup didn't wear off, and the wind wouldn't dare muss her hair. She had never looked limp, dusty, worn or tired. She had never given the impression of anything less than absolute perfection.

Just being around her had made *him* tired.

"If she cared anything at all about the Cameron name," Darla went on in that conspiratorial tone, "she would save them further heartache. She would leave and never come back."

"And you think losing their daughter again wouldn't cause them further heartache?"

The look she gave him was patronizing and reminded him of who she was and who he was, and how important that had always been to her—and people like her—before he'd gained respectability. "They would get over it, just as they did before."

"Uh-huh." Leah and Bryce hadn't gotten over anything. They had just learned to live with it.

Like him.

"So..." All thoughts of Laurel out of her mind, Darla gave him a bright smile. "Are you coming to the wedding?"

"Probably." He shouldn't, because of Laurel, but he probably would, because of Laurel.

"I'm maid of honor, you know. I went into Asheville yesterday for the final fitting of my dress. It's absolutely gorgeous—satin the exact shade of my favorite champagne, almost off the shoulder, a little daring. I'm going to be the most beautiful girl there—with the exception of the bride, of course." She smiled that big, perfect smile again, then turned coy. "You know, a handsome man like you should escort the most beautiful girl there."

He looked at Laurel again. Instead of escorting her, he would be sitting at the back watching her try to become invisible for the sake of her perfect—and perfectly selfish—sister. The way she was trying to be invisible right now, while checking the flowers as if each and every one must be flawless, rejecting the ones that—like her—failed to measure up to impossible standards.

"Beau?" Darla followed his gaze, and irritation crept into her voice. "Beau!"

Finally he looked at her. If she'd been catty before, she was downright lionish now. She looked supremely annoyed—and supremely dangerous because of it.

"For God's sake, Beau, after everything she did to you, you can still look at her like that?"

"Like what?"

"Like you did when she was wild and you were—" She broke off, and splotches of color appeared in her cheeks. Darla could be petty, sarcastic and cutting with the best of them, but there were some lines—such as a face-to-face insult to someone she claimed as a friend—that even she preferred not to cross.

So he crossed them for her. "When I was what? No good? Trash? A punk?" he asked quietly, feeling no sting, no insult. "Sometimes you manage to forget that, don't you?"

"I'm sorry, Beau. I didn't mean—"

He didn't care what she meant—really, honestly didn't care—and the reason, he suspected, was still picking through yellow and orange-red flowers thirty feet away. If the words had come from Laurel's mouth and not Darla's, then they would have had some bite. But Darla didn't have the power to hurt him. She never had and never would.

"It's okay," he said and meant it. "Don't worry about it." Maneuvering his cart around her, he started toward the shrubs. "I'll see you at the wedding if not before. Take care."

Halfway to the end of the grounds, he pivoted and returned to the middle, turning onto a wide aisle, parking the cart next to a display of brilliant flowers. He circled around Laurel to a safe distance on the opposite side, then crouched. "Hey."

The look she gave him was wary, just a quick glance, then away. Because of Wednesday night? Because she'd seen him with Darla? For reasons totally unrelated to him, or a combination of the above? He hoped it was the last. He didn't want complete responsibility for the hopelessness that darkened her eyes, but he would like to think he had some effect her. Even if it proved he was a damn fool.

"Want to give me some advice?"

She selected one last six-pack, wedged it into a tray with others and stood up. Moving warily past him, she loaded three trays into the cart, then looked at him. "Sure. Give up any hope of ever being able to discuss anything not directly related to Darla, and watch out when you get close. She bites."

"I already know that. I'm talking about my yard."

Her carefully blank expression didn't change. "Fertilize a couple times a season and water as needed, and it'll be fine."

When she would have pushed past, he stepped in front of her cart, blocking it. "You've seen my house. Help me pick out some bushes to plant around it."

Wariness eased into surprise that wavered, then disappeared. "I can't. I've got to get the truck back to the inn."

"So take it back. I'll follow you, and you can come back here with me."

Again that little waver, as if she was tempted to say yes, but wouldn't. Instead she gestured to the mass of flowers. "These have to be planted."

"I can help you." The suggestion was out before he could stop it, and he wondered where it came from. Probably the same place that had conjured this sudden desire to seek out her help, to spend time with her.

"No." Her refusal was neither polite nor graceful, and it lacked conviction.

"Come on, Laurel. Don't make me wheedle. It's not a pretty sight."

A ghost of a smile almost appeared, but didn't quite. "I'm sure Darla would be happy to help you."

"All Darla knows about yards is that you hire gardeners to take care of them. Besides, she's never seen my house. No one has besides the crew that built it and you."

For a long moment, she looked at him, then made a point of checking her watch. "All right," she said on a reluctant sigh. "But make it quick. I've got to get the truck back. What kind of shrubs do you want?"

"Ones that don't require a lot of maintenance."

"You want flowers? The forsythia's pretty. So's the rhododendron. The azalea. The pyracantha." She gestured to samples of each as they walked. "For non-flowering types, the red tip is nice. A lot of people plant junipers so they'll have green all year round. How about vines? Wisteria, clematis, climbing rose, honeysuckle?"

"Honeysuckle? Hell, why don't I just plant kudzu and be done with it?"

"Not all types of honeysuckle spread like weeds, and any type can be controlled. You plant it to grow around a railing or on a trellis and cut it back when it tries to escape."

"You choose," he said with a shrug.

She gave him another of those long looks, then shook her head. "It's not my yard, my money or my responsibility. You have to live with whatever's planted there, so you make the choices."

"If it *were* your yard, what would you choose?"

Another look, followed by a shrug of surrender. "I'd put a line of red tips along the driveway on the side away from the house. I'd plant a big forsythia in the corner closest to the driveway where the house extends beyond the porch. In the opposite corner I'd put some junipers, and in the front I would plant azaleas. I would put lots of flowers on the porch and the back deck—bright red geraniums in baskets or old clay pots. And at the base of some of the bigger trees, I would plant wisteria."

"Okay. What do we need?"

By the time she finished selecting plants, he'd traded his shopping basket for a big wheeled cart similar to the type found in a lumberyard, and it was overflowing. They paid for their purchases, then loaded them into their trucks, parked only a few spaces apart. "How about telling me what to do with all this stuff?" he asked as he lifted the last bag of mulch over the side. "I'd do the work. You would just supervise."

"Why?"

"Well, if you want to do the work while I watch—"

"Why are you doing this? Are you trying to make up for the other night?" She didn't give him a chance to answer. "Because you don't have to. I know that being invited to your house didn't mean anything. I wasn't trying to make something out of it when I offered to cook. I know you just wanted to show me how much better your life is."

There was some truth in her last statement, but it wasn't the whole truth. She'd already seen—from his truck, his job, the way her parents treated him—that his life had changed for the better. He had issued the invitation because...

Because he was crazy. Self-destructive. A damn fool.

Because he'd wanted just once to walk to the Cameron door and be treated like any suitable young man come to claim their daughter for an evening.

Because he'd wanted her to see where he lived. Wanted her to see how he lived.

"You don't have to feel bad. You don't have to make up for anything. Under the circumstances, no one expects it of you, least of all me." She forced a wobbly smile. "So go home and plant your plants and forget about me. The last thing you need in your life is my kind of bad luck and trouble."

When she started to walk away, he stopped her with his hand on her elbow. "Where did you hear that?"

There was a faint sheen to her eyes that made him feel sick. "It doesn't matter. That's what you call me, isn't it?"

"Not— Just—" Giving up, he swore. "I'm sorry, Laurel."

"Don't be. Those four words pretty much sum up who and what I am. *I* should be sorry that I earned such a nickname, and I am. I am so damned sorry." For one brief moment, she wrapped her fingers tightly around his arm, then she let go and walked away.

"It did mean something," he said to her back, pitching his voice so it carried. When her steps slowed, he moved forward. "Inviting you to my house. I wanted you to see—" He broke off, lowered his voice and rearranged the words. "I wanted to see you."

She gave a soft sigh, shook her head. "You should keep your distance."

"I know. But it's not that easy. We have a history. We can't just pretend that it never happened." He gestured impatiently. "Hell, I was in love with you. That's kind of hard to forget."

She turned to stare at him. She looked stricken, surprised, totally overwhelmed. For a moment he thought she might cry, or laugh, or fall back on old habits and simply run away. She stood her ground, though, and made a serious effort to control her emotions. "Knowing that five years ago might have made a difference." The sorrow and regret were heavier in her voice than ever before.

"Of course you knew. How could you not know?" he asked, still impatient, but the instant he voiced the words, her own words from a few days ago echoed in his mind. He hadn't been pining away for her, he had insisted—had lied—and she had replied in that same quiet voice. *I know that whatever you felt ended that night.* Not "I know that you stopped loving me that night," just *whatever you felt*. A catchall phrase that could cover anything from casual affection to pure lust to soul-stealing love.

Could she really have been so blind that she couldn't recognize what he'd felt for her? Of course she could have. Her self-esteem had sunk past zero. She had deemed herself unlovable, had honestly believed that her family found her so. When she had believed that even her own mother couldn't love her, why would she have thought that someone else could?

"You never said anything," she gently reminded him.

"I didn't think I needed to say it. I thought you could tell." But that was only partly true. He'd thought he was different from everyone else in her life, had thought that he was reaching her in ways no one else could. He had just assumed that she saw what was so very obvious to him.

But there was more. He had never, to the best of his recollection, said "I love you"—not to her, not to anyone. Not his mother, not his father, not the teenage girls who had come before her or the women who had come after. The words had been as foreign to him as another language—scary, mushy, ill-fitting and unnecessary. She *knew*, or so he'd convinced himself, and so there was no need to humble himself with an alien declaration.

But she hadn't known, and it might have made a difference. She might not have gone out with McCandless. She might not have run away with Buddy. She might not have broken his heart.

She offered a pain-filled smile. "I was an idiot back then. There were a lot of simple truths I needed to be convinced of. I know the words are inadequate, but I'm sorry. I am *so* sorry."

"I don't want your apologies, Laurel."

"What do you want?"

Before the wrong answer could pop out, he grabbed the opportunity to lighten the conversation a bit. "A little help planting all these shrubs?"

For a long time, she remained silent before finally offering half a smile. "All right. I'll come out to your place as soon as I get these flowers planted."

He started to offer a trade—his help for hers—then thought better of it. Instead he agreed to her plan, then watched her drive out of sight before heading for his own truck and home.

She had been right about one thing—he *should* keep his distance. But he had been equally right in claiming it wasn't so easy. In a perfect world, her return home would mean nothing to him. He would be able to see her and feel nothing, to remember her with nothing more than nostalgia for the past that was meaningless in the present. Hell, in a perfect world, there would be nothing to feel or remember because he never would have known her in the first place.

But their world wasn't perfect, and her homecoming did mean something. For a few sweet months she had been the most important part of his life. The way those months had ended couldn't change that. Her leaving couldn't change it.

Her coming home could change a lot. It could resurrect the past or put it to rest. It could make his life sweet again. It could put him in a world of hurt or give him something to fill all the empty spaces. It could destroy him or heal him.

If he had any sense, he would take a page from her book and run far and fast away. But a Walker didn't survive in Angel's Peak by running. A Walker had to take his chances where he found them and make the most of them.

This—a second chance with Laurel—just might be the most important chance of his life.

On her hands and knees, Laurel moved slowly along the edge of the flower bed, pushing the cut-open bag of mulch in front of her, spreading it by handfuls around each of the newly planted marigolds. She'd been out here for an hour, mindlessly digging, planting, tamping down and now mulching, but her mind was stuck on permanent replay back in the nursery parking lot. Back where Beau had so carelessly tossed out his little bombshell.

Hell, I was in love with you.

In love. She was twenty-five years old, and no one had ever been *in love* with her. So many people in her life— Buddy included—hadn't even liked her very much. So many people still didn't. But Beau had loved her. *Loved* her. She didn't know whether to laugh with joy that at her worst time, someone had found something about her worth loving or to cry because she'd been loved and hadn't known it.

She had thought... Well, frankly, she'd thought that Beau had liked her well enough. She'd thought he had especially liked having sex with her. And she'd thought that what she mostly was to him was a symbol, his way of thumbing his nose at the society that looked down on him. She'd thought any of a dozen girls in town would have served his purpose equally well—Meg, if she'd been old enough, Darla if she would have let him near, all the other little princesses of Angel's Peak's most prominent families.

But he had *loved* her, and she'd been too full of self-loathing to notice.

She was really sorry she hadn't, because she might never experience the feeling again.

"Those colors certainly brighten up this side of the house."

With a glance at her mother, Laurel sat back and slipped off her gardening gloves. "I didn't ask whether you wanted something softer here. I could move these around back and get some periwinkles or impatiens—"

Leah interrupted her. "It wasn't a criticism, darlin'. I love marigolds." She offered her hand, pulled Laurel to her feet, then slid her arm around her waist and turned her away from the house. "Next Saturday is Meg's big day. The ceremony's going to be right out there. Chairs will be set up on either side of a carpeted aisle leading to the dais where the minister will perform the ceremony. We're having a big tent over there, and there will be tables under the trees for the reception. It seems as if we've invited everyone in the county.''

Everyone but *her,* Laurel thought with bittersweet regret. Of course her mother had made it clear that she was welcome, but the bride had made it even clearer that she wasn't.

Leah drew her to a bench underneath the nearest live oak. ''I always hoped you'd be the first of my children to marry—at least, until...''

''Until I took up with Beau?''

After a moment's hesitation, Leah nodded. ''You have to admit, he wasn't any mother's dream back then.''

''And what about now? Meg says he's considered quite a catch.''

''He's polite and respectful. He makes good money and does wonderful work. He's widely sought after. He doesn't run around, he stays out of trouble, and—let's face it—'' her mother grinned ''— he's darned good-looking. So, yes, there are a lot of women who would like to take him home.'' The smile disappeared, and after a time, Leah looked at her. ''Are you one of them?''

To answer the question truthfully required more from Laurel than she was willing to give at the moment. So much of her had been tied up with Beau five years ago. Because of the intensity of the relationship, because of the way she'd caused it to end so badly, so much of her still was.

But she had other, more important obligations right now. She had a baby to consider, to plan for, to—if necessary—sacrifice for. Everything she did, everything she wanted, had to be in the baby's best interests.

And Beau wasn't.

''I just got out of one bad relationship, Mom. I'm not looking for another.''

''How bad?'' Leah asked, her expression dark and concerned. ''Did he hurt you? Did he hit you?''

"No, nothing like that. We fought a lot, but it was just words."

Her answer didn't reassure her mother. "Sometimes words can be more devastating than blows."

That was true. The ugly words Beau had thrown at her that last night had hurt far more than getting slapped or punched could have. The calculated insults Buddy had directed her way for five long years had been more damaging than most beatings.

"We broke up, got back together, broke up again. I couldn't stay away from him. He was all I had, and I needed him."

"But you finally managed to leave him. How?"

Of course you'll have an abortion. The words echoed in Laurel's head and made her place one hand protectively over her stomach. But she couldn't tell her mother about that, not yet. "One day we had a fight, and he walked out. And for the first time, I didn't care. I watched him go, and I wasn't sad or sorry or frightened or hurt. I only felt free."

Leah squeezed her hand. "Don't think that because things weren't good with Buddy, they can't be good with someone else."

Laurel knew better than that. She would never be one of those I-got-burned-once-so-I'll-never-go-near-the-fire-again sort of people. She didn't want to live alone the rest of her life and had great hopes for falling in love and getting married. But the road to happily-ever-after was strewn with obstacles, and she had a major one in the baby.

After a moment, Leah stood up. "What are your plans for the rest of the day?"

"I'd like to borrow the car if I could."

"Sure. The keys are in the office. Where are you going?"

Laurel's answer made her feel guilty, made her face warmer than the morning shade could account for. "I ran into Beau at the nursery this morning. I agreed to help him plant some shrubs at his house."

Leah gave her a look that made her want to squirm, then squeezed her hand once more as she stood up. "Be careful."

Be careful you don't get hurt? Be careful you don't hurt Beau? Though Laurel was fairly sure one or both of those was her mother's meaning, she preferred to think it was something more routine—*Watch out for traffic, don't be reckless, don't get too much sun, take care and come back in the same shape you're leaving.* "I will."

After Leah went inside, Laurel finished her chores, storing the leftover mulch in the storage shed and dumping the plastic packs in the trash. She went inside long enough to wash up and debated changing clothes. In the end, she wore the same khaki shorts and T-shirt. She was going to work, after all, not on a social visit. She did tuck in the shirt, though, roll up the sleeves a time or two and slide a belt through the loops on her shorts.

She made the drive to Beau's house with the air conditioner off, the windows rolled down and the stereo turned loud. While with Buddy, she had walked most places, ridden on his Harley or relied on city buses. She had missed the sheer pleasure of driving, and so she had renewed her driver's license each time it expired, just in case the opportunity arose. Now that it had, she enjoyed every minute of it.

Or was it her destination that made the trip so pleasurable?

The deep purple truck was in the driveway, its cargo unloaded and waiting nearby, and its driver sat in a rocker on the porch, boots propped on the railing, head back and eyes closed. As she approached, she thought for one tempting moment about stopping where she was and simply watching—appreciating—him for a while, but she forced herself to keep walking.

She climbed the steps and seated herself in the rocker on the opposite side. A board squeaked softly with each rock, a comforting sound.

"Did you get everything planted?"

She kept her gaze on the mountains in the distance. "Yes." Then she asked, "How did you know I wasn't some stranger? Did you look?"

"Didn't need to. I always get this feeling..."

She always did, too, a quivery, teenage-girl-with-a-crush sort of feeling. She imagined his was more along the lines of a sick feeling in his gut.

His feet hit the floor with a solid thud, and he straightened in the chair and looked at her. "Pick a place for the Chinese maple."

She looked across the yard, all too aware of him in her peripheral vision. If this were her house, she would plant the tree outside the bedroom window, where she could lie in bed on lazy mornings and see its vibrant foliage every time she looked out. But if he wanted to see a maple from his bedroom, he would have planted it there without asking her advice.

She blindly picked a spot in the front yard, and he moved the tree there. She followed with a shovel and fertilizer.

"Where did you learn about gardening?"

She stood back and watched him dig. "I worked at a nursery in Louisiana. I needed the job badly, so I lied and said I was experienced. I bluffed my way through the days and spent my evenings at the library, absorbing everything I could about plants. I liked the job a lot."

"It might not have been the life you expected," he said, wiping his forehead on his sleeve, "but it doesn't sound too shabby. At least you discovered some things you enjoyed."

"Five years with Buddy to find out that I have a knack for growing flowers? It doesn't seem like a fair exchange to me."

"No one made you go with him."

"How could I have stayed here after everything that had happened? What could I have done?"

He tossed out two, three, four more shovelfuls of dirt,

then braced one foot on the shovel and looked at her. "You could have stayed with me."

She stared back as she said politely, "I'm sorry. I missed that invitation. Did it come before 'lying bitch' or after 'You make me sick'? Or maybe it was between the part about how much you despised me and the part about what a worthless, cheap—" Abruptly she stopped, choking up, unable to repeat his insult after five years.

His face flooded with shame, and his fingers tightened around the shovel handle. "I didn't mean—I was angry. I wanted to hurt you."

The way she had hurt him. She understood. She had deserved every bit of that anger and more, so much more. "And you stayed angry for a very long time," she said gently. "You never would have taken me back."

"I would have the very next day. If you had come out here again. If you had told me the truth. If you had asked."

She didn't believe him. Between her and Skip Mc-Candless, Beau had been left with nothing but his pride. He wouldn't have sacrificed it just to have her back. Rather than point that out, though, she mildly said, "See? This is what you get when you insist on hanging out with someone with whom you have a history."

His grin was slow to come, didn't form completely and was rueful. "We had some good times. Why is it easier to remember the bad?"

"Because they came last, and they were so much worse than the good times were good."

"Maybe for you. Not for me. The good times were the best." Without a pause, he asked, "Is this deep enough?"

She gauged the size of the tree's root ball against the hole. "I think so."

Laying the shovel aside, he removed the twine that encircled the burlap, cut four slashes in the fabric, then settled the tree in the hole. He held it while she stepped back to make sure it was straight, then she traded places with him so he could scrape the dirt back into the hole. It was an intriguing sight—Beau on his knees in front of her, his dark head bent, the muscles in his back bunching and relaxing under the thin cotton of his shirt.

After one long, greedy look, she forced her gaze up and away to the valleys and peaks that stretched off to Tennessee. Everything in the near distance was green, light and dark, gradually giving way to hazy blues and muted purples that blended into a sky of blue and white wisps. Subconsciously she gave a heavy, satisfied sigh, aware of it only when she felt Beau's gaze flicker to her. "I think you win the prize for the most beautiful view in the state."

"I know," he smugly agreed. "Like I said, this place is worth the effort."

"The autumn color must be fantastic."

"You can see for yourself come October."

She didn't acknowledge his offhand invitation but continued to look out. Come October, she would be six and a half months pregnant, and there would be no hiding it from anyone. Beau's interest in her would be nil once he found out about the baby, especially once he found out that Buddy was the father. He would feel awkward and would avoid her, and she would be sorry, but she would have more important things on her mind. Like her baby. Feeling her move inside her. Planning for her birth, going to childbirth classes, maybe even knitting little booties and blankets.

Come October, she would be that much closer to the biggest day of her life, to accepting the most awesome responsibility, to experiencing the most incredible joy.

Then, come December, she would be a mother, and for the first time in twenty-five years, her life would be perfect. Purely, sweetly perfect.

Chapter Six

What was the reason for that serene little smile? Beau wondered. Memories of Octobers past, of cooler fall weather, wiener roasts, the festival in town? Simple appreciation for the mountains where she'd lived the better part of her life? Anticipation of being home in four months, and four months beyond that, and another four?

The reason didn't really matter. The fact was, she was smiling, and it was sweet. That was a rare enough occasion in her life even now that she was home. Most of her smiles were full of sorrow, regret, apology. He wanted to see more like this.

At his suggestion, they moved to the driveway and evenly spaced the red tip shrubs a few feet from the edge of the gravel. "Someday I'm going to build a workshop over there," he said with a nod toward the tangle of wild-flowers and vines off to the side. "Your mother's let me take over her workshop at the inn, but most of my jobs don't have a convenient place like that. Then I'll be able to do the moldings, balusters and trim work here.''

"You really like what you do," Laurel commented as she turned a shrub on its side and worked it free of its container.

"About as much as you like what you do. Maybe you should start your own nursery someday."

"And go into competition with Redfern's?" she asked dryly. "I don't think Angel's Peak can support two nurseries."

"So find some specialty aspect of the business and focus on that."

She handed him the shrub, then brushed a strand of hair back. He had watched Darla Wells do that this morning, a calculated move designed to return order to her perfect hair and, in the process, to display her perfectly cared-for hand. Laurel did it without thought, a simple, straightforward move to comb back her hair without a moment's consideration of how she looked doing it, of whether her manicure was flawless or her movements graceful. Darla had done it for effect, Laurel with purpose.

There was no question which he found more enticing.

He tamped the dirt around the bush and moved to dig the next hole. "What prompted you to cut your hair?"

She touched it again, self-conscious this time. "Was I really so vain about it before?"

"Well, let's say the only time you didn't worry about how it looked was when we were—" he wanted to break off and trust her to understand, but he forced himself to finish "—making love. And when we were done, the very first thing you always did was brush it." He had spent many a pleasant time deep in the forest on a lazy afternoon, naked, watching her as she sat also naked, her spine perfectly straight, her body perfectly beautiful, brushing her hair until it blinded him in the sunlight. As soon as she'd laid the brush aside, he'd always reached for her, and they had tangled it all over again.

His voice husky with remembered heat, remembered desire, he asked again, "So why did you cut it? When did it stop being so important to you?"

"When it became so important to Buddy," she said, and in an instant, his arousal turned unpleasantly achy and unwelcome. "When he walked out the last time and I knew I would never take him back, I celebrated by cutting my hair and going back to my natural color."

"Could we maybe agree on something here?" He waited for her to look at him before continuing. "Could we not mention Buddy anymore?"

"Like it or not, he was a part of my life for five years."

"Well, I don't like it. I don't like *him*. He was and always will be trash—and trust me. I'm a Walker. I know trash. He couldn't possibly have given you anything worth having or remembering. I don't understand why you don't want to forget that you ever knew him."

For a long moment she stood still, her expression impossible to read. When finally she spoke, her voice was impossible to read, too, her words carefully couched in quiet, emotionless tones. "And what am I supposed to do if you ask a question and he's part of the answer?"

It was a legitimate question. The bastard *had* been with her all those years. Was it fair to ask her to pretend that that part of her life hadn't existed?

Was it fair that she'd run away with Buddy in the first place?

Was it fair that, after everything else Beau had endured—the betrayal, the beating, the heartache—he'd also had to endure the knowledge that she was with Buddy? That she had chosen Buddy over him?

He planted the next red tip with more energy than required, breaking one small branch in the process. Once the dirt was tamped down, he faced her. "I'd been told all my life that I was no good because I was a Walker, because I lived out here, because my old man was no good, and his old man before him. But I never really believed it. I knew I was a better person than the people in town gave me credit for. I knew that being a Walker and being poor didn't automatically make me trash. I *knew* that." The insistence left his voice, lowered it. "And then you left me for Buddy Jenkins. For the first time in my life, I felt like the most worthless, no-good nobody that ever lived."

She flinched, and her eyes grew a shade darker, but she didn't speak.

"Maybe it makes me petty, but I've heard as much about Buddy—" he gave the name a derisive twist "—as I can stand. Under the circumstances, I'd rather forget that he exists. I'd rather pretend that you never knew him. You're a smart woman. You can talk around him without talking about him. Is that too much to ask?"

She shook her head in a careful, controlled way that made her look fragile, as if something was about to wear her down. Stress? Unnatural restrictions on what she could and couldn't say? This emotional minefield that was their lives?

He wanted to offer some reassurance, wanted to convince her that getting past their pasts, both shared and unshared, might lead to a present—maybe a future—worth the effort. Instead, he moved to the next place they'd marked, planted another bush, and another and another. She followed along, unpotting roots, steadying plants, saying absolutely nothing because he'd jumped down her throat when she'd offered an innocent answer to his own question.

Finally, when they finished with the red tips and the forsythia, when the junipers were in the ground and the azaleas formed a border across the front, when nothing was left but the flowers to be potted, he gestured toward the house. "Come in and we'll fix some lunch."

"That's not necessary."

"I know. Please..." He touched the back of her hand, felt the muscles tighten, the nerves quiver. She didn't pull away, though—not then, not when he curved his fingers around her palm, not when he twined his fingers through hers and pressed his palm against hers.

Holding hands. It was about as chaste as physical contact could get. Little kids on the playground did it. Teenagers who'd never shared anything more than a clumsy kiss. Old folks who'd been married so long that they couldn't share much more than a kiss. It was innocent.

Yeah, right.

Innocent, like the thoughts going through his mind, of other places he'd like to touch, places he would like her to touch.

Innocent, like the memories of the first time they made love, when he'd discovered too late that she was a virgin, when she'd wrapped her fingers tightly around his and held on through the pain.

Innocent, like all the times he'd touched her, claimed her, possessed her.

Not so innocent.

He pulled her up the steps and to the door, where he released her to enter the house ahead of him. "You can wash up in here," he said, stepping past her and into his bedroom, past the bed and into the bathroom.

Approval of the room pierced the melancholy that had settled over her, bringing a soft sound of delight from her, making her smile once more. "This is beautiful."

"I'm fond of it myself." He had wanted the room to be as different from the same room in the old house as possible, and he had succeeded. There were no warped, scarred wooden floors here, no layers of peeling, faded wallpaper, leaky faucets, rust stains on the porcelain or grimy, ill-fitting curtains on the window.

The floor was rough-hewn stone, as were the walls. The counter top was of the same stone, polished to a high gloss, solid and massive, with the sink carved right in. The glass-enclosed shower filled one corner, with an antique armoire for linens opposite. The whirlpool tub was big enough for two and centered in front of the window, which filled the outside wall and framed a view as impressive as the one that had given Laurel pause outside. It was a hell of a place to relax after a long day's work.

It would be a hell of a place to rejuvenate after a long night's lovemaking.

She turned the water on and reached for the soap. He would like to stand there and watch as she lathered her hands, would like to see her bend over the sink and splash cool water over her warm skin. But propriety insisted that he give her privacy, and so he murmured, "I'll be in the kitchen," and left.

After a stop in the hall bath to wash his own hands, to splash cold water over his face, he went to the kitchen and pulled an assortment of items out of the refrigerator, adding to them an assortment from the cabinets. He was washing bell peppers and celery at the sink when he got that feeling he'd mentioned to Laurel on the porch.

When he turned, she was standing on the opposite side of the island. Her face looked scrubbed fresh, her hair just a bit damp. She looked beautiful. Wary.

"Do I have everything we need?" he asked.

Her gaze swept the counter. "For what?"

"Stir-fry." There was rice, spices, sauces, pork, vegetables and oil.

"Sure. You can use practically anything."

"Teach me something wicked."

The smile that slowly curved her lips was warm, womanly, and made his blood hot. For the first time since her return, he saw a glimpse of the old Laurel, the wild one, the one who had waited until him for sex and had enjoyed it tremendously. "Every wicked thing I know, I learned from you," she said, her voice low, unintentionally husky.

He had to swallow hard to clear the lump from his throat. "You said you do some wicked stir-frys and a sinful salsa." Another hard swallow. "Teach me one."

And she did. She gave him a cooking lesson, wielding a knife with ease, directing him through each step of the dish. When it was done, they took their lunch to the only set of two chairs on the place—the rockers out front—and ate in what was most likely the first companionable silence they'd ever shared.

Finished with the meal, she laid her plate aside and turned her chair to face him. "Of all of the houses you've worked on, which one was your favorite?"

He was about to name his own when she raised one hand.

"And you can't pick this one."

"There aren't that many. The work I do tends to be time-consuming. Most projects take months—sometimes even years."

"But you must have a favorite."

He shrugged. "I guess the ones we're doing now."

"Why?"

"Because your parents hired me before they'd even bought the houses. I've been involved from the beginning. And each house is different enough from the other to keep my interest. And it's close to home." And for the last two weeks, he'd been around to see her.

"Don't you like to travel?"

"I did. I do."

"But you don't like being away from your house, especially on long-term jobs. And it's hard on relationships."

"I don't have any relationships," he said automatically.

"You could. With Darla."

"Been there. Done that."

"What happened?"

He remembered Laurel's warning at the nursery about the other woman. "She was too self-centered. Too perfect.

Too easy.'' He grinned. ''I like women who are a little more difficult.''

Her cheeks turned pink, and she looked away. ''So you had a—a thing with Darla.''

''Not 'a thing.' Six dates. Six perfectly groomed, perfectly planned, perfectly executed dates, where we talked about Darla, Darla and—oh, yeah, Darla.'' He turned his own chair to face her, then stretched out his legs, his feet only inches from hers. ''You two are about the same age, aren't you? You must have gone to school together.''

''Yes, we must have,'' she said dryly.

''So you weren't friends even before you ran wild.''

''We were never friends. She stole my boyfriend when we were thirteen. And when we were fourteen. And fifteen.''

''Is that how you ended up with me at nineteen? Because you knew she wouldn't want me?''

She gave him a chastening look. ''Oh, she wanted you. All the girls did. They were just afraid to have you.''

''Except you.''

''I was afraid, too.''

He thought back to that night. She had played and teased and tormented him for weeks, first giving him nothing, then a kiss but just a kiss, then bit by bit more until there was only one thing left to do. *He* had been afraid—just turned twenty-three, a Walker from the wrong side of town, about to do the deed with the elder Cameron daughter, princess by birth, wild child by nature. By the time he'd discovered the secret she'd kept from him, it had been too late. He had taken her virginity, and she had taken his heart, and nothing had ever been the same since.

''You weren't afraid,'' he disagreed. ''Not the way I remember it.''

''With all that knees-knocking and hands-shaking, if I wasn't afraid, then what was I?''

He gazed into the distance, as if he could see through

the hills and the years to that spot at the end of County
Line Road, to the blanket, the pile of clothes, her long, pale
body, her thick blond hair. "Beautiful," he murmured.
"Perfect."

For one brief, wistful moment, she looked as if she
wanted to say something—something important. Then the
moment passed. "We'd better get those flowers planted and
mulch and water everything."

Leave the flowers where they were, he wanted to say,
and tell me what brought you that look. But he let the urge
pass, too, and instead stood up. "I'll bring them up here
out of the sun."

They worked efficiently and quickly—too quickly. Before long, all the flowers were in their pots and spread about
on the porch and the back deck. The newly planted beds
were mulched and watered, and there was no other reason
for her to stay.

He walked to the car with her, where he slid his hands
into his hip pockets and rocked back on his heels. "Thanks
for your help."

"You're welcome."

That took care of the niceties. Beau tried to think of
something to say. Laurel waited nervously beside the open
car door. He felt like a kid again, asking his first serious
girlfriend for a real date. Rose had been a year older and
two years more experienced—at least, until that night.
She'd taught him all the things that he'd later taught Laurel.

Putting Rose out of his mind, he cleared his throat.
"Want to do something tomorrow?"

Reluctantly she shook her head. "If Mom doesn't mind,
I'm going to borrow her car to go into Asheville. I need to
get Meg and Kevin a wedding gift."

"I can take you. I need to get something, too."

She gazed past him for a moment, then shyly glanced
his way. "All right."

"I'll pick you up around ten. We can have lunch before the church crowd gets out, then do the shopping."

With a nod, she climbed into the car. As he'd done this morning, a few nights ago, a few years ago, he watched her go.

Sunday morning found Laurel sitting in the booth by the kitchen window, nursing a glass of orange juice and a queasy stomach. She'd been blessedly free of morning sickness since she'd returned home, but this morning even the faint aromas of bacon and eggs were enough to make her swear off food for a while. She hoped this was just an aberration. She wasn't sure she could handle this last week before Meg's wedding and bouts of nausea at the same time.

The sound of rubber soles on wood flooring brought her gaze up from the juice and to her sister, scuffing her feet along. When Annie saw Laurel, she changed directions, climbed up to stand on the bench beside her and gave her an accusing look. "You're not dressed for church."

"No, sweetie, I'm not going."

"Why not? Everyone's going but Daddy, who has to stay an' watch the inn an' won't let me stay with him. Why aren't you going?"

"Because I've got plans." Before Annie could ask what plans and plead to tag along, Laurel tugged her sister's curls. "Has anyone ever told you how pretty you are?"

"Of course." Annie sighed heavily as she seated herself on the table, smoothed her ruffled white sundress, then swung her feet in small white sandals, kicking the back of the bench on each swing. "Everyone tells me I'm pretty, an' Mrs. Thompson, who teaches Sunday school, always pinches me an' says, 'Oh, you're so sweet.'" She demonstrated on Laurel's cheek, leaned close and shifted into a falsetto for the last word before settling back. "Sometimes I don't want to be sweet."

"Well, I've got news for you, munchkin—sometimes you're not. Sometimes you're a real little stinker."

Annie giggled. "Good. I *like* being a stinker."

"Oh, great. Encourage her to misbehave. That's just what this family needs. Irresponsible as always, aren't you, Laurel?" The intrusion came from Meg, dressed for church and, judging from her expression, sending un-Christian thoughts Laurel's way. She subjected Laurel to a thorough, disapproving look, as if her jeans and camp shirt weren't fit for public wearing. "You're obviously not going to church. You know, it might do you some good."

Laurel lifted Annie to the floor, then stood up. Eye to eye with Meg, she returned the long look, then mildly said, "It doesn't look as if it's done *you* much good. Your tongue is as sharp as any."

"I save my polite behavior for people who deserve it."

"And God made you the judge of that? I seem to remember something about 'Judge not lest ye be judged.'"

"Do you also remember 'Do unto others...'?" Meg's smile was malicious. "I'm simply doing unto you the way you've done us. If you don't like it, you're free to leave."

"That would make you happy, wouldn't it, if I left and never came back?" Laurel smiled tightly. "Sorry to disappoint you, Meg, but I'm here to stay. I don't plan to ever leave again."

Her sister's response was scornful. "Oh, right. You'll get tired of playing your games. You'll discover that being responsible and putting other people's needs ahead of your own aren't nearly as much fun as living for the moment. You'll lose interest in pretending to be grown up, you'll track down your worthless boyfriend again or hook up with some other nobody, and you'll run away again."

Hearing their parents in the hall, Laurel lowered her voice. "You're wrong, Meg. I'll be here in six months, six years and sixty years. I'm here to stay."

As Leah and Bryce came through the swinging doors,

Laurel stepped away from Meg and took her juice glass to the sink. Much as she hated these conversations with her sister, this one seemed to have accomplished one good thing—one queasiness had canceled the other. She felt safe enough to sneak a cookie from the tray Colleen had baked this morning for the guests.

"Want to come to church with us, Laurel?" Leah asked. "You still have time to run up and change."

"It would make us late, Mama," Meg interjected. "Changing isn't that easy."

Laurel turned from the counter with a smile firmly in place. "For some of us it isn't so hard. Some of us don't require all the fuss and bother others do. But no, thanks, Mom. Not today."

After calling Matthew downstairs, Leah hustled everyone out to the car. Laurel was left alone in the kitchen with Bryce. He watched her for a moment, then quietly asked, "Are you okay?"

"I'm fine."

"Whoever would have guessed that sweet, malleable Meg could hold such a grudge?"

She finished the cookie and took an orange from the fruit basket, scoring the skin with a knife, then peeling it. "I didn't think either you or Mom had noticed."

"Your mother hasn't. She's got so much on her mind, between your coming home, the wedding and summer being such a busy season. Is there anything I can do?"

Laurel shrugged. "It'll be okay as long as I stay out of Meg's way and don't do anything to upset her big day. I'm not planning to cause any trouble or embarrassment for her. I promise."

"I didn't think you were," he responded with a grin. "You've been properly repentant—just not enough for church, huh?"

"I would have offered to take care of things around here so you could go with the rest of the family, but..." She hesitated, feeling selfish even though there was no reason. Bryce and Leah had taken turns accompanying the family to church ever since they got married. They were used to it. Besides, they might not have wanted her taking sole responsibility for the inn, even for only a few hours. They might not trust her that much yet. "I'm going to Asheville. With Beau."

Bryce acknowledged that with a nod and nothing else as he filled a cup with coffee.

She watched him stir in sugar and cream, then peel the paper baking cup from a blueberry muffin and slather it with butter, before finally asking, "Don't you have anything to say?"

"Have a good time."

"Wednesday night you and Mom were none too happy that I was going out with him. Mom said she didn't want to see him hurt. She thinks I might do that."

He offered her half the muffin, and she took it, as hungry as if she hadn't just eaten a cookie and an orange. "Your mother does worry about Beau, and about you. Under the circumstances, I think that's only natural."

"I didn't mean to hurt him before. I certainly don't plan to do it again." Her smile was rueful. "I keep promising both him and myself that I'll keep my distance."

"But he doesn't want you at a distance, does he?" he asked without expecting an answer. "What do you want?"

Wiping her hands on a napkin, she turned to stare out the window. That was an easy question. She wanted a man to love, who would love her in return. Someone to live with, laugh with, make a future with. A home of her own, a family of her own. Happily-ever-after.

Nothing less than perfection.

And she couldn't have it, because loving her meant loving her baby. She certainly couldn't have it with Beau, who didn't even want to hear Buddy's name, who was convinced that Buddy couldn't possibly have given her anything worth having.

"I want a second chance," she said at last.

"With Beau?"

She watched the subject of their conversation park his truck at the edge of the driveway and start toward the back door. Dressed in jeans and a white cotton shirt, with his hair combed back and his jaw clean shaven, he looked like the answer to Bryce's question, the answer to her dreams. But under the circumstances, all he could be was her fantasy, short-term and sweet. In another week, Meg's wedding would be over, and her secret would be a secret no more.

And she and Beau would be history. Again. For the last time.

"With all the Camerons," she said at last. "With myself." With Beau and with her baby.

"You've got it with your mother and me." Bryce hugged her, then picked up his coffee again. "Need an advance on your salary?"

She shook her head. She had enough cash to buy a decent gift. She would like to splurge on a new dress for the wedding, something lovely and feminine, but the floral dress upstairs in her closet would do. She had too many upcoming expenses—maternity clothes, baby clothes, doctor bills and so on—to waste money on a dress for ego's sake.

"Then have fun."

Bryce disappeared into the hallway just as Beau came through the back door. He hesitated, looking after her father before his gaze settled on her. "Good morning."

She looked at him and heard Bryce's question repeat in her mind. What did she want? Everything. The man, the baby, the dream. Too bad she had to settle for less.

"Morning," she said without a hint of the faint sorrow that had crept over her. "Want some breakfast before we go?"

"Not if we're eating lunch when we get there. Are you ready?"

She took two more of Colleen's cookies, claimed her purse from the coat tree near the back stairs, then followed him outside.

The silence that kept them company most of the way down the mountain was companionable. Since she'd returned, the atmosphere around them had been charged with tension. In the past there'd been such sexual tension between them. But today there was quiet. Not quite peace, but almost.

They were only a dozen miles from the city when he finally spoke. "I half expected you to send a message through someone saying that you'd changed your mind about going with me."

"It never crossed my mind," she lied. All the way home yesterday she'd thought this trip would be a mistake. She'd lain in bed last night watching the sky and wondering if she was setting herself up for heartache. When she'd awakened this morning feeling nothing but sheer pleasure at the prospect of spending the day away from Angel's Peak with Beau, she'd known it was a risk.

But she hadn't been able to even consider canceling. As Bryce had pointed out, Beau didn't seem to want her at a distance. And as she had admitted to herself if no one else, that wasn't where she wanted to be. She had one week left to enjoy his company, to tempt herself with things she couldn't have, to feel free, as if life were full of possibilities.

One week. Seven days. It wasn't long enough for things to progress beyond friendship, beyond mutual attraction. It wasn't long enough for either of them to get hurt. But it was enough to provide her with dreams to sustain her until they one day became reality.

With somebody else.

But what if he surprised her? What if he didn't mind that she was pregnant? What if he wanted to see her anyway?

She scowled at such a fanciful thought. Buddy had minded that she was pregnant, and he was a hell of a lot more involved in it than Beau was. Buddy should have been glad. He should have recognized the baby for the miracle it was. He could have taken a few days to adjust to the idea—even she had needed that—but then he should have been happy. He should have started planning for their future, their family.

But he had minded, and Beau would mind, and thinking that he might not was the surest way to get her hopes up and her dreams shattered.

"What are you going to get Meg and Kevin?"

Laurel blinked, looked at Beau and tried to focus her thoughts. "Meg and…" She blinked again. "I don't know. I've never met Kevin, and I don't know Meg anymore. I don't know where they're going to live or what kind of jobs they'll be doing or what their hobbies are. I don't really know anything."

"Kevin's a good guy. He's a lawyer. He's been practicing in Asheville with his father, but he's going to set up an office in Angel's Peak after the wedding. Meg's going to teach fourth grade at Lincoln Elementary. They've got a house over on Willow. As far as hobbies, Kevin plays poker and skis, and Meg does volunteer work." At her wry look, he chuckled. "I know. Whoever would have thought that the day would come when you'd have to ask me about your family?"

"Some things have changed since the old days," she said with a wistful sigh.

"Everything's changed."

"Everything but me. I'm still making people unhappy without even trying. I still can't manage to do the right thing."

His expression was faintly sympathetic. "You must have had another run-in with Meg this morning."

She nodded.

"What is the 'right thing' she wants you to do? Run away and hide until she and Kevin are safely off to Cozumel or St. Thomas or wherever the hell they're going?"

"Is it really so much to ask? This is her wedding—hopefully the only one she'll ever have. She wants it to be perfect."

"It'll be perfect, whether you're there or not. Besides, you can't afford to disappear until after the wedding. Whether you lied or told the truth, it would break your mother's heart."

He was right about that. If she admitted to Leah that she was leaving at Meg's insistence, her sister's relationship with their mother would suffer. If she simply let Leah believe she was too selfish, too self-centered, to stick around for the wedding, her own relationship with Leah would suffer. Considering that she was still trying to heal the wounds inflicted five and eight and ten years ago, further harm might be irreparable.

"I don't know why I'm even talking about it. I don't have anywhere to go. Angel's Peak is it for me. If I can't be there, then I might as well not be anywhere."

The look he gave her was sharp, the words dismissive. "Meg will get over it someday, and you'll both be glad that you didn't miss her wedding." He exited the interstate onto a heavily traveled thoroughfare, then pulled into a restaurant parking lot. "My favorite place to eat in Asheville. You do still like Mexican, don't you?"

She thought about it a moment. On the drive down, she'd polished off the two cookies, and her stomach remained fairly settled. "Yeah," she said with a grin. "I can handle some Mexican."

The restaurant lobby was crowded with diners waiting for tables when Beau followed Laurel out. For the first time since he'd known her, she'd shown a healthy appetite. The teenage Laurel had been too body-conscious to ever do more than pick at her food. Today she'd eaten like a normal person—not an uncomfortable, uneasy, couldn't-relax-with-present-company sort of person, but just a regular person sharing a meal and enjoying it.

Now she walked out into the hot June sun and gave a lazy, satisfied sigh. ''Wouldn't this be a perfect day to go swimming out past Lavender Hill?''

Innocent words to make his body tighten and his temperature rise a dozen degrees. He had shown her the place, where a creek coming down the mountain had been diverted by a rock slide to form a deep, clear pool. On a few sunny afternoons they'd gone swimming there, stripping down naked, then making love while their skin was wet and cool.

''The pool's dried up,'' he said, his voice sounding almost normal with great effort. ''Someone diverted the creek upstream. All that's there now is weeds.'' He'd discovered that three, maybe four, years ago on a particularly melancholy day. Unable to get Laurel out of his mind, he'd driven to one of the last places he'd been with her and had found only rocks, dirt and weeds. He'd followed the stream bed for a half mile up the mountain before reaching the homemade dam that sent the water on its new course.

At the time, the destruction of the pool had seemed fitting and only fair, considering the destruction of his life.

Now he wished it was still there, wished for just one more afternoon to while away there.

''Where do you want to look for a gift?'' he asked as he unlocked, then opened the truck door. ''Meg and Kevin are registered at a couple of department stores at the mall.''

''Of course they are,'' she said snidely before sliding onto the seat.

He controlled a grin as he circled the truck and got in.

"Five years ago you would have looked down on the practice of registering for wedding gifts because it was traditional, and you tried so damn hard to not be traditional. Is that the problem you have with it now?"

"I have no problem with people registering at hardware or cooking or discount stores, where you can get things you really need. But I promise you, Meg's chosen fine china and delicate crystal and gorgeous silver—all very expensive and all guaranteed to sit in a cabinet or drawer for the next fifty years except for the occasional holiday spent at home. It just seems pointless to me."

"But if fine china and delicate crystal are what she wants..."

After a moment, Laurel shrugged. "Then I guess it's what she should have."

Beau took that as agreement to head toward the mall. They hadn't gone more than a few miles, though, when abruptly she straightened. "Can we stop there?"

He looked at the block of shops, just opening for the afternoon's business, and found a parking space around the corner.

The stores were mostly small and were packed with merchandise—some functional, some purely decorative and some just plain weird. Laurel shopped in a way he could appreciate. She didn't linger, didn't browse. Anything that caught her attention did so quickly, or she moved on.

They had worked their way through half the shops when abruptly she stopped. She was standing in front of a display of glass sculptures, her gaze riveted on one in particular, a flowing form of a mother and child. Her touch was almost reverent, her fingertips gliding lightly across the surface, coming to rest at the base.

Beau stepped closer to her and murmured, "You have the look on your face that makes salesclerks' eyes light up."

His voice startled her, made her jerk her hand back and step away.

"Meg's not pregnant, is she? Because if she's not, it doesn't seem quite appropriate."

"No. No, as far as I know, she's not." She glanced at the statue again. "Would it matter if she were?"

"Not to me," he teased. "I've never gotten close to her." He shifted his gaze back to the statue. He could see why it had caught Laurel's eye. It was simple, elegant, and made a powerful statement about the love of a mother for her baby.

Conspicuously missing from the shelf, though, was a similar statue of father and child. Probably because the artist knew what Beau knew—that good fathers were rare and lousy ones plentiful. Hell, with the long history of rotten fathers in the Walker family, he was probably predisposed to become one himself.

Which was why he never intended to become one at all.

With one last look at the statue, Laurel moved on, and he followed, gazing disinterestedly at handmade earrings of beads, feathers and stones, at leather bags, quilts, crocheted doilies, beeswax candles. When she stopped again, at first he thought they were back at the statue of mother and child, but a glance showed that it was a different display by the same artist.

This time she picked one up, a large, heavy piece of softly rounded mountains stretching off into infinity. The glass was textured in places, frosted in others, crystal clear in yet others. It would blend perfectly with the contemporary style Meg had chosen for their house.

"What do you think?" she asked.

"It's nice."

"It's the view from your deck."

He moved behind her, studying it from her perspective. She was right. There was a valley here, a peak there, twin balds over there. There was even a textured ribbon of bubbles in glass exactly where a narrow, unnamed river wended its way down the mountainside. It wouldn't look bad in Meg and Kevin's new old house.

It wouldn't look at all bad in the rustic stone-and-wood of his place.

"Are you thinking of getting that for Meg?"

"Oh, no. She wouldn't appreciate it." She started to return the piece to the shelf, but he stopped her.

"Then I'll get it. For me. My house can use a few more things in it." He paid for it, waited while the clerk boxed it, then took it to the truck before meeting Laurel again in the next store.

When they left the last shop, she sighed. "I may have to settle for a wine glass or butter dish or something. I just wanted to get something that she might look at or actually use once in a while."

It was just a wedding gift, he wanted to remind her, and only one out of dozens. It wasn't a big deal.

But to her it wasn't *just* a gift. It was restitution, making amends, asking forgiveness, and for that it needed to be special. A wine glass or butter dish, picked off the same wish list made available to strangers who'd never met Meg, just didn't qualify.

"There are other stores in town," he said. "I'm in no hurry."

But after wandering through more than two dozen shops all over the city, offering everything from one-of-a-kind crafts to antiques to flea-market junk, he was tired, and it was approaching closing time at the mall.

They went straight to the department store, where he spent an obscene amount on a matched set of beer steins. Looking glum, Laurel chose a set of hated wine glasses, handed over the cash and reluctantly accepted the shopping bag the clerk offered.

"Look at it this way," Beau suggested in an effort to cheer her. "At least she can't fault your taste."

"Don't count on it. These days Meg's able to find fault in everything I do."

Once they were settled in the truck, Beau headed out of the city and back toward Angel's Peak, with one large box and two fair-sized bags between them. There'd been a time when Laurel had never sat farther than an inch or two away, when they'd gotten more intimate than any car seat was ever intended for, when every hello and goodbye in her mother's car or his took long, hot minutes and bordered on indecent.

A time when anything—everything—had seemed possible in his life. After all, he'd already done the impossible in winning the affection and favors of the elder Cameron daughter.

Lately it seemed he was remembering that feeling more and more. As if old wrongs could be righted, old wounds healed and old dreams fulfilled. As if anything *was* possible.

Including regaining the affection and favors of the elder Cameron daughter.

"I appreciate your patience," she said. "Bud— Most men don't like to shop."

Buddy didn't like to shop. That was what she'd started to say before catching herself. For whatever it was worth, Beau wasn't fond of the pastime, either, but he couldn't imagine a better way to spend a summer Sunday afternoon than following Laurel wherever she wanted to go.

Well, one better way did come to mind. Maybe next Sunday or the Sunday after that. Maybe every Sunday until they were both too old to manage.

"I don't care much about shopping, either," she went on, her cheeks still pink from her near-slip. "It's been so long since I've had the money for more than the essentials that it's not much fun. But I love these places that call themselves antique stores but really just have old junk. I've found some great old pottery bowls for a dollar or two, and

I had this wonderful serving platter that I picked up for a few bucks—'' She stopped suddenly, and her expression took on a distant look. When she spoke again, her voice was softer. ''I only brought what clothes I could carry when I came home. I left everything else behind. The landlady probably took what she wanted and trashed the rest.''

He remembered the two bags she'd had when he'd given her a ride home that first morning. Both had been torn and tattered, and not big enough to hold more than a few outfits. Five years away, five years of working tough, dirty jobs for minimum wage and sometimes tips, and that was all she had to show for it: a couple of small bags of ill-fitting clothes.

He'd definitely had it easier.

''Where did you leave everything else?'' he asked, keeping his gaze on the road.

''Arizona. Tucson.''

''It gets awfully hot there.''

She laughed. ''You aren't kidding—and it's *dry* heat. All my life I've heard people complain about the humidity in the South, but I missed it. Once we—once I got into the desert, I felt as if I were going to shrivel up and blow away. I couldn't breathe. I'd walk outside and feel the sun sucking the moisture out of my body. It was such a relief to get back to the South.''

''What was your favorite place?''

She didn't hesitate. ''New Orleans. I'd love to go back.''

''What was your least favorite?''

Again, there was no hesitation. ''California.''

''Why?''

She looked out the window at the mountains around them, and her voice took on a wistful note. ''Because it was so far from home.''

''If you were homesick, why didn't you come back?'' When she didn't answer, he prompted, ''Was it because of me?''

"Partly. After what Skip did…" Her shrug was eloquent. "I couldn't stay. I couldn't live with what I had done."

Beau's fingers tightened around the steering wheel as he forced the tension there and out of his voice. "You had it right the first time. *Skip* did it. Not you."

"He did it because of me. That whole night was my fault—standing you up, going out with him, knowing there would be trouble. I just didn't think…" She let the words trail off, then shuddered. "I didn't think, as usual, and you had to pay for it."

Trouble. It was a mild word for one of the two worst times in his life. He had left the restaurant that night in a jealous, wounded rage and driven aimlessly around the county. He had been back in town and on his way home when McCandless had flagged him down. Because he'd thought Laurel might still be with the guy, he had stopped. But it hadn't been Laurel waiting in the bastard's car. It had been his friends, and between the four of them, they'd given him a beating more brutal than any his old man had inflicted. Bleeding and battered, he'd made it home, as far as the couch, where he'd spent the night in a world of hurt, where he had still lain the next morning when she came to see him.

Trouble. Yes, there had been trouble.

Part of him wished he could absolve Laurel of her guilt, but the truth was, she wasn't blameless. She'd made a deliberate choice to stand him up that night and to go out with McCandless instead. Not a malicious choice, by any means. He knew her well enough to believe that she truly hadn't wanted anyone hurt, that she'd had no idea when McCandless had taken her home what his plans were. She would have tried to warn Beau if she'd known. That whole night had simply been one more of the confused, bewildered, bad-judgment mistakes that had filled her life back then.

"It wasn't a reason to leave home."

She smiled sadly. "It left me with no other choice. And what happened the night I left ensured that I couldn't come back."

He didn't remember anything about the night she'd left—didn't remember anything about a lot of nights back then—but he remembered the next day. The news couldn't have spread quicker if the Camerons had posted a banner over the main street downtown announcing that their daughter had run off with the most worthless, no-good bastard to ever set foot in Angel's Peak. Jenkins's friends had bragged about it. Laurel's enemies had snickered over it.

That was the other, the absolute, worst time in his life.

"What happened that night?"

She opened her mouth, closed it and, he suspected, was seeking a way to answer his question without disregarding his foolish request of yesterday. He gestured impatiently. "You can use his name."

Ironically, she didn't. "I was desperate to leave Angel's Peak. I asked him the first time we met to take me away, and he finally agreed. We went to the house so I could pack. When I came out, his Harley was parked under the tree where I'd left him, but there was no sign of him. He came out a few minutes later with a bag filled with stuff he'd stolen from the house. Among other things, he took silver that had been in the Cameron family for generations and the diamond earrings Bryce gave my mother on their anniversary. And I let him take them because I was afraid that if I didn't, he wouldn't take *me*." When she looked at him, she resembled nothing so much as a lost, frightened little girl. "Mom and Dad think *I* took those things. They think *I* stole from them."

"I don't believe that. Whatever else you were then, Laurel, you weren't a thief. They know that."

"But Meg says—"

"Meg, who thinks she wants nothing more than to chase

you away? You're going to take Meg's word for anything?"

"But—" For a moment, she looked confused, then resignation claimed her features. "She said she would tell Mom and Dad the truth if I went away until after the wedding. She was watching from her window that night, and she saw him come out with the bag. Douglas saw us, too. He was coming home from a date. But when he saw us, *I* was holding the bag. *I* was the one looking so damn guilty."

Beau slowed for a red light ahead and realized that they were back in Angel's Peak. He hadn't even noticed the passage of the miles. About four and a half more, and their time together would end.

For today. But there was always tomorrow.

The conversation lagged until he pulled to a stop near the inn's back door. There he faced her. "Probably the only thing you're guilty of, Laurel, is bad judgment. Your parents know that."

Her only response was a faintly hopeful smile that disappeared too soon. Then she opened the door, clutched her shopping bag to her chest and left the truck. Turning back, she politely said, "Thank you for lunch. And for taking me to Asheville. And for being so patient."

This time he was the one who responded with just a gesture—a nod. If things were different, he would walk her to the door. Maybe she would invite him inside. Maybe he would kiss her goodbye. Definitely they would make plans to be together again.

But things weren't different—not that different, not yet. With another of her timid little smiles, she closed the door and crossed the yard to the steps. A moment later that door closed behind her, too. There would be no lazy evening together, no sweet kisses, no definite date to look forward to. But all in all, it hadn't been a bad way to spend a day.

Not bad at all.

Chapter Seven

Laurel was on her knees weeding a bed of bright fuchsia periwinkles Tuesday afternoon when a shadow fell over her. Wiping her sleeve across her cheek, she looked up, grateful for the temporary shade but not thrilled by who provided it.

As usual, Meg looked angry with the world—or, at least, Laurel's place in it. "It's one thing to work as a gardener, particularly when it's the only skill you have," her sister said, "but do you have to look the part?"

She *did* look a sight, Laurel imagined. It was a hot day, and she'd spent most of it in the sun. Her cotton gloves had made her hands sweat, so she'd discarded them hours ago, and now her hands were caked with dirt, her nails black with it. Her hair was wet underneath the ball cap, her clothes were damp and limp, and she smelled more than a little rank.

Ah, the rewards of a hard day's work.

"You know, gardening has long been considered a perfectly suitable hobby for genteel Southern ladies," she said, keeping her voice even, her tone mild.

"Well, you're a Southerner. One out of three..." Meg moved a few feet into the shade cast by a live oak, laced her fingers together and said, "My friends are giving me a shower tonight. Mama insists that I take you with me, so be ready at six."

Laurel thought longingly of a long bath and a quiet evening curled up in bed in her nightshirt. She was tired, bone tired, and couldn't imagine anything less appealing than an entire evening with Meg, Darla Wells and the other perfect little princesses who rounded out their circle of friends. She would have nothing to say to them, nothing in common with them.

Except Meg. For Meg she could do it. But that wasn't her sister's intent at all.

"I'll drop you off in town, and you can amuse yourself until the party is over. That way I can enjoy my own wedding shower, you won't have to try to relate to my friends, and everyone will be happy—most especially Mama."

Laurel leaned forward to pluck an imaginary weed, smoothed the mulch, then sat back and fixed her attention on her sister. "Why are you being so difficult, Meg? I've given you my word that I won't disrupt your wedding."

"And I've told you that your mere presence is a disruption."

"I know I've let you down—"

"You never let me down. I learned at a young age not to count on you for anything but trouble, so how could I be disappointed by anything you did?"

"I was your big sister, and we were close—"

"Not that close," Meg interrupted. "It's hard to be close to someone who cares only about herself."

Laurel resisted the urge to point out that she was learning that firsthand. Instead, she took a deep breath, curbed her tongue and tried again. "I know I made some major mistakes, but I'm trying to get past that. I'm trying to start over again, and I need to do it here. I need to be a part of the family again. I need to belong again."

For a moment she thought she might have reached her sister, but hope died as mockery crept over Meg's face. "Typical Laurel," she said scathingly. "You never gave a thought to this family when you were breaking Mama's and Daddy's hearts, when you were making life miserable for everybody. No, you only care when it's convenient for *you*—when you need a family, when *you* can benefit."

Laurel's sigh was weary. She was wasting her breath. Meg wasn't ready to believe her. She certainly wasn't ready to forgive her. She might never be.

In the meantime, the least Laurel could do was grant Meg's wish for tonight. "What do you want me to do?"

"Clean up, dress up, pretend you're going to the party with me. I'll drop you off in town, and I'll pick you up when the shower's over. When we get home, you tell Mama we were together all evening and had a reasonably pleasant time."

"And what if someone tells her I wasn't at the shower?"

"These are my friends. None of them will tell anyone." Meg's gaze narrowed. "Will you do it?"

"I'll be ready at six." Affecting a casual shrug, Laurel turned back to her work, concentrating hard until Meg was gone. Then she sank down again and sighed. She had no one to blame but herself. She had disrupted everyone's lives ten years ago, had kept them disrupted right up to the present. If she didn't like the way any of them treated her now, it was her own fault.

But of all the people she'd expected to hold grudges, Meg was the last. She had always been so sweet, had always adored her big sister, no matter how she might deny it. Now she was the angriest, the most bitter, the least forgiving.

At last, legs and back aching, she got to her feet. How

much longer would she be able to handle the physical demands of this job on a full-time basis—the bending, the lifting, the kneeling? At least through the summer, she hoped. She wanted to see the garden and lawn through its winter preparations, wanted to live up to every one of the obligations she'd taken on with this job. If she could manage that, then by next spring, she would be strong again, ready to begin the work all over again.

But today her back hurt, and she was in need of a long, hot bath.

By a quarter of six, she was feeling better and looking it, too. No evidence of her day digging in the dirt remained, except for the pink that crept across her sunburned nose and cheeks. All the grime had been soaked away, along with most of the aches and the fatigue. She felt ready for an evening doing...whatever. Eating in a restaurant alone. Sitting in a park. Wandering the streets of Angel's Peak. Being someplace she didn't want to be while pretending to be someplace she wasn't wanted.

One last time before going downstairs, she checked her reflection in the mirror. Her hair looked fine—as short as it was, it had no options—and her sunburn was barely pink. Her dress, left over from five years ago, was a simple cotton sundress, nothing special. She was probably underdressed for a shower with Meg and friends, but since she wasn't going, what did it matter? She wouldn't embarrass herself in the plain yellow dress.

On the way out of the room, she picked up her purse. Downstairs she found Leah and the kitchen staff preparing for dinner. "I can stay and help with this," she volunteered, hoping against hope that her mother would accept her offer.

Of course she didn't. "No, thanks, hon. You and Meg have a good time tonight."

Her mother's obvious pleasure at the thought of her elder daughters spending an evening together pricked Laurel's conscience. She hated misleading Leah, but what choice did she have? She could lie, or she could ruin one more of Meg's special occasions. It really wasn't a major lie, she rationalized, and telling the truth—that Meg would go to such lengths to keep Laurel out of her life—would only hurt their mother. The deception was for the greater good. This way only *she* got hurt.

"With both of your waitresses gone, who will handle the dining room?" Laurel asked in one last, halfhearted effort.

Leah laughed. "I've waited a few tables in my life. Besides, all those teenage girls with us this week think Matthew's just about the cutest thing around. They'll be thrilled to have him as their waiter."

And he, being a typical male, would be happy with the attention. Laurel accepted defeat with half a smile as Meg came down the stairs. She wore linen shorts and a matching, fitted vest, with her hair pulled back in a French braid and no jewelry but a gold chain around her neck and Kevin's engagement ring on her finger. She looked cool and beautiful and aloof enough to make Laurel's heart ache.

"You girls have fun," Leah called as they left.

"We will," Meg dutifully answered.

A corresponding lie couldn't clear the lump in Laurel's throat.

The drive into town was silent. Meg stopped in front of Angel's Peak's sole movie theater, tossed a twenty-dollar bill into Laurel's lap and waited impatiently. "I'll meet you here at nine-thirty."

And what was she supposed to do in the meantime? Laurel wanted to ask, but it would be pointless. All that mattered to Meg was that Laurel stay out of her way. Whether she did it by having dinner, seeing a movie or twiddling her thumbs on the street corner was inconsequential.

She climbed out of the car, stepped onto the sidewalk and watched as her sister drove away without so much as a glance back.

With a sigh, she looked around. The movie wouldn't start

until seven-fifteen, and, judging by the violent colors and explosive action depicted on the posters, it wasn't something she had the stomach for. She could go window shopping over on Main Street, one block over, but Sunday with Beau had been enough shopping to last her awhile. She could simply walk around town—Angel's Peak was safe enough for that, even after dark—and reacquaint herself with sights she had once known well, or she could cover the short distance to any of Angel's Peak's restaurants and treat herself to a leisurely, solitary dinner.

A grumble from her stomach settled the question. Dinner first, and some other way to pass the evening later.

The town didn't suffer from an overabundance of restaurants, but most of them were good and, thanks to Meg, she could afford dinner for one in the best of them. She settled on one at the lower end of the scale, though, an old-fashioned hamburger drive-in that offered the best burgers in three counties and the best memories of her rebellious life.

She ordered the burger basket and a chocolate malt and carried the tray to one of a half dozen empty picnic tables out front. The table was wobbly, its fake redwood planks warped from sun and rain, and the bench was warm from the day's heat. She had spent many an evening right there, with food in front of her and Beau beside her, surrounded by their friends while the other kids in town—the good kids—stayed close to their cars.

Five years later, and she was still relegated to the outcasts' seating.

She was halfway through her meal when a tray appeared on the table across from her. An instant later Beau swung his leg over the bench and sat down. He took his time—sliding a straw into his drink, salting his fries, scraping shreds of lettuce from his burger—before looking at her.

She gestured to the pile of greens. ''Did you finally give

up asking them to hold the lettuce, or is their motto still 'Have it your way—as long as your way is *our* way'?''

"I gave up. What are you doing here all alone?''

She considered a simple lie—just having dinner, revisiting old memories, passing time—then told the truth. "Being a good sister and giving Meg the best shower gift she could have.''

"What is that?''

"My absence.'' Her answer made him look uncomfortable, and she shrugged. "It's all right. The last way in the world I wanted to spend my evening was with Darla Wells and that bunch. I'd much rather have dinner all alone.'' Not that she was alone now. With Beau might be the *best* way in the world to spend an evening.

"So if you didn't want to go with Meg, why didn't you just stay home?''

"Mom insisted that Meg invite me. It would have hurt her feelings if either of us had refused.''

"So the Cameron girls are lying to their mother.''

She didn't need the reminder. She felt guilty enough about it. "I'm sorry to say, I've done it before. It's probably a first for Meg, though.'' She dipped her last French fry in ketchup and ate it before asking, "What brings you here?''

"I was on my way home when I recognized a familiar face in a familiar place. Since a man's gotta eat...'' He finished with a shrug.

"It hasn't changed at all, has it?'' she said with a look around. Large plate glass windows looked in on the activity inside, cars came and went from the parking lot, teenage girls on inline skates delivered orders and picked up trays, and fifties music played from crackly speakers overhead.

"Only the faces are different,'' he agreed. "We're the ones who've changed.''

"We spent a lot of time here,'' she remarked softly, wistfully.

"At this very table—though usually not on opposite sides."

No, usually they had shared the same few square inches. Depending on the number of friends who had joined them, she had sat anywhere from next to him to snuggled right up on his lap. They had eaten, talked, socialized, partied and necked right here.

Sweet memories from a sad time.

Forcing herself back into the present, she locked her gaze on him. He wore jeans and a T-shirt, with a sprinkling of plaster dust across the right shoulder. He looked handsome. More than handsome. He looked dangerous to any woman's heart. "How was your day?"

He shrugged. "The reproduction plaster medallion that we ordered for the chandelier base in the blue house's living room got broken in transit, so we had to send it back to Savannah. One of my men smashed his hand with a hammer and broke it—the hand, not the hammer. Half the crew wants vacation at the same time, and we're having a hell of a time finding some of the fixtures we need. Just a typical day." Then he grinned. "Oh, yeah, and the crew spent half their days going back and forth to their trucks hoping to catch a glimpse of the new gardener over at the inn who spent the whole day outside in shorts and a little T-shirt."

"That shirt was perfectly modest," she said, her cheeks pink from the fact that she'd been noticed. She'd spent entirely too much time looking in the direction of the construction site, hoping for a glimpse of *him*, but she hadn't noticed any of his crew ever looking back.

"Maybe, but we've all got good imaginations. In fact—" his voice turned a shade husky "—some of us don't need to imagine."

The pink turned to red as heat washed over her. "*One* of you," she corrected. "Only one of you." After a cooling drink from her melting malt, she cleared the huskiness from her own voice. "What is the gardener supposed to wear in this heat? Long sleeves and overalls?"

"That would be a shame. Most of the crew voted for a swimsuit but figured that was out of the question."

She thought of her body, the changes it was undergoing now and the changes yet to come. In her two weeks home, she had gained about ten pounds that everyone attributed to Colleen's cooking. Since she'd been underweight to start, it wasn't a lot. She looked at herself naked every morning and saw no telltale signs of pregnancy—no rounded belly, no swollen breasts, no pale stretch marks. But all that would come.

And when it did, no man in town would be interested in looking. Not Beau, not his crew, no one.

"Definitely out of the question," she said dryly.

He accepted her answer if he'd expected no other and changed the subject. "How's the garden project between the three houses coming?"

"Slowly. I've done some sketches, but we can't actually do anything until after Meg's wedding. Mom wants everything to be perfect for that. No uprooted trees, no clear views to the work site, no exposed dirt to muck things up."

"You want it to be perfect, too, don't you?"

"I'm just trying to earn my salary," she replied, but it was far from the truth. Money wasn't the reason she'd spent the last two full days working outside, weeding every bed, watering and fertilizing the flowers so they would be at their peak. She had cut off every dead blossom, trimmed back plants run wild and pruned shrubs, and she planned to spend several more days mowing, raking, making everything just *so*. Whatever other flaws Meg found in her, she wouldn't find *anything* wrong with her work. The setting for her wedding would be, like her, perfect.

"You're a good sister," Beau said quietly.

The comment both warmed and saddened her. "I used to be. We were very close as kids. We shared a room even when we didn't have to. When she moved into her own room, she still slept in mine half the time. We used to lie in bed with the moon lighting the room and make wishes on stars and talk about what we were going to be when we grew up. Meg wanted to stay right here in Angel's Peak, to be the umpteenth-generation Cameron to make a contribution. She wanted be a schoolteacher, a wife and a mother.'' Her smile quavered. ''It looks like she's going to have it all.''

''And what were you going to be?''

She looked away into the past, remembering, then shrugged, her tone becoming dismissive. ''I had a dozen dreams. I wanted a career, travel, excitement and glamour. I wanted to do whatever my heart desired and do it in a hundred different places. I wanted to speak exotic languages, eat exotic foods and live my life with no responsibilities to anyone but myself.''

But those were only a few of her dreams—the few she had nurtured because they were different from everyone else's dreams. Her other desires had been simpler and similar to Meg's. She'd wanted to stay close to her family, to marry and live out a fairy-tale romance, to have babies and a home all their own. *Those* were the dreams she'd nurtured in the last five years. Such ordinary dreams easily attainable by practically anyone.

Except her.

''It's not too late to do those things.'' Again he spoke quietly, almost cautiously.

She shook her head with a smile that was part regret for things she no longer wanted and answered instead about the dreams she did want. ''It is for me. For a while, at least.'' She doubted that there really was a fairy tale out there with her name on it. Her mother had found one, though, and Meg seemed to have one of her own. Of course, much of Meg's whole life had been a fairy tale, except for the parts that Laurel had touched.

Maybe somewhere down the line, when her baby was grown, when she'd proved with long years of quiet, responsible living that she really had grown up, that she could be trusted, that she had changed... Maybe then, when she had more to offer than another man's child and a reputation for bad luck and trouble, she would be lucky enough to meet her own Prince Charming and they would live happily ever after.

Of course, she'd already met one Prince Charming in Beau. How many was a fallen princess allowed?

Across the table, Beau recognized the brief flash of despair that crossed her face and wondered at its cause. Regret for the dreams she'd lost, for the excitement she'd missed, the exotic languages she'd never learned?

There wasn't much excitement or glamour in Angel's Peak. It was just a nice little town, a great place to be from, but maybe—for her—not a great place to be. Maybe she was already getting restless, in spite of her claim that she was home to stay. Maybe she was realizing that twenty-five was too young to give up her dreams.

Maybe she was thinking about leaving.

"Why is it too late?" he asked, though he really didn't want to know. "Why do you have to wait awhile?"

For a few moments too long, she busied herself with gathering the remains from her dinner into a neat wad and stuffing it inside the empty cup that had held a malt. Chocolate had always been her favorite, and she'd liked her fries crispy and cooked with thin strips of onion and jalapeño pepper. Concerned about adding an extra pound here or there, she'd eaten little more than rabbit food the rest of the time to make up for her indulgences, which made them that much better, she'd claimed.

He knew now that she'd been right. *She* had been *his* indulgence, and though she'd cost him a lot, he'd never regretted the sacrifices.

Unable to avoid his questions any longer, she finally

looked at him. "Things have changed. *I've* changed. I've seen enough of the world. I've had enough excitement. And I've learned that a life without responsibility isn't much of a life, because the only way to have that is to have no one in your life, and that's awfully sad."

It was a better answer than he'd expected—enough to make a man hopeful. "Then maybe you need some new dreams."

"Or maybe just a few old ones," she murmured with a distant look in her eyes.

He would like to think he was part of those old dreams, but the answer was difficult to guess, the question impossible to ask.

Flipping the plastic cap off his cup, he drained the last of the soda, crumpled the top of the cup and sent it sailing into the nearby garbage can. It'd been five years, but he hadn't lost his touch. "What are your plans for the rest of the evening? You just going to sit here until Meg finishes with her party and comes back for you?"

"Actually, I'm supposed to meet her in front of the theater at nine-thirty. She suggested I pass the time seeing a movie—in the dark, out of sight of the entire community—but frankly, I'm not up for mayhem and death tonight."

"I was planning to go by the nursing home this evening to see my dad. Want to come?" As soon as the words were out, he gave a wry shake of his head. "I know. Weird invitation. Forget—"

"I'd like to go." Her smile was wry, too. "I worked in a nursing home for a month or so in Texas, until—" she caught herself before Buddy's name slipped out "—until we moved on. I like old folks." She rose from the table and emptied her tray, then returned it to the counter beside the order window. By the time he got to his feet, she was waiting near his truck, hands clasped, looking incredibly young and beautiful.

After a quick stop at a convenience store, he drove the

half mile to the nursing home. It was situated on a quiet side street with the hospital two blocks in one direction and a funeral home two blocks in the other. It was the better of the two facilities in Angel's Peak—nothing special, but clean, neat, with a staff who genuinely cared about their patients.

Which made it pretty special, after all.

The grass had recently been mowed, leaving clippings sprinkled over the sidewalk. Between the lawn and the cinder-block building were a few sad flower beds, in desperate need of a little expert care. Laurel's attention went straight to them.

"If someone deadheaded those marigolds every few days and watered and fertilized them regularly, they would be big, gorgeous plants instead of those spindly little yellowing things."

"If someone volunteered her services to do that, I bet the folks inside—staff and patients alike—would be thrilled," he remarked as he shifted the bag he picked up at the store to one hand and held the door open for her.

She said nothing, but the look she wore as she passed through the door was thoughtful. He wouldn't be surprised to see the flowers in better shape the next time he visited. That wild Cameron girl volunteering at a nursing home. Whoever would have believed it?

Inside she looked around the large lobby with its vinyl couches, hard molded chairs and plastic plants and pointed toward a corner. "I'll wait over there."

"Come on back. He'll be happy to see a new face." Then he grimaced. "Actually, *my* face is new every time— at least, to him. Come on. He may be senile, but he hasn't lost his appreciation of pretty women."

With no hint of reluctance, she accompanied him past the reception desk and all the way to the end of the hall. He heard the television before reaching the door and knew what he would find before opening it—a room lit only by the TV and smelling of disinfectant, old age and death. There were two homey pieces of furniture—a dresser and a comfortable chair that was seldom used—along with the hospital bed that made a once-strong man look even thinner and frailer than he really was and an over-the-bed table on wheels. There would be a small bouquet of flowers from the garden, faded and losing their petals, and a ratty bathrobe of red and green plaid draped over the foot of the bed for visitors who rarely came and walks rarely taken.

This was his father's world—eight by ten dreary, grim feet. But with one look into Jim's face as he approached the bed, Beau amended that. His father's world was inside his head, where he lived a life that no one else could share, a life probably much better than the real one.

"Dad?" He switched on the overhead fixture, sending fluorescent light into the room, banishing shadows to the corners. "How are you, Dad?"

The eyes that met his were similar in size, shape and color to his own, but they were empty. Occasionally there was confusion, bewilderment or annoyance. Never recognition. Never affection.

But he had never seen affection when his father looked at him.

"I brought you a visitor, Dad. This is Laurel."

She circled to the opposite side of the bed. "Hello, Mr. Walker."

After a moment, the old man's gaze shifted her way, and he reached out with one trembling hand. "I know you." His voice shook as badly as his hand, was as weak and insubstantial as his body. Only ten years ago he'd had the power to lay Beau out flat on the floor with one punch, and his voice had been strong with anger, bitterness and derision. Now he wasn't even a shadow of his former self.

Laurel accepted his hand, holding it gently between both of hers. "How are you, Mr. Walker?"

"I've been better, and I've been worse."

She glanced across the bed at Beau, and he knew she knew he was agreeing most emphatically. Jim Walker had definitely been worse.

"Who are you?" the old man demanded, his voice quavering.

"My name is Laurel. I'm a friend of Beau's."

"I've got a son named Beau. Do you know him? I never see him. He never comes here."

Beau touched Jim's arm, drawing his attention. "That's not true, Dad. I come to see you at least once a week."

His father looked at him—looked through him—then turned fretfully back to Laurel. "His mother spoils him rotten. Says I'm too strict on him. A boy needs rules, and when he breaks them, he has to deal with the consequences. She's turned him against me—turned everyone against me. That's why he never comes to see me." Without warning, he changed the subject. "Do I know you? Who are you? What are you doing in my room?"

"Mr. Walker, I'm going to leave now so you can visit with Beau." She laid his hand on the quilt tucked tightly around him, gave Beau a faint smile and left the room.

As the door closed behind her, Jim started muttering again. "I've got a son named Beau. I never see the boy. He never comes to see me."

Beau spent fifteen minutes with the old man, answering the same questions a dozen times or more, listening to thoughts that rambled and meandered through the last thirty years. He gave him the cream-filled cake that the doctor allowed once a week, along with the chocolate soda, and wiped his mouth when he was done, and wondered all the while why the hell life was so unfair.

Finally, when his father dozed off, he turned off the light, lowered the volume on the television and went looking for Laurel. He found her in the lobby with a white-haired woman about four times her age, chatting as if they were the best of friends. He paused at the door to catch her eye, signaled for her to continue her conversation, then went outside to wait.

He was leaning against the truck, breathing deeply to clear his lungs of the nursing home smells, when she joined him. He wasn't sure why he'd wanted her to meet Jim, wasn't sure if he regretted it. He wasn't sure of anything except that he didn't want to find himself in his father's shoes someday—old, frail, alone and bitterly regretful of the love that had let him down a lifetime ago.

He didn't want to hate himself and everyone else for losing Laurel a second time.

She stopped beside him, wrapped her fingers around his and squeezed tightly for a moment. When she backed away, she spoke in a soft, gentle voice. "There's a little park across the street from the theater. Let's go there and wait for Meg."

At his nod, she circled the truck, climbing in as he did, closing the door as he did. He drove back downtown, parked and walked to the park with her. Not even a quarter of a block, the patch of ground had a pretentious name—Centennial Garden—and little to recommend it. There was no playground equipment to attract children, no blooms for the floral-minded, not much grass. Just one wooden bench underneath a spreading oak.

Laurel sat sideways at one end of the bench, her feet drawn onto the slats, her skirt tucked around her. She didn't ask any questions, didn't offer any opinions, but merely waited for him to speak.

He blew his breath out in a heavy sigh. "I'm not even thirty years old. I'm too young to have a father like that."

"When Annie's thirty, Bryce will be pushing eighty."

But he wouldn't be like Jim. Beyond the fact that they were both men, they'd never been alike and never would be.

"Seeing him usually doesn't bother me. I'm long past regretting the relationship we could have had, and I haven't

needed a father for years. It's just..." Just that he didn't
want to end up like Jim. Just that he'd spent enough of his
life alone, without responsibilities—the way Laurel had
once thought she wanted to be—and he knew too well what
she had finally learned: that having no one in your life was
sad.

And he was damn tired of being sad.

"Do you suppose family relationships have always been
so complicated, or have we made them that way?" she
asked, laying one arm on the back of the bench, tilting her
head to rest on her hand. "I mean, when the first Camerons
and Walkers settled in Angel's Peak, do you think they had
the same problems with their sons and daughters? Did their
children find their parents impossible to deal with? In thirty
years will *our* children find *us* impossible?"

Our children. He knew she was speaking in generali-
ties—his children and her children, not of the children they
could someday have together—but his mind insisted on a
literal interpretation. He could well imagine the intimacy
required to create such children, but the rest was beyond
his grasp. He couldn't imagine himself a father, not with
the visit to his own father so fresh in his mind. He couldn't
imagine accepting such awesome responsibility, of risking
such tremendous potential for damage.

Five years ago he couldn't have imagined Laurel taking
on such responsibility, either. The brash, self-centered, insecure girl he had known then had been the candidate least
likely to put herself second to anyone. But the woman she
had become, the woman who wanted people in her life...
It was easier to see the mother in her, easier to envision
her with babies.

That was something she would want. He felt fairly certain of it. Was it something he could learn to want?

In the warm dusk, with street lamps buzzing nearby,
quiet broken only by the occasional passing car and his

father's querulous voice still in his mind, he found no easy answers.

"I think the first Camerons and Walkers were too busy trying to survive to worry about anything else," he said at last. "As for the ones who came between them and us, who knows? Maybe family was more important a hundred years ago. Maybe relationships were easier. And maybe it only seems that way from the distance of a hundred years."

For a time silence settled between them—easy silence, the kind he imagined two people who knew each other well often shared. He didn't feel the need to talk—to rehash the past, speculate about the future or avoid mention of either one. Just sitting there on the same bench was enough.

After one long, lazy moment had stretched into another, she offered him a smile. "You don't have to stay here until Meg comes. I don't mind waiting alone."

"I'm in no hurry." What did he have to go home to? An empty house, a few hours of television, a long night in bed alone.

He shifted on the bench, not enough to face her but enough that she was more than just a blur in his peripheral vision. "Want to go to a wedding with me Saturday?"

"It's hardly necessary to ask. You know I'm going to be there."

"But I'm asking you to be there with me."

She turned her head away, as if the shadows behind them were of great interest, and softly asked, "Why?"

Was she concerned with what people might think? There probably would be talk, but, considering her reputation, that was a given anyway. Wouldn't such talk be easier if she wasn't alone and feeling like an unwelcome guest? Besides, maybe Meg wouldn't make her so unwelcome if she *was* with someone. Maybe her sister would count on that to keep her quiet and well behaved.

He didn't mention that, though. Instead he replied, "Be-

cause Darla Wells suggested that I should escort the most
beautiful girl there.''

''But she didn't mean me.''

''No. Darla has no shortage of ego. But I *do* mean you.''
He hesitated, then decided to play dirty. ''Are you ashamed
to be seen with me there?''

Her sharp gaze met his. ''Of course not.''

''Then you'll go.''

''If you don't mind sitting at the back and staying way,
way out of Meg's way.''

''I don't mind at all.''

A smile slowly curved her lips. ''Then I would like to
go with you.''

''Good. After the reception we'll go someplace for dinner.''

She nodded in agreement before looking away. Almost
immediately her features formed into a frown. Looking toward the street, he saw the reason. Meg had just pulled to
the curb. As they watched, she got out and looked at them
over the roof of the car. She looked impatient, put out
and—on seeing Beau—just a little bit ashamed.

''She's early,'' he remarked.

''After lying to Mom and dumping me here, her conscience probably wouldn't let her enjoy the party. One
more thing she can blame me for.'' Laurel dropped her feet
to the ground and slid to the edge of the bench. ''Thanks
for the company. I enjoyed it.''

For a moment she sat there, reluctant to rise and walk
away—but no more reluctant than he was to watch her go.
Finally she stood up. So did he, and they followed the path
to the sidewalk and the Cameron sedan. ''Hello, Meg,'' he
greeted her.

''Hey, Beau.'' Her shame was more obvious up close
and under the streetlight. Her face was flushed, and her
hand, resting on the car roof, was knotted in a tight fist.
Part of him felt sorry for her. Hostility and bitterness were

foreign to her. She no more knew how to handle them than Laurel had known how to handle her own emotions all those years ago.

But the stronger part of his sympathy lay with Laurel. All those years ago she'd been a confused, messed-up kid. Meg was an intelligent, responsible adult who should have better control than a troubled teenager.

The three of them stood in awkward silence for a moment, then Laurel touched his arm, the tips of her fingers brushing lightly over his skin. "I'll see you."

The words were quiet, a polite promise. They were enough to carry him through the next few days, but so much less than he wanted. He wanted more—more of a touch, more of a commitment, more of a goodbye. He wanted to take her home himself, to never take her home, to keep her with him until all this wanting was fulfilled.

He wanted everything. He settled for a quiet promise of his own.

"Yes, you will."

Chapter Eight

Saturday was as perfect a June day as any Laurel had ever seen. The temperature hovered in the mid-80s in the shade, and the humidity was only mildly uncomfortable. The sky was the perfect shade of sky blue, the clouds perfectly puffy and white. Meg couldn't have asked for a better summer day to get married.

Laurel sat on the window seat in her room, wearing the pretty kindergarten-teacher dress. Her hair was combed, her makeup done, and her ballet slippers lay ready to step into for the trip downstairs. She intended to put off that trip until Beau had arrived. She wouldn't risk running into curious townsfolk or a hostile sister until it was absolutely necessary.

The yard outside had been transformed in the last twenty-four hours. Rows of white chairs had been neatly arranged before a flower-decked dais. A gaily striped tent had been pitched off to one side, and more white chairs circled matching tables underneath the trees. Inside the tent, the kitchen staff was laying out service for a few hundred. Two tables were set up for the bar. Another was ready for Colleen's magnificent wedding cake, yet another for the groom's cake.

She caught occasional glimpses of her mother, beautiful in a mint-green dress, and her father, needing only his tuxedo jacket before escorting the bride. Douglas and Matthew were dressing in their own tuxes down the hall while, across the hall, Meg was preparing for her big day.

Everyone was busy. Everyone had something important to do. Except Laurel.

A knock at the door drew her attention that way. It was probably Annie, tired of being overlooked and in need of a little attention. That was fine, because Laurel was in need of giving a little. "Come in."

It wasn't Annie. She would have burst in, a ball of energy, and thrown herself across the bed or barreled right onto Laurel's lap. No, her guest opened the door with restraint, hesitated a moment, then came inside and pushed the door up—but not quite closed—behind him. "Your grandmother said I could find you here," Beau said with just a touch of awkwardness.

Laurel allowed herself a few long moments for the sheer pleasure of looking at him. He was dressed in khaki trousers and a white cotton shirt, open at the collar, the sleeves turned back. It was just the right touch of casual for a hot afternoon wedding, the sort of clothes the Cameron men no doubt wished they could wear. Of course, as guests, she and Beau didn't have to be as formal as the wedding party.

As guests. She was about to be just another guest at her own sister's wedding. The thought was enough to make her heart ache.

"I'm in hiding," she said as lightly as she could, though she heard the faint wobble in the last word.

"I thought it was the bride who hid."

"That's who I'm hiding from." She gestured carelessly. "Have a seat."

There was only one chair in the room, currently home to a tall stack of gardening books. He ignored it and sat instead at the foot of the bed. "So this is where you grew up."

"No. I grew up in Alabama. Texas. Arizona. This is where I lived."

"And dreamed all those dreams." He took a good look around. "It's awfully sweet. Not at all what I imagined for you."

It *was* a sweet room. The walls were lavender, the trim white. The coverlet on the twin bed was a patchwork of a dozen lavender fabrics. The curtains were eyelet, the pillows behind her back lace, and the lamp on the bedside table, with its beaded fringe, was as romantic as they came. "It's been this way since I was fifteen."

"And your parents kept it for you."

She nodded, then curiously asked, "What would you have imagined?"

"I don't know. Bold colors—red, maybe. No lace. No frills. A few signs of rebellion."

The walls in *his* bedroom, the parts that weren't stone or raw wood, were tomato red, as bold and rich as the green in the living room and kitchen. There was no lace, no frills. Just a strong, aesthetically pleasing room.

It certainly pleased her.

In response to his suggestion, she shook her head. "This room suited me. It was comfortable. I didn't feel quite so lost in it."

"A twin bed. No room for fun."

She laughed. "I was a teenage girl. I wasn't supposed to be having any fun—at least, not that sort."

"I always wondered about this room. I had this fantasy about sneaking in here at night and making love to you, with your brothers and sister next door and your parents downstairs. Of all the places off-limits to me back then, this was the *most* off-limits. I wasn't even allowed to come to the house. Setting foot in this room probably would have gotten me thrown in jail.'' He grinned. ''But it would've been worth it to know what I'd done and where I'd done it and that you had let me.''

''Worth it?'' She gave a shake of her head. ''You were a deluded young man.''

His grin faded. ''No. I was a man in love with a girl whose primary interest in me was shocking the hell out of her family.''

''That's not entirely true, Beau.''

''No, not entirely. But true enough.'' He moved to sit beside her on the window seat. ''What's so interesting out there?''

She turned to look out again. Guests were arriving now, some taking seats in the few shaded chairs, others standing in groups under the trees. She knew most of them—family friends, acquaintances from school and church, one-time friends of her own—but she felt little pleasure at seeing them. She wasn't looking forward to facing anyone she'd known before and during her wilder years, which ruled out virtually everyone except the groom's family.

Maybe she should have done as Meg asked—gone away and stayed away until after the wedding.

''Everything looks great.''

She murmured her agreement.

He shifted to face her. ''Having second thoughts?''

Her nod was solemn. ''People will talk.''

''So?''

''It's the most important day of my sister's life. She has a right to not have it disrupted by gossip about me.''

''People always gossip. If it's not about you—and probably me—it'll be about someone else.''

''She doesn't want me there.''

''Yes, she does,'' he said calmly. ''She just can't admit

it to herself. You're right, Laurel. It's the most important day of her life. If she forced you to stay away, she would later regret it. She's just not ready to make you feel welcome. She's not ready to— '' He stopped, leaving the sentence hanging, as his gaze shifted toward the door.

Laurel looked, too. She hadn't heard the door swing open, but Beau hadn't closed it behind him, she remembered. The subject of their conversation stood there, wearing a white cotton robe and looking as beautiful as she would in her wedding gown. She was stunning—and nervous. "I—I need some help with my dress."

Laurel bit back the urge to offer her own help. She wasn't up for rejections right now. "I'll find Mom or Grandma."

Meg's nervousness increased a few notches. "I thought maybe you..."

Beau nudged Laurel to her feet. "Go on. I'll wait in the kitchen for you."

Meg stepped aside to let him pass, then waited for Laurel's answer. She gave it with a nod and a gesture toward her sister's room.

"I thought your bridesmaids were helping you," she said as she closed Meg's door behind them.

"They're busy getting themselves ready." Meg discarded the robe and stepped into the dress she'd left lying across the bed, then turned to face the mirror, her back to Laurel. "If you could do the buttons..."

There was a long line of them, satin-covered and fitting into narrow loops, closely spaced down the back of the dress. Laurel started from the bottom and worked her way up, brushing her fingers lightly across the rich white fabric. It was a gorgeous gown, far more elegant and sophisticated than she would have expected. There were no yards of rustling fabric, no billowing lace, no ruffles and few frills— just a sprinkling of seed pearls on a sleeveless, fitted sheath depending on the drape of its fabric and its wearer to make it stunning. Meg did.

As Laurel finished with the last button, Meg finally spoke. "I've been so angry with you."

"I know. I caused a lot of problems. I disappointed everybody. I made the whole family so unhap—"

Meg interrupted. "You were supposed to be my maid of honor. Remember?"

All those long years ago, when they had planned the weddings they would someday have, many details had changed, from the groom to the setting to the wedding dress. But one thing had always remained constant—they would each be the other's maid of honor. Friends could be bridesmaids, but maids of honor *had* to be sisters. It had been a non-negotiable sisters pact.

"You promised to be my maid of honor, then you left. By the time you came back, it was too late. I was too angry."

Laurel met Meg's gaze in the mirror. "I'm sorry. If I'd had any idea you were getting married, I would have come back sooner."

"Didn't you have any idea that we missed you? That we wanted you back?"

"No," Laurel said softly. "I thought you were all better off without me. I thought you'd be happier without all the trouble I'd caused. I thought no one could ever forgive me, and Buddy agreed."

"Buddy? You listened to Buddy Jenkins instead of what you knew in your heart?"

Her heart had been broken over what she'd done to her family, what she'd done to Beau, and it had known nothing but pain, guilt and loss. "All I knew was that I was a lousy daughter who had hurt everyone who ever cared about her. I knew that I had brought a great deal of unhappiness to my family, and I had brought into their lives a man who would steal from them. I knew that I couldn't forgive myself, so how could anyone else forgive me?''

"Because we loved you." Meg's dark eyes welled with tears. "How could you not know that?"

Laurel's throat grew tight. "I was a very troubled kid. I didn't love myself, and I didn't believe that anybody else could."

"Well, you were wrong, and if you had stayed here or if you had come back sooner, you would have seen that and we wouldn't have worried about you and I wouldn't have gotten angry with you and I wouldn't be getting married today without you."

"You're not getting married without me. I'm here. I'll always be here."

For a long time Meg studied her, then—for the first time reminding Laurel of the younger sister to whom she'd been so close—she hesitantly asked, "Promise?"

"I promise."

After another long moment's study in the mirror, Meg turned and hugged her. In her sister's arms, Laurel felt as if a great burden had been lifted, as if everything would turn out all right, after all.

She felt as if she were really and truly *home.*

After a while, she eased away. "We're going to wrinkle your dress and make you late for your wedding."

Meg's smile as she drew back was supremely confident. "Kevin will wait."

"Then he's a smart man." Laurel picked up the headpiece from the dresser, a length of frothy tulle attached to a tiny-silk-rose-adorned band that fitted across the forehead and over the hair. As she worked it into place, careful not to disturb Meg's softly upswept hair, she asked, "Do you love him?"

"More than anything."

"I hope you two are always as happy as you are today."

She straightened the tulle so it floated down Meg's back, then stepped back. "You're gorgeous."

"So are you. It must run in the family." Meg's smile faltered, then disappeared. "I'm sorry for the way I've treated you. I've acted like a spoiled brat."

"Well, after twenty-two years of being perfect, I guess you're entitled," Laurel teased. "It's okay."

"For what it's worth, I had a lousy time at the shower the other night."

Laurel had suspected as much, but before she could say so, there was a rap at the door.

"Meg? It's time, honey." It was Bryce, come to escort his middle daughter down the aisle and give her away.

With one last adjustment to the tulle, Laurel wished her sister luck, opened the door to their father and slipped down the stairs to find Beau. He looked the slightest bit anxious as she approached him.

"Everything okay?"

She gave a great sigh of relief, followed by an equally big smile. Everything was much better than okay. Things were close to normal with her sister, she was no longer dreading this wedding, and she was feeling incredibly hopeful. If Meg could forgive her at the last minute, who knew what else was possible?

Slipping her arm through Beau's, she drew him toward the back door. "Everything's fine," she said. "Come on. We have a wedding to attend."

Beau didn't consider himself particularly sentimental—though others might disagree—but he had to admit that the wedding was quite an event. The ceremony had come off without a hitch. All the women, including flower-girl Annie, were beautiful, and all the men were solemn and handsome. It had been an oddly touching service for someone like him, who had no family but a father who didn't remember him, who had recently reconnected with the woman he'd once wanted to spend the rest of his life with.

He was beginning to suspect that he still did.

The bride and groom had taken leave a half hour earlier on their way to Asheville to catch a plane for the Caribbean, but the party was still in full swing. Beau leaned one shoulder against a tree, taking advantage of the shade, and watching the guests with idle curiosity. Some were eating, others dancing, but most gathered in the shade, like him, and talked. He'd seen a few curious gazes following Laurel, had heard a few voices drop into whispers when she came near. Either she didn't notice, or she was doing a fine job of pretending not to care. More likely, she was so relieved by and grateful for her apparent truce with Meg that she couldn't be bothered by what the local busybodies had to say.

She came toward him now, moving with the slow, easy grace that threatened to cut him off at the knees. She looked so lovely, so *womanly,* and she moved as if she knew all the secrets of her body, of his body. She said hello to a few people she passed, but her attention was primarily on him. Her sweet, satisfied smile was for him alone.

"What did you think of the wedding?" she asked, claiming a wide spot of bark to lean beside him.

"It was nice. The first one I've ever been to."

"It was my second in ten years." She smiled faintly. "With the first, they were friends of—of ours in Louisiana. They got married in jeans and T-shirts in the gravel parking lot of the bar where they'd met, and the only flowers in sight were the ones tattooed on the bride's arms."

Friends of Buddy's, Beau thought grimly, which meant the guy was a biker, a bum, a criminal or all of the above. Then he forced Jenkins out of his mind. There was no cause for jealousy. She wasn't with Buddy anymore. She was with *him.* "It didn't make you want to run out and get your own tattoos?"

"I'm not into pain," she said lightly. But that hadn't stopped her from experiencing a tremendous amount of it.

"A gravel parking lot," he repeated. "I suppose they rode off into the sunset on his Harley."

"Actually, as soon as the vows were exchanged, the party moved inside the bar, where they proceeded to drink each other literally under the table. They were passed out there when we left."

"Whoever said bikers weren't romantic?" he asked dryly. Watching her grandparents on the patch of grass serving as a dance floor, he asked a question that surprised himself as well as her. "Did he ever ask you to marry him?" *He. Him.* Buddy.

"No."

"If he had, would you have said yes?"

For a moment, she looked away, too, then shifted her gaze to him. He saw it in his peripheral vision, felt it in the heat that warmed his skin. "I honestly don't know. If I was lonely enough. If I felt lost enough. If he convinced me that I should."

It wasn't the answer he wanted—an unqualified no, not only *no* but *hell, no.* But it was a fair answer. It told him that she hadn't been in love with Jenkins. She hadn't run away with him because she needed him, hadn't followed him across the country because she couldn't live without him. If someday he came riding back into town looking for her, she wouldn't go running to him.

It was an answer he could appreciate.

"Want to go for a walk?"

Her question drew his gaze to her face. There was a little more peace in her eyes, a little less sorrow. She was a happier woman than he'd found in her room before the wedding.

He wondered if he could make her happier still. Could she ever look at him the way Meg looked at Kevin, the way Leah looked at Bryce? Could she ever commit to him the way her sister and mother had committed to the men in their lives?

Could she ever love him?

Drawing back from the serious path his thoughts were taking, he answered her question with a nod, pushed away from the tree and walked beside her toward the back of the property. They passed his truck and entered the woods that separated the inn from the two new additions, that offered shade from the midafternoon sun and privacy from the party behind them. The sounds carried—the voices, the laughter, the music—but they were shielded from view by distance and woods.

Laurel smiled apologetically. "The wedding was wonderful, and the reception is fun, but I needed a break from the crowd. I'm not very crowd friendly."

He pushed his hands into his pockets. "For your first major public appearance since your return, it's gone well."

"Not too many behind-the-hand whispers and pointed fingers," she said with an agreeable nod. "Enough of them, but not as many as I'd feared."

They walked a short distance in silence. When they came to a fallen pine blocking the path, she moved ahead of him. She didn't climb over or duck under but chose instead to use it as a bench, pushing against the bark with both hands to lift herself the few inches necessary to take a seat. With her hands folded in her lap, her feet swinging in midair, she looked young and carefree, like a child.

But she was no child. One look at her body, one glance into her dark eyes, one moment's reflection on the hunger stirring in his own body, were enough to confirm that.

Once again he chose a tree for support, hands in his pockets to hide the tension that knotted his muscles. A dozen feet separated them—a dozen feet that could be crossed in seconds if he gave himself permission, if she issued an invitation. For the moment he waited.

"We used to play in these woods when we were children," she said, her voice soft, her attention years distant. "Hide-and-seek or explorers or pioneers in the great wilderness. We were so young, so innocent—and so fortunate. After the way she was raised, Mom was determined that we would have absolutely, perfectly normal childhoods. And they were. Storybook perfect."

Like most of the town, Beau knew the basic details of Leah's upbringing—abandoned at the local orphans' home when she was about five, the fruitless search for her family, her teenage marriage to Terence Cameron. He'd given her four children, this property and not much else before leaving her a widow at the age of twenty-nine.

Through the family ties, though, Leah had met Terence's estranged cousin Bryce, and the rest was history of the happily-ever-after kind.

Just what did it take for a person to earn the happily-ever-after stuff? Luck? Fate? Right place, right time? He would like to know, because he thought he was entitled to a little of it himself.

Starting with Laurel.

A cooling breeze rustled through the leaves, bringing with it woodsy scents and swelling the music before it settled once more into distant strains. The band was playing a slow song now, one that called for intimacy, shared space, privacy. It was the sort of song that, danced with the right woman, could lead to things far more pleasant, more intense, more rewarding, than a simple waltz.

"Want to dance?"

For an instant he wasn't sure whether he'd asked or she had. But his throat was too tight to squeeze three small words through. His voice would have been huskier, thicker. His question would have been more intimate.

Slowly she slid to the ground, her slippers making no more than a rustle of sound on the pine needles that carpeted the forest floor, and took a few steps toward him. He met her halfway, already hot, already aroused, always needy. She stepped into his arms as naturally as if he'd last held her yesterday, not five years ago, and her body fitted there perfectly.

They moved in time to the faint music, needing little of the narrow clearing. Beau held her close, breathing deeply of her scents, remembering other dances, other times. Every time he'd held her like this, life had been better than good. With her in his arms, he'd held everything he'd ever wanted.

Some things never changed.

When the last strains of the song faded away, he murmured in her ear, "The music's stopped."

She didn't draw back, didn't lift her head from his shoulder, didn't open her eyes. "It'll start again."

"Laurel." Cupping his palms to her face, he lifted her head. Her lashes fluttered, revealing brown eyes dazed with sensation, with need and desire. He whispered her name again, soundlessly this time, then touched his mouth to hers. So sweet, so hot, so achingly familiar. He longed to take his time, to reacquaint himself with the shape of her lips, the taste of her skin, the texture of her innocent kisses, but his need for her—his hunger—had gone too long unfulfilled.

He slid his tongue into her mouth, taking this new first kiss to deeper levels immediately, but she didn't object to the sudden intimacy. She welcomed him, raising her hands to cling to his shirt, kissing him back, matching his desire, his impatience, his demand, with her own.

When the music began again, Beau found himself leaning against the log where she had sat, his feet braced apart, with Laurel between his thighs. He was hard. She was shivery. He wanted this contact—mouth to mouth, hips to hips—more than he wanted to breathe, more than he wanted anything. Still, when she pressed tightly against him, when he thought she just might crawl inside him, he ended the kiss and forced an inch or two between their bodies.

"We can't do this." His voice was harsh, barely functional.

First disappointment, then embarrassment, crept into her eyes, and she tried to wriggle free, making him groan at the effort. Abruptly she became motionless. Color flooded her face, and her gaze lowered to his chest. "I—I'm sor—"

"Come home with me."

Slowly she raised her head, bringing her gaze into contact with his. "But you said we can't—"

"Not here. Do you know how many times we've made love in the woods, on the ground or in the back seat of my old car?"

A shy smile touched her mouth. "I remember every time."

"I always wanted to do it right, to take you someplace that was worth going, but I never had anyplace." He brushed his fingers lightly across her hair. "Now I do. Come home with me, Laurel."

She studied him for a long moment. Debating the wisdom of agreeing to his request? Determining whether she wanted him enough to make the decision coolly, rationally, not in the heat of passion? That was what he wanted—clear thinking, logic and sense, no regret. It was easy for him. He wanted her. The dancing was nice, and so was the kissing, the touching, but even without all that, he wanted her.

He always had.

He always would.

"All right." Once the quiet words were out, she gently pulled free, turned and walked away.

He rested his hands on the log, the bark biting into his palms, and admired the view. She moved so easily, so unconsciously erotically. Watching her do simple things— brush her hair, walk, talk—had always turned him on more than the most overtly sexual actions of any other woman. This afternoon was no exception.

After a few yards, she turned back to look at him. "Are you coming?" she asked innocently.

He didn't try to resist the grin that spread across his face. "I'm right behind you, darlin'."

He caught up with her in three strides, then walked beside her out of the woods and back to his truck. They didn't hold hands, didn't touch at all. It wasn't necessary. The intimacy was there anyway.

At the truck she stopped and faced him. Her hands were clasped tightly together, and the shyness was on her face again. "I need to tell my mother I'm leaving."

"I'll wait for you here." He let her get a short distance away, then abruptly, though he didn't mean to, he spoke. "Laurel? Don't change your mind."

The self-assured, full-of-promise smile came back, doing wonderful things for her and wicked things to him. "Five minutes. I'll be back."

He waited beside the truck, his gaze following her progress through the crowd until he lost her in the shadows of the tent. Restlessly, he walked a short distance away, turned, then paced back.

Today's wedding had been a big success all around. Meg had had her dream day. Laurel had found some peace with her sister. And *he* had been invited to what was probably the social event of the year. He, who for years had never been welcomed in this house, who had been looked down on by many of the guests present today. He had finally become fully, completely acceptable.

Five years ago, ten, even fifteen, he had wanted very much to belong. He'd wanted to be anyone in the world besides who he was. Walkers were worthless, lazy, drunks, good for nothing. He'd had to work twice as hard to prove himself half as good. Too often he'd dreamed of being one of the privileged kids whose lives had seemed blessed.

Now he'd celebrated a wedding of two of their own with those same privileged kids. He'd dated some of them, considered others friends.

Only now it no longer mattered. Now the only thing he wanted was Laurel, who had also been privileged, though not so very blessed.

The back screen door banged close, drawing him around as Laurel came down the steps with a straw purse slung over one shoulder. All she needed now was a big straw hat tied with ribbons and a giant floppy bow to match her dress, and she would embody the quintessential Southern belle.

All she needed was nothing at all to embody every fantasy he'd ever had.

He helped her into the truck, watching as she tucked her long skirt out of the way before he closed the door. Once behind the wheel, he started the engine and carefully backed into the driveway.

Trying to ignore the nervousness settling inside her, Laurel looked out the window as he drove. The small parking lot was filled with cars, and the overflow stretched out in neat rows across the far end of the front lawn. Matthew's buddies had been hired as parking valets for the afternoon. Her younger brother was with them now, his tux jacket and cummerbund discarded. He waved as they drove past, and she returned the wave.

Silence accompanied them into town and all the way to the turnoff onto Beau's narrow, potholed road. Finally he looked her way. "You're awfully quiet. Having second thoughts?"

"No."

"You can change your mind if you want. I won't be angry. Disappointed as hell, but never angry."

Her smile trembled as she gave the same sure answer. "No."

Maybe this wasn't the best idea she'd ever had, not when she was going to break the news of her pregnancy to her parents tonight or tomorrow or the next day. Not when she would tell Beau immediately after that and, in response, he would tell her goodbye. Taking this next step in their relationship could be a surefire road to heartache.

Or maybe it was merely taking a chance—on him, on herself, on their future. Maybe it was believing in him, trusting him to be a better, kinder, more generous man than any she'd ever known. Maybe she was making her best effort at capturing a dream.

She'd argued the point with herself from the moment she'd left him at the truck to find her mother, and the bottom line remained the same: she wanted this. Whether it was good or bad, right or wrong, pleasure or heartache, she needed these few hours. She needed the intimacy, the affection, the pleasure, the satisfaction. She needed for a while to be just a woman, not a mother-to-be with responsibilities, obligations, limitations.

She needed Beau.

And, after her earlier talk with Meg, she was feeling awfully hopeful.

He drove between the fence posts that marked his property line and up the hill, parking next to the fledgling red tips. Surrounded by silence once again, they left the truck and went inside the house. She waited on the landing as he closed and locked the door.

When he turned, he looked faintly nervous. "Want something to drink?"

She shook her head.

His half smile was endearing. "Want to see my bedroom?"

She nodded and led the way into the room. The walls *were* tomato red, as she'd recalled, and everything was bold and rich. It was a wonderful room for what they were about to do, a perfect room for the memories she would treasure.

She walked to the tall windows and looked out over the

mountains. Beau came to stand directly behind her, his hands warm on her shoulders. "Nice view."

"Hmm," he agreed, but he wasn't looking out the window. She knew because his head was bent, his mouth brushing over her ear, her neck, her jaw. She shivered but didn't pull away. Instead she tilted her head back and to one side, giving him better access. His tongue touched her skin, his teeth nipped at it, and she gave a soft, shuddery sigh.

"Tell me what you want, Laurel," he murmured, his voice throaty.

"This. You. Everything."

He chuckled. "You've got me, darlin'. I'm here for the duration."

And how long was that? her little voice wondered. This afternoon? Tonight? Short term, long term or forever? As long as he got what he wanted? Until he found out that she carried another man's baby?

It didn't matter, not right this very moment. All that mattered was that he was here now and he was kissing her, seducing her. All that mattered was that *right now* he wanted her. Right now he needed her. Right now he probably even loved her.

Right now, that was enough.

And later… Later was soon enough for regret.

His hands slid down her arms, over her breasts, and made her moan. "Do you like that?"

"You know I do," she whispered. His hands were strong and warmed her skin through the thin fabric of her dress. He rubbed back and forth, gently squeezing, caressing, coaxing her nipples into hard peaks.

"What about this?" He deftly unfastened the top few buttons of her dress and slid his hands inside, callused skin to exquisitely sensitive flesh.

Her only response was a sound, a breathless, helpless, pure-pleasure sort of sound.

When he spoke again, the teasing was gone, leaving his voice intense, erotic, hypnotic. "Do you know how much I've missed you? How many nights I've wanted you? How much I've hurt over you?"

He didn't give her a chance to answer, but she couldn't have to save her life. All she could say was please. *Please.*

"Sometimes I thought I would never see you again— never kiss you, never hold you, never love you. Sometimes I thought I would die..." His voice grew hard, thick. "Turn around, Laurel. Kiss me."

She did as he demanded—turned in his arms, slid her arms around his neck, claimed his mouth. It was impossible to tell who controlled the kiss, who was more eager, more desperate. It was impossible to care.

The kiss went on forever, hungry, hard, feeding her arousal and robbing her of strength. She didn't know which of them made the decision to discard their clothing. She simply knew that suddenly her hands were on his shirt, fumbling over buttons, while his made quick work of her dress, opening it just far enough, sliding it off her shoulders, tangling her arms in it. While she tried to work free of it, he transferred his kisses from her mouth to her breast, to each straining nipple in turn, and she no longer cared about the dress. She no longer cared about anything but *this*—this exquisite sensation, this pleasure and pain, this emptiness and anticipation.

With the frenzied skill he'd developed five years ago, Beau worked his clothes off, then hers, without releasing her, without breaking contact with her body for more than an instant. His need for full contact—to slide inside her, deep, deep inside, and never pull out again—was strong, but years of ingrained caution were stronger. Leaving her for only the space of a breath in spite of her murmured protest, he took a condom from the drawer, dealt with it, then followed her down onto the bed and buried himself inside her in one long, endless movement.

Holding himself motionless, he closed his eyes. The setting was different, but the feeling... Oh, hell, yes, he knew this feeling—this sense of rightness, of belonging, of homecoming. He'd been here a hundred times before, had lost himself here, had found himself here.

He braced himself on his hands, knotted into fists and sinking deep in the soft covers, and gazed down at Laurel. She wore a faint, sweet smile, but when she felt his gaze and opened her eyes, the smile turned womanly and wicked. "Make love to me, Beau."

She'd made the demand—the plea—many times before, from the very first time right up to the very last. He had always had been happy to indulge her.

Today was no exception.

He set an easy rhythm and felt her hips rising to meet his, felt her fingers curling around his shoulders with surprising strength, pulling him to her, kissing him, seducing him all over again.

The need was strong, the hunger raw. He'd waited so long, wanted so long, and now the having was incredible. Amazing. Frightening. It had never been like this with any other woman. Never this sweet. This intense. This important. Never with anyone but Laurel.

But he had never loved any woman but Laurel.

Her breathing quickened, and her body tightened where it sheltered him. She forced him to move faster, took him deeper, held him tighter, as a flush crept over the long line of her throat to her face. She was close, so close, and so was he. All he needed was one more thrust, one more clenching of muscles deep in her belly, one more instant of pure, sweet torment, and then...

The thought slipped away as she cried out and arched beneath him, against him, and the trembling and quivering of her body proved to be exactly what he needed. With a moment's brief regret for the barrier of the condom, he surrendered to the release that rocketed through him. It tightened his muscles, robbed him of air and set off tiny explosions of light behind his tightly closed eyes, and it set one undeniable truth echoing in its wake.

All he needed was Laurel. In the past. In his present. Forever.

Five years ago, Laurel had been vain enough to think that her body was something to be proud of—the right weight with the right curves and exactly the right fullness to her breasts and hips. After all, she'd worked hard enough to ensure that.

Today, at the grand old age of twenty-five, pregnant and with the late-afternoon sun streaming across the bed through the west-facing windows, she was all too willing to turn onto her side with her back to Beau, with one arm tucked close, with one knee bent and drawn up. He was willing to let her.

He lay behind her, close enough that she could feel the heat radiating from his body, but not against her. His fingers trailed lazily over her back, making her shiver, leaving trails of goosebumps in their wake. "Do you have any idea how much I've missed you?"

She did, but she wanted to be told. "No. How much?"

"More than I can express. More than you can imagine."

"I can imagine a lot."

His fingers slid around her rib cage, brushed her arm away, stroked the curve of her breast. "Not enough. You were every dream I ever had, everything I ever wanted. You were the best and brightest part of my life."

His words saddened her. She could imagine a lot, but not that. Not being that important to anyone. Not back then.

She blinked back tears. "Then why are you here with me now? After what I did, after everything I destroyed, why are you here?"

Cupping her chin, he turned her face so he could look at her. "Because you're still the best part."

Her heart ached—and filled with hope. Maybe there was a chance for them, after all. If he could forgive her past, then maybe he could accept her future. Maybe he could love her *and* her baby. Maybe he could be a father—the kind he'd never had, the loving, generous, devoted kind every child deserved—to her child.

To Buddy's child.

Buddy, whose name she wasn't even supposed to mention.

Turning her face away again, she murmured, "You're a better man than I ever deserved."

His hand returned to her breast as he disagreed. "I'm exactly the man you've always deserved."

"You're pretty sure of yourself, aren't you?"

He squeezed her nipple and made her gasp, drew his hand across her belly and made her breath catch, slid his fingers lower for an intimate caress that turned her body to liquid. "I'm sure of you. I'm sure of this."

This made her eyes drift shut, made her blood pump heat throughout her body. *This* made her nerves hum and her muscles taut and sparked her desire as if it hadn't just been satisfied, as if it had gone unsatisfied for a sinfully long time.

He pressed against her, his body strong and hot, his arousal swollen against her hip. "I'm sure I can make you weak. I'm sure I can make you plead. I'm sure I can make you writhe—" he drew the word out, long, sinuous, sensuous, as his talented fingers drew the matching response from her body "—underneath me."

She had to struggle to get air into her lungs, to form coherent words, to issue a husky challenge. "Prove it."

His chuckle was deep and resonant in her ear. "I thought I'd already started."

For a time he simply continued to stroke her, sometimes intimate, sometimes not, as he spread lazy, damp kisses across her back, up her neck, across her jaw, down her arm.

Before long, it didn't matter where he touched because every caress had become intimate. His fingers tickling across her nipples or rubbing with slow, firm pressure down her thigh, his hand pressing against her hip or sliding between her legs—all were erotic, sending little bursts of heat and need through her. Before long, she was pushing back against him, opening more to his questing caresses. She tried to capture his hand, to guide his fingers to the one place she needed them most, but he resisted, using his free hand to imprison hers above her head.

"I know you're weak," he whispered in her ear between kisses, "because I can feel your body tremble. I can feel you writhe, too. What does that leave?" He bent over her, dragged the rough surface of his tongue across her nipple, dragged a ragged cry from her. "Oh, yeah. Pleading. Are you going to plead for me, darlin'?"

She did, breathlessly, eagerly. "Oh, please, Beau... I want you... I need you..."

The instant the last word was out, he was gone. Her hands were freed, her back cool where he had lain against her, her body one long ache from top to bottom. "Oh, please," she moaned, her voice vibrating with the same frustration that racked her body. "Please don't leave me, Beau."

And in an instant he was back, sliding in behind her, lifting her leg higher, positioning her to accept him from behind. He filled her slowly, so slowly, while his fingers continued to work their magic, creating pleasure so intense that she thought she might die. She begged him with words, with actions and soft little sounds, but still he teased her, tormented her, until finally, his voice little more than a rumble, he growled, "Okay, darlin'. Now."

Her completion was swift, powerful, numbing. The roaring in her ears muted the sounds of her own harsh cries. Her vision turned dark, her breathing stopped, and her mind went on sensory overload while great waves of pleasure washed over her.

Dimly aware of Beau's own finish, she mustered the strength to reach back, to touch his face, to feel his shudders. Once they'd passed, once he was still and spent inside her, he pressed a kiss to her palm, held her tighter and cooled her shoulder with an exhausted, satisfied sigh.

He'd said he was exactly the man she deserved.

She should be so lucky.

She'd gotten the man she deserved the night she'd ridden away from Angel's Peak with Buddy. But Beau was the man she wanted. The man she needed.

For whatever it was worth, Beau was the man she loved.

Chapter Nine

The sunsets must be spectacular, Laurel had said the first time she'd visited the house, and she'd been absolutely right. The sun bathed the sky in every shade from palest pink to deepest purple and shone gold on the tops of cloud banks thousands of miles above them. It created a show of light and color so breathtaking that, when it was over, she felt as if she should stand and applaud.

She didn't get to her feet, though. Instead she gave a great sigh, snuggled closer to Beau and murmured, "Wonderful."

"Thank you."

"The sunset," she said with an exaggerated roll of her eyes, then thought about the time they'd spent tangling the sheets on his bed, and amended her comment. "And you, too. You're pretty darn impressive."

"Only with you, sweetheart."

She scoffed at his answer, though deep inside, it pleased her immensely. "Oh, please—"

"I've heard that before," he teased. "You plead very nicely."

"You please very nicely." She rolled over on the quilt he'd spread over the rough-hewn boards and stared up into the sky. With the setting of the sun, everything around them changed. The sky grew darker and the stars became more visible. The temperature dropped a few degrees. The night songs of tree frogs competed with whippoorwills and an occasional owl's hoot. A lazy, comforting sense of satisfaction settled around them.

She *was* satisfied. Right this moment, she needed nothing that wasn't within arm's reach. Later she could come up with a few requests, but for this moment she was supremely content.

"You're a fortunate man, Beau Walker."

He didn't deny her assertion or offer a glib response. In fact, he gave it some serious thought before agreeing. "You're right. I am."

"You have your work. Your health. This house. Gorgeous sunsets. These mountains."

Before she could go on, he interrupted. "You."

She lay quietly. From bad luck and trouble to good fortune. That was quite a leap. Once she told him about the baby, would she fall back into the bad-luck category?

He nudged her with his elbow. "That's where you're supposed to agree."

Sitting up, she scooted closer to him and rested her elbow on his up-drawn knees. "Actually," she said, forcing a light tone into her voice, "I was trying to remember if anyone has ever considered himself fortunate to have me around. I don't believe so."

"I always did."

"And, as I told you in my room, you were a deluded young man."

"You're avoiding the issue."

"What issue?"

"Whether I have you. Whether you wanted me this afternoon or just sex. Whether we have something here or you're just occupying your time."

She gazed at him in the ever-darkening night, saw the vague insecurity, the need for reassurance. "All right," she said softly. "How is this for an answer? I'm falling in love with you. I don't know whether anything will come of it. A lot of things have happened between us. A lot will happen. I might break your heart. More likely, you'll break mine."

His gaze turned dark with a challenge. "Or maybe we'll live a long, happy life together."

That was her dearest, sweetest dream. The dream that seemed more possible with each moment. The dream that would make everything that had gone before worthwhile—all the pain, the sorrow, the guilt. It was the dream that could make her life perfect.

Or turn it into a perfect hell.

"Maybe," she agreed, her throat tight. Or maybe not. In another day or two, they would know. But tonight they would make the most of what remained of the best day of her life. Tonight she would pretend that he was right, that their happily-ever-after was just around the corner. Tonight she would pretend that their future was sunny and bright.

Tomorrow or the next day, she might pay for it.

The quiet between them was broken by a growl from her stomach. She grinned. "You promised me dinner after the wedding. Instead we got sidetracked."

"Who needs food when you can do what we did?"

"I need food *so* I can do what we did."

He sat up and got to his feet in one easy movement, then gave her a hand. "Want to go into town?"

She shook her head.

"Want to see what we have in the kitchen?"

This time she nodded. He shook out the quilt, folded it carelessly, then followed her through the French doors into the bedroom. While he returned the quilt to the closet, she went ahead into the kitchen, making her way through darkened rooms, switching on lights as she went.

She found chicken and walnuts in the freezer, onion, celery and mayonnaise in the refrigerator, bread in the pantry. When Beau joined her, they tossed together a quick chicken salad to fill thick sandwiches. For lack of anyplace better, they ate their dinner standing at the island.

"You need furniture," she stated, pointing out the obvious.

"We'll go shopping next Saturday."

Choosing sofas and chairs, tables and lamps, items of wood and cloth that would remind him of her every time he saw them, that would mark his house with her taste. She liked the idea tremendously. She liked the homeyness of it, the togetherness, the for-the-future-ness of it.

But it was *his* house, not hers. His furniture, not theirs. She was merely a guest whose welcome might too soon run out, and then he would be stuck with reminders of her that would diminish his pleasure in his own home. She couldn't be responsible for that.

"Buying furniture is a very personal thing," she said. "You have to choose what feels right for *you,* not someone else. You might not like my taste. Remember my lavender and white bedroom?"

He grinned. "That room all but shouts 'innocent virgin child.' But you're not a child anymore. You're not innocent, and I know for damn sure you're not a virgin."

"You don't have to look so pleased with yourself," she said, feigning a pout.

"If I recall that night clearly, *you* were looking very pleased with me."

"And as I recall," she countered, "you were looking very surprised."

"Of course I was surprised. With your reputation, to discover that you were a virgin... I was stunned—and very,

very grateful.'' After a moment, as if it didn't matter, he asked, ''Why were you?''

She prefaced her answer with a shrug. ''Everyone thought I was easy. My mother believed I'd been sexually active for years before that. The misconception suited me. It enhanced the reputation I was trying to build, and it was an easy lie to sustain. You know how boys are. They could never admit that they'd gone out with me and failed to score, especially when rumor said I would do it with *any-one*. So they lied, and I let them, and I waited for...''

The right time? The right man? What had made her give in to Beau when she'd refused everyone else? What had she sensed about him, felt for him, that made sex with him not only permissible but desirable? How had she'd known that he was right when all those others were wrong?

Instinct, perhaps. Intuition. Fate.

''I waited for you,'' she finished simply.

She could see that her answer touched him. Whatever her reasons for waiting for him, he was grateful that she had. So was she.

''I think the more interesting question,'' she said quietly, ''is why you were there to be chosen. You believed my reputation. You believed I'd been promiscuous with all those boys, but you wanted me anyway. Why?''

''From the first time we met, I thought there was more to you than the reputation. Underneath the bleached hair and the tight clothes and the oozing sexuality, I saw a sweet, confused, frightened girl who needed someone to take care of her, and I wanted to be that someone.''

''And that was why I chose you,'' she said with a faint smile. Because he had, at least in part, seen through her act. Because he'd treated her better than anyone else. Because he'd wanted to give to as well as take from her. Because he'd had feelings for her that went beyond the sexual.

And that was why, eventually, she'd ruined things between them. Because she couldn't deal with the intensity of those feelings.

She hoped against hope that Beau could deal with his feelings for Buddy. If he couldn't, this sweet new relationship was doomed to fail just as painfully as the first.

Across the island, Beau watched the emotion—brief panic—flit across her face and wondered what caused it. Old memories? Or new fears? *I might break your heart,* she'd said earlier. *More likely, you'll break mine.* Maybe he should have told her, promised her, that that wasn't going to happen, not now, not ever. She was all he'd ever wanted five years ago, and that hadn't changed.

Maybe he should have told her he loved her. Hadn't he lost her once before in part because she hadn't known how he felt? Hadn't she said it might have made a difference?

The moment for saying it had passed, but it would come again. When they returned to bed, when they made love again, before he took her home... He *would* tell her. He wouldn't trust her to understand what he refused to put into words. He would make sure she understood exactly what he felt for her. He would leave no room for doubt.

When they made love again... The mere thought was enough to stir his blood. Simply looking at her was enough to start the need building.

There was nothing provocative about her stance, her clothes, her behavior. She was leaning on the island, her arms folded and resting on the white tile. To accommodate the island's height, her feet were some distance back, her spine a graceful curve. The position would easily accommodate *him.* All he had to do was walk around behind her, lift her skirt, open his jeans...

He swallowed hard on a groan, felt the prickle of a cold sweat. Such nothing little thoughts to get so hard, to create such need. It was as if they hadn't spent the best part of the afternoon in his bed, as if they'd never satisfied just such hunger.

But a lifetime of wanting couldn't be quenched in one afternoon, and that was how long he'd wanted her. How long since he'd had her. How long before he would have her again.

With a soft sigh and a sweetly unaware expression, she looked up at him and became still. She knew. She could look at him and see that he wanted—needed—her, just as he could look at her and watch the same desire take hold. Her eyes grew darker, softer. Her breasts swelled beneath the soft fabric her crossed arms pulled taut. Her breathing shifted, changed, became shallow and irregular.

"What were we talking about? I forget." Her voice was insubstantial, her thoughts occupied elsewhere.

"Why you remained a virgin until you met me." He didn't sound much stronger, much steadier. "Did I ever tell you how much I appreciated that?"

She shook her head. "But you showed me."

He had, he recalled. That night and every other night, right up through this afternoon. In about five minutes, he was going to show her again.

"We—" She broke off to clear her throat, but the attempt failed. Her voice was throatier, more enticing, than ever. "We need to clean up."

"That can wait. I can't."

She looked at him—just looked—then slowly straightened. She circled the island and left the kitchen, flipping the lights off on her way, leaving him standing in darkness. The living room lights went off next, but he didn't need light to see. He could follow her blindly—could smell her fragrance, could, he fancied, feel the heat of her that charged the very air.

When he reached the night-darkened bedroom, the first thing he saw was her dress, a splash of subdued color on the moonlit floor, and the only thing he heard was the rustle of covers, of sheet sliding against bare skin. He stripped off his own clothes, grabbed a condom from the drawer and joined her on the bed.

She was eager to help with the condom—or maybe just eager to torment him. Her always graceful movements turned clumsy, her fingers fumbling over his swollen flesh, her hands forgetting their task and stroking, rubbing, petting, instead. When at last the latex was in place, he rolled onto his back, and she settled over him, taking him, giving a soft sigh when he'd filled her completely.

"Laurel." His face was in moonlight, hers in shadow, but he could feel her gaze lock with his. "I—"

She must have suspected what he was about to say, because she laid her fingers across his mouth. "Don't say anything in the heat of passion that you might regret later," she gently warned.

He pulled her hand away and indignantly asked, "Do I look as if I'm in the heat of passion?"

She moved lazily, thrusting her hips, sliding with agonizing slowness along the length of his arousal, then taking him deep again. The sensation was incredible, making him groan, making his body arch involuntarily against hers. "I think so," she replied, sounding both amused and further aroused by his response.

Sliding his hands to her hips, he held her motionless and treated her to the same shuddering pleasure. "So I am. But I know what I'm saying. I know what I feel." In truth, though, his mind was getting hazy, his words becoming more difficult to put into order. Maybe she was right. Maybe this wasn't the best time, not with her sitting naked astride his hips, not with their bodies so intimately joined.

Taking advantage of his silence, she slid his hands from her hips to her breasts, guided his fingers to her nipples. Then she began the torment for real, riding him, controlling him, taking him faster, harder, deeper, pushing him to the edge, then leaving him behind as release exploded through her. Unable to endure the helpless clenching of her body around his, an instant later he found his own satisfaction with a guttural cry.

When her body was no longer racked by shudders and his muscles stopped their spasmodic trembling, when her sobs subsided into manageable breaths and his heart settled into a nearly normal rate, he wrapped his fingers around the back of her neck and pulled her to him, nose to nose, gaze to dark gaze.

"I know what I'm saying, and I know what I feel," he repeated. He drew a deep breath, gentled his hold on her and said the words he'd never said before, words he'd never meant more.

"I love you, Laurel."

This wasn't the way she had imagined a declaration of love would feel.

Laurel sat on the window seat in her room, her arms wrapped around a once-favored stuffed bear who'd grown threadbare over the years but still managed to give comfort. It was Sunday morning, all the wedding guests had gone home, and the family had gone to church, except for her mother. Leah was downstairs in the office, preparing for the guests scheduled to arrive later this morning.

And Laurel remained here in her room, torn between sheer joy and enormous regret. On the one hand, she was thrilled—honored—that Beau had said he loved her. She knew he didn't use the words lightly, knew the admission was so rare that it must be true.

On the other hand, what if he didn't love her enough to accept her baby, too? Losing him would be hard enough if she believed that he merely wanted her. Now that he'd said the magic words, it would be impossible. *I love you*s didn't come along often enough in life. This was her first.

It could be her last.

She heaved a great, dramatic sigh that seemed to echo

through the room, weaving into the soft surfaces, seeping into the hard ones, until it surrounded her.

"That was a world-class sigh."

She looked up to find her mother standing in the open doorway, and a little of her hopelessness faded away. She was grown up and soon to be a mother herself, but she still found instant and immediate comfort in her mother's presence. The old Laurel would have scoffed. The grown Laurel hoped her daughter or son felt the same way in twenty-five years.

"Do you have any idea how many times I've seen you sitting exactly like that?" Leah came into the room, brushed Laurel's feet aside and sat down at the opposite end of the padded seat. "Maxwell saw you through a lot of problems."

Laurel looked down at the fuzzy bear. She'd slept with him, talked to him, cried on him. Maybe her baby would do the same.

"You were out late last night."

A flush warmed Laurel's face. Beau had awakened her around four o'clock, helped her into her clothes and brought her home. He'd kissed her thoroughly at the back door, fully awakening her and her desire yet again. She had watched from the kitchen window until he'd driven away, then tiptoed upstairs and to bed. She'd made little noise, and there'd been no hint that anyone was awake.

"Is everything okay with you and Beau?"

Laurel ignored the question, set the bear aside and sat straighter on the bench. "I need to tell you something."

For one moment, dismay was clearly visible in Leah's face. She looked as if she was running a list of all the worst-case scenarios through her mind. Was being pregnant on that list?

"You can tell me anything, darlin'," she said at last, her voice carefully tempered. "What is it? What's bothering you this morning?"

Laurel tried a few beginnings in her mind. *Remember back when you were seventeen and you got pregnant with Douglas and Daddy had to marry you?* No. She wasn't seventeen—she was old enough to know better—and Buddy wasn't going to marry her no matter what the reason.

With five kids, two of them young men, you know that no form of birth control is a hundred percent effective, don't you? No again. That was making excuses, and she was old enough—hopefully mature enough—to accept responsibility for her own actions.

Taking a deep breath, she opened her mouth, hoped the right words came and settled instead for a blurted confession. "I'm pregnant."

Leah stared at her, blinking, obviously trying very hard to show no reaction at all until she knew what reaction Laurel wanted from her. "I—I see," she said, sounding as off-balance as she looked. "Is this good news or bad?"

"I guess that depends on your point of view. How do you feel about being a grandmother at your age?"

"My age? Honey, I'm on the downhill side of forty. Ask me how I felt about becoming a *mother* at my age." Suddenly she smiled. "Annie will be an aunt before she's five. She can grow up with her niece or nephew." Then the smile faded, and she took Laurel's hand in hers. "How do you feel about becoming a single mother?"

"Terrified. And excited. I can be a good mother, I know I can, but... I can't do it by myself. I don't have a steady job. I can't manage a place of my own. I can't even pay the medical expenses. I know all that makes me a pretty poor candidate for motherhood, but... I don't have much choice. The baby's going to be here in six months or so, and I've got to be ready."

"We'll help with all that, of course. You've got a home here, and we can turn Meg's room into a nursery," Leah said absently. "We've got Annie's baby furniture in the attic, and a lot of her baby clothes, too. That's no problem.''

No problem. Her grown daughter had just dropped herself and her illegitimate child into her lap for the family to take care of, and it was no problem.

"It's a problem for me," Laurel said quietly. "I'm twenty-five years old—old enough to be with a man, old enough to get pregnant. I should be better prepared for this. I should be able to handle it on my own."

Leah's look was both wise and amused. "Did you get pregnant on purpose?"

"No."

"So how could you have been better prepared for it?"

Laurel wasn't sure. Maybe by getting decent grades in school. By going to college and earning a degree that would qualify her for a good job with the benefits of health insurance. Maybe by swearing off sex until she was married and in a better position to bring a child into the world.

"What about the father? Does he know?"

"Yes. Does he care? Not in the least. Buddy's not exactly the paternal type."

Leah looked a little surprised. Obviously, she hadn't imagined her daughter as the steady type. She would be surprised to hear that there'd been only two men in Laurel's life.

Then Leah's surprise grew into a smile. "I'm going to be a grandmother and while I'm still young enough to enjoy it. Isn't that amazing?"

That was exactly how Laurel felt sometimes. But her mother's next question made her feel sick.

"Does Beau know?"

"No."

"Oh, honey, you should have told him. As soon as you realized that things were getting serious between you, before you spent last night with him, you should have told him. A lot of men have strange ideas regarding other men's children."

"I wanted to tell him, but I wanted to tell you first, and I had to wait until after Meg's wedding, and by then..." By then, things had already gone way beyond "getting serious."

"Honey, you've got to tell him. Right away."

"But, Mom, what if he hates the idea? What if he doesn't want anything to do with us?"

Leah slid across the bench and wrapped her arms around Laurel.

"If that's his decision, honey, you'll have to live with it, even if it breaks your heart. That's why you should have told him *first,* then fallen in love with him later."

Laurel knew her mother was right. She just didn't know when she could have told Beau. After all, she hadn't *meant* to get involved with him.

But she should have told him. Here in this room before the wedding. Sitting on the bench in town Tuesday evening. While they were planting the bushes at his house a week ago. At some point she should have told the truth and given him the option of walking away.

No matter how hopeful she'd felt.

"You'll tell him today." Her mother's words were part statement of fact, part question.

Numbly Laurel nodded.

"Who knows? He might not be like most men. Bryce certainly wasn't. Beau might not care at all."

"You don't know how he feels about Buddy."

The forced optimism left Leah's voice. "I can imagine." She held Laurel a long time, then gave her a tight squeeze. "A *baby.* This is good news."

Laurel was tempted to peek at her to see if she was sincere, then decided she didn't need to. The baby was inevitable, so even if Leah wasn't thrilled with the idea, she would make the best of it. She would welcome her first grandchild and never, ever give the child reason to suspect that news of her impending birth had been met with anything less than joy.

After a time, she drew back. "Can I borrow your car?"

"Of course. I'll get the keys."

Downstairs Laurel took the keys, then left before she could change her mind. Beau was supposed to spend the afternoon with her, but she didn't want to wait. One way or the other, she needed an answer now.

His truck was in his driveway, and through the open second-floor windows, the whine of a power saw was clearly audible. She waited on the porch until it stopped, then rang the doorbell. A moment—an eternity—later, he opened the door.

He wore jeans and no shirt, was sweaty, dusty and incredibly handsome. Leaning forward he kissed her mouth, then stepped back so she could enter. "I thought I was picking you up after lunch."

"I know. I decided to save you a trip into town." She gestured toward the second floor. "You're working upstairs."

He nodded. "Come and see."

Grateful for a moment's reprieve, she followed him up the stairs and into the first room. What had been stud walls on her first visit were Sheetrocked now, giving the room and closet definition. It was a nice size and shape, with two dormer windows and a sloped ceiling under the eaves. Benches with storage underneath had been built under each window, and bookcases had been recessed into the walls on each side.

The room would make a great nursery with pale yellow walls and a ceiling of sky blue. She would stencil bunnies and bears all the way around at a child's eye level and cover the bench pads with fabric sponged with the same design. She would fill the seats with stuffed animals and the shelves with books and would place a rocker between the windows and a crib along the opposite wall.

But it wasn't her room to do anything with. It probably never would be.

"It looks great."

Her simple compliment pleased Beau and made him grin. "Not bad for a room that will probably never be used."

"Of course you'll use it. It could be an office or a guest room. Someday, when you have a family, it will make a great kid's room."

Feeling a twinge of something—panic?—deep inside, Beau considered changing the subject. They had an entire day to spend any way they wanted. There was no reason to spoil it with serious talk. Last night they had gotten serious enough to last awhile.

But things between them *were* serious, and this subject— more than even the question of marriage—was the most serious of all. In fact, if they couldn't find common ground here, there might be no marriage. There might be nothing left at all.

He walked close to the nearest wall and ran his palm over the coat of mud that covered the joint between two pieces of Sheetrock. It was relatively flat, in need of only a minor sanding. He would do all that later, get the trim up and be ready to paint before too long.

He wondered what colors Laurel would choose if he asked.

Finally he looked at her. "You want a family, don't you?"

"Of course. Don't you?"

Of course. It was that simple for her, that easy, that expected. Not so for him. "Yes. No. Not exactly."

She backed up until the window seat that he'd built this morning was behind her. Without taking her eyes from him, she sank down, folded her hands in her lap and carefully pointed out, "It's a simple question, Beau. Either you want a family or you don't. Yes or no."

"It's not that simple. I want *you,* and I kind of like the idea of in-laws—the parents, brothers and sisters I never had. So, yes, a family would be nice. But as far as a family of my own—children…" He broke off, unable to continue, to put into words something that so clearly went against her own desires.

"You don't want children." Her expression was as flat and blank as her voice, as if she were parroting words whose meaning she couldn't comprehend.

"Honestly? It's never been on my list of things to do. Give me a few years to think about it. Take a few years to persuade me—" he accompanied the words with a grin "—and I'll probably change my mind. But not right now. I'm just not ready."

She sat still for a long time, looking pale and disappointed and hurt.

He crouched in front of her, took her hands in his. "It's something we'll work out together. I'm not saying you can never have any children. I just have to get used to the idea. I have to learn to want it." Anxiety crept into his voice at her lack of response. "I'm just asking for a little time, Laurel."

"A little time is all I've got."

"What do you mean?"

Looking exquisitely sad, she tightened her fingers around his. "I should have told you days ago. I should have been open and honest from the start."

"About what?"

She gazed into his eyes for a long moment before smiling sorrowfully. "I'm pregnant, Beau. My baby is due in December."

His fingers went numb. "You're…pregnant." Now *he* was the one speaking a foreign language, the one who didn't—couldn't—understand. "But— Who—?"

"Buddy."

With a shudder of revulsion, he pulled his hands free, got to his feet and walked away. *Pregnant.* He had made love to her three times yesterday, had used a condom every time to prevent something that had already happened. She was *pregnant.*

With Buddy Jenkins's baby.

Oh, God.

"I know I should have told you sooner. I just never found the right time. I needed to tell Mom first, and I couldn't do that before yesterday because I didn't want to spoil Meg's wedding, and then—" Her voice softened, lost hope. "Then it was too late."

Too late. Damn right. By then they'd been kissing, naked and sweaty. By then he'd admitted that he loved her, and she had claimed something of the same. She'd just forgotten to mention that one small detail. The deal breaker.

"I had a right to know," he said flatly.

"I know."

"If I had known, I wouldn't have—" Sought her out. Spent time with her. Dreamed about her. Fallen in love with her. If he had known, he would have looked at her and known that she was bad luck and more trouble than ever, and he would have kept his distance.

Though he didn't say any of that, she knew. It was in the sorrow that etched her face, in the bleak disappointment that darkened her eyes. "I'm sorry, Beau. I'm so sorry." Clumsily she got to her feet and started toward the door.

"Wait a minute." He'd watched her walk away too many times before. If he let her go now, she might not come back, not ever. "Maybe... Maybe we can work this out. We're intelligent adults. Maybe..."

"We're intelligent adults who want very different things."

He forced a grin that he didn't feel. "I want you, and you want me. That's a start."

"But you *don't* want a baby, and you especially don't want Buddy's baby. So what do we do? Do you refuse to acknowledge the fact that I'm pregnant? Do you pretend that the baby doesn't exist, that he's some nuisance to be neglected and ignored? Do I separate my life into two halves, one to be spent with you and one with my baby, and never the two of you together?"

"No," he said quietly. That would be impossible for her and unfair to her child.

But asking him to raise Buddy's baby was unfair, too. Any child would be a problem, but Buddy's... How could he treat Buddy's child as his own when everything that made Jenkins a man to despise was also a part of the kid?

But so was everything that made Laurel a woman to love. And the worst things about Buddy were unique to Buddy, not things that could be passed along through genetics. The chances were remote that a child raised in a stable home by loving parents would develop the character—or lack of—of the man who had contributed only sperm to his existence.

And the chances were equally remote that *he* could be a loving parent to a child who would provide a constant reminder of the worst time in his life.

Laurel stepped over a stack of cove molding and quarter-round trim and took his hands in hers. "I really am sorry, Beau. I do love you, but my first responsibility is my baby. His father's already rejected him, and now you don't want him. I'm all he's got." Rising onto her toes, she kissed his cheek. "I'm so sorry." And then she left.

He listened to her leaving—to her footsteps echoing on the stairs, the closing of the door, the sound of the car driving away. He stood exactly where she'd left him and listened until there was nothing more to hear.

Nothing but the sound of his life crashing around him.

Later, much later, he drew a deep shuddering breath, gave himself a mental shake and returned to the trim job she had interrupted. He should have expected something like this. Life had been too good lately, too easy, and if there was one lesson he'd learned, it was that a Walker's life was never easy. He should have known fate was playing another dirty trick on him. He should have been prepared.

But, damn it, he wasn't. He'd thought things were finally going his way. Just once in his life, he was going to get it all—love, a future and Laurel.

But only if he was willing to take Buddy's baby in the bargain.

And he wasn't.

He picked up the piece of trim he'd just cut, held it in place and realized that the two feet he'd cut off were necessary to reach the joint. He had cut the damn piece to length before Laurel arrived. Muttering a curse, he tossed it aside, unplugged the saw and left the room. He was in no shape to be working with power tools this morning.

As he went downstairs, he smelled the lingering scent of her perfume in the air. It was stronger in his bedroom, strongest of all on his sheets. In the few hours he'd slept this morning after taking her home, the fragrance had surrounded him, had been a part of the erotic dreams that haunted him.

With another curse, he stripped everything from the bed and dumped it in the washer down the hall. Once the machine was running, washing away the last trace of her, he returned to the bedroom and sprawled in front of the television.

The satellite dish out back picked up more stations than any sane person needed, but he couldn't find a single program that interested him. He shut off the TV, scooted lower in the chair and stared out the French doors.

He couldn't even be angry with her. Sure, she should have told him from the start that she was pregnant. Then it would have been his decision to spend time with her and fall in love with her, and he'd have no one but himself to blame.

But *he* should have told *her* that he didn't have the slightest desire to ever bring kids into this world. If she'd known that, she would have stayed away from him, and they wouldn't be where they were now.

Nowhere.

It really wasn't fair.

But life wasn't fair. A person either accepted that and dealt with it, or he lived a miserable existence. Beau had had enough misery.

But what exactly did accepting and dealing with it mean in this case? Forgetting that he'd never wanted kids? Dealing with the fact that the woman he loved was pregnant? Accepting his worst enemy's child as his own?

Or forgetting that he loved her—had always loved her and always would? Dealing with the choice between being stubborn and alone or changing his attitude and having someone—multiple someones—to share his life? Accepting things he couldn't change—her pregnancy—or things he could—his fear?

There were no easy answers but one. He loved her. She hadn't been gone even an hour, and already he missed her. He wanted to go after her, wanted to make whatever promises she required to bring her back to his life, his house, his bed.

But he couldn't make promises he might not be able to keep.

Restless with the need to do something, he showered and dressed, then left the house. Though he wasn't sure where he was going when he left, the instant he turned into the nursing home parking lot, he knew it had been his destination all along.

Sunday was a popular day for visitors, maybe because of the guilt inspired by morning church services or because it was still considered around here as a day for family. Beau had spent hundreds of Sundays alone.

It looked as if he would spend hundreds more that way.

The nursing home was exactly the same as always. The flowers were sickly. Yellowed grass clippings were scattered across the sidewalk. The inside smelled of disinfectant and death. And his father didn't have a clue in hell who he was.

"Hey, Dad." Beau shut off the TV and opened the shades on both windows, letting in sunshine so bright that it was blinding. "How are you feeling?"

"I've been better, and I've been worse."

"So have I." A hell of a lot better. Not too much worse.

"What day is it?"

"Sunday."

"I watch TV on Sunday."

"Come on, you have the television on all the time. You can do without it while I'm here. You can talk to me instead."

The old man looked petulant and confused. "I don't know you."

"Of course you know me. I'm Beau."

"I got a boy named Beau. He never comes here."

"*I'm* Beau. I'm your son."

Jim shook his head. "He's a rotten kid. His mother ruined him—spoiled him, then left me to deal with him. It's her fault he turned out the way he did. Everything's her fault, and that kid's."

"And the fact that you were a mean son of a bitch doesn't change anything, does it?" Beau asked bitterly.

His father looked at him, and for a moment, Beau thought there was a flash of recognition—just a flash—and then it was gone. So was the resentment, leaving nothing but easy-to-live-with confusion. "Who are you visiting, son? You got family here?"

Son. His father thought he was talking to a complete

stranger, and he called him *son*, while he referred to his own son as a rotten kid.

"No," he said with a weary sigh. "I don't have any family at all."

"A man your age should be married and raising a family."

"Why? You have a son, and he won't even come to visit you."

"I was hard on the boy. Hard on his mama, too. It's a fact—I wasn't cut out to be a father. Didn't have what it takes."

Was that true of him, too? Beau wondered. Like father, like son? "Too bad you didn't figure that out before you became one."

Jim pointed a shaky finger at him. "What day is it?"

"Sunday."

"I watch TV on Sunday. And why are those shades open? The sun hurts my eyes."

"I'll close the shades, Dad." As he crossed the room to do so, Jim clicked the television back on and turned the volume up another notch.

Beau returned to the bedside, though the old man didn't seem aware of him, and used the next few moments to study his father. Like father, like son? Other than their eyes, there was little physical resemblance. Their personalities were nothing alike, either. At his best, Jim had been quick to anger, quick to violence and unforgiving. He'd resented everyone in his life and blamed everyone in the world except himself for his own failings and unhappiness. He'd been lazy, harsh and mean, had never given a damn about Beau other than as an outlet for his temper. He'd never been able to maintain one decent relationship, never had one generous thought or committed one kind deed.

They were nothing alike, and yet Beau had granted this hate-filled old man more influence over his life than anyone else. He'd let their dysfunctional relationship shape his past and threaten his future. Maybe he wasn't cut out for fatherhood. Maybe he could never get past his feelings for Buddy Jenkins and accept his child. But those were discoveries he would have to make for himself, not accept as fact simply because of his own father.

During a commercial, Jim scowled at him. "You can go now. Go see whoever it was you came to see, and let me watch my television in peace."

Beau touched the old man's hand. His fingers were thin, misshapen with arthritis, cold. He couldn't make a fist now, couldn't beat out his anger and frustration. He couldn't offer a hand in friendship, either. But he'd never been able to do that.

He was a sad old man.

Beau felt equally as sad.

"I'll be back later in the week, Dad."

He was halfway out the door before Jim spoke again. "Bring that girl with you—that Laurel. I don't see pretty girls every day."

Now there was one thing they had in common. Neither did he. If she had her way, he might never see her again.

And that would be too sad to bear.

Chapter Ten

Laurel was up and working outside early Tuesday morning. Bryce had recommended that she give up the gardening job, but Leah had sided with her in claiming that work was good for her, as long as it wasn't too strenuous. The doctor she'd seen yesterday afternoon had agreed.

Without something to keep her busy, she would probably sink into a deep depression. She was about halfway there already and trying hard to keep the disappointment and hurt from dragging her in deeper.

She had known all along that Beau would want nothing further to do with her once he knew the truth. She'd been prepared for that, hadn't she? She'd given herself all the warnings, had convinced herself that she could spend time with him, enjoy his company and walk away with nothing more than sweet memories when it was over.

But she hadn't been prepared for those sweet memories to include hours of lovemaking. She certainly hadn't been prepared for them to include a declaration of love. She hadn't been prepared for the heartache, the disappointment, the incredible hurt caused by loss of hope.

So now she had to deal with it. She had to put him out of her mind and focus all her energy and hope on the one thing left her—the baby. She had to forget dreams of Beau, love and a family and reacquaint herself with those other dreams that included only her and the baby. She'd been content with those dreams before she'd come home. She could be content with them again.

Maybe.

In another lifetime.

She swung open the wide doors that led into the storage shed, took her work gloves from a shelf and shook them out, then pulled them on. It was too early to start mowing— mustn't disturb the guests who preferred to sleep past six-thirty—and the flower beds were in as perfect order as they would ever get. The shed, though, could use a thorough cleaning and rearranging so that she knew exactly what was there and what she needed to buy on her next trip into town.

She was moving tall bags of pine bark mulch outside when a voice interrupted her.

"Should you be doing that?"

For a moment she stood still, her eyes closed on a fresh wave of pain. Then, with a deep breath for fortification, she turned and dropped the bag she held at Beau's feet. "Why shouldn't I be doing it?"

Rather than make reference to her pregnancy, he chose not to answer at all—proof, she thought sadly, of just how much he hated the idea.

"You're in early."

He nodded.

"I didn't see you here at all yesterday."

"I had some things to take care of."

She wondered if first on the list hadn't been avoiding her. In all the weeks since she'd come back, he hadn't missed a single day at the site, even though he'd always had things to take care of.

"How long can you do this job?" he asked, awkwardly gesturing to the shed behind her.

"Until there's snow on the ground. How long can you do yours?"

His gaze narrowed. "It's hardly the same. There's nothing wrong with me."

"There's nothing *wrong* with me, either. I'm pregnant, Beau, not sick." She forced her voice into gentler tones. "Was there something you wanted?"

For a moment she could see in his look exactly what he wanted—her, but only her, not any additional baggage—and then his eyes turned dark and unreadable. "Why didn't you stay with Jenkins?"

"When I told him I was pregnant, he demanded that I have an abortion. When I refused, he left." She paused. "He wanted me only as long as it was just me. He didn't want a baby. Seems the two of you have something in common after all."

"That's not fair, Laurel. If it'd been anyone but Jenkins—"

"You still would have hated the idea. You just wouldn't be so repulsed by it."

He started to walk away, then swung back around. "Look, I don't want to fight with you."

"You don't want to be with me. You don't want to fight with me. What *do* you want?"

For a moment he looked as if he might give an answer she could appreciate; then the look faded into uncertainty. "I don't know."

"Well, until you figure it out, could you please stay away from me?" Despite her best intentions, her voice wobbled on the last words. "If you're not going to be a part of our lives, I've got to get used to that. I've got to get over it and focus on what I do have."

"*His* baby."

"*My* baby. He lost whatever claim he might have had when he ordered me to get rid of it."

He flinched at the harshness of her words. Whatever his feelings about fatherhood, at least that was something he never would have demanded. Like her, he would have needed some time to get used to the idea, and then he would have made the best of it.

If this were his baby instead of Buddy's.

But it wasn't his child, and he would never allow it to be.

"I'm sorry, Beau," she said with a soft sigh. "I'm sorry for the way this has worked out. I'm sorry I didn't tell you that very first day. Most of all, I'm sorry that you don't think any better of yourself than you do. You're not your father. You're nothing like him, and you never could be. You have so much to give, and there's no one more deserving than a child. I'm sorry you can't see that."

He looked as if he wanted to speak but could find neither the words nor the courage. Instead, after one long, tense moment, he turned and walked away.

Laurel wanted to follow him, to hold him and make promises, offer reassurances, that everything would be all right. But she had no such promises to make, no sweet reassurances to offer. Those could be found only within himself.

"Hey, Laurel, whatcha doin'?"

She watched one moment longer, until Beau was out of sight in the trees, then shifted her gaze as Annie skipped barefooted across the yard to her. Her dark curls bounced about her head, and the hem of her white nightgown dragged in the grass, leaving a broad trail in the dew.

"I'm cleaning out the shed," she replied as her sister drew near. "What are you doing?"

"I want to help."

"Okay. But first you have to put some clothes on. No self-respecting gardener works in her nightgown."

"Okay." But she showed no inclination to return to the house. Instead, she hiked the gown up over her knees, then climbed up to straddle the side of the utility cart hitched to the riding mower. "Want to take me for a ride?"

"Maybe later, but not now. The guests are still sleeping."

"But it's morning. Time to rise an' shine."

And Annie certainly did, Laurel thought with a rush of love and longing. Her arms felt so empty while her heart felt so full, so she remedied that by giving the girl a big hug. "You're a doll, Annie."

Annie rested her head contentedly on Laurel's shoulder. "Will your baby be a doll, too?"

"Absolutely."

"Will it be a girl doll like me or a boy doll?"

"I don't know, sweetie. It's a surprise."

"I hope it's a girl so I can play with her. Or, hey, maybe you can have both a boy *an'* a girl. That would be pretty neat. Maybe? Please?"

Laurel chuckled. "I don't think so, babe. At least, not this time." Her choice of words made her humor quickly fade. At the rate things were going, there might never be a next time. This baby might be her one and only chance at motherhood.

Then she stiffened her spine. If that was what fate had in store for her, then so be it. She would put all her energy, all her creativity and all her love into doing the job right, and if she succeeded, neither she nor the baby would ever notice the one thing missing from their lives. They would be perfectly happy together, and they would never care that Beau wasn't a part of them.

And that was a world-class fantasy with no basis in reality, because she would never be perfectly happy without Beau.

Not ever.

From the protective cover of a live oak, Beau watched the sisters cuddle together and felt a curious longing burn through him. Annie could be Laurel's child—the age was right, the resemblance, the love. Hell, if she were just a few months older, she could have been *their* child. And would he have run away from her, too?

He didn't know.

Laurel held Annie close, brushed her hair back and gave her a big, exaggerated kiss that made her giggle. Then abruptly Annie kissed Laurel, though not in any of the usual places. She wriggled free, stood in the cart and bent to press a kiss to Laurel's stomach. She seemed to be talking, probably saying hello to the new family member who rested within, probably urging him or her to hurry his appearance into the world so she would have someone to play with and they could become best friends.

It was hard to believe that Laurel carried a new life within her—a tiny little creature who would grow and thrive until he was able to live on his own. It was nothing less than amazing. Wondrous.

But he'd never wanted to be amazed. He'd never wanted such wonder.

Had he?

A memory from Saturday afternoon worked its way into his conscious mind. It had been the first time they'd made love, and he had been on the verge of a release that had rocked him through his soul. Yet amid all the sensation, all the need, all the intensity, he'd had one brief thought, one sincere regret for the condom that separated them. He'd wanted to fill *her,* had wanted to empty into her all those possibilities for creating tiny little creatures of their own. Not risks. *Possibilities.*

And if, in four weeks' time, she'd come to him with

news of a pregnancy, how would he have reacted to that possibility?

Differently than he had Sunday, he suspected, though maybe not with the joy such news deserved. But not with the revulsion, either.

Babies were the most helpless, blameless creatures that ever lived. What did it say for him that he couldn't accept one, that he could give up the woman he loved more easily than he could deal with the presence of an infant in his life?

No, that wasn't exactly right. More easily than he could deal with the awesome responsibility of playing father to that helpless, blameless infant. What lessons of fatherhood had he learned from his old man? Might makes right. When in doubt, hit. Destroy the good and wallow in the bad. Never dream. Never hope. Never love.

Lessons he would rather die than pass on to any child.

In front of the shed, Laurel lifted Annie out of the cart and swung her around. Without thinking, he took a step forward, his hand extended in warning. Annie was small but sturdy. Surely such activity couldn't possibly be good for either Laurel or the baby.

But before he could speak, before he could draw attention his way, he caught himself. She didn't want his warnings or his concern over what was good for her. She wanted him to act like the intelligent adult he'd claimed to be. She wanted him to change a lifetime's way of thinking. She wanted him to take big chances that he just wasn't sure he could risk.

For his sake, for her sake, for her baby's sake.

With a sigh, he turned his back on her, closed his ears to the laughter she and Annie shared and headed to the site. He unlocked both houses and opened the windows, letting hot air out and slightly cooler humid air in, then walked through the blue house's first floor rooms. The echo—the emptiness—reminded him of his own house. He'd been telling himself it was because of the high ceilings, bare floors and the lack of furniture to absorb noise, but he'd been wrong. He could cover the floors with wall-to-wall carpet, could fill the rooms with enough furniture for three houses, and it would still be empty. As long as he lived in it alone, it would remain that way.

So would he.

By the time his crew began arriving, he was working at the most mindless task he could find—installing batts of insulation in the attic. Unfortunately, he found himself drawn to the tall windows too often for his peace of mind to stare out toward the inn. Tall pines and oaks blocked his view, but he knew Laurel was over there. Through the open window he could occasionally hear the grumble of the mower as she cut a swath through this end of the yard. Then the sound faded away as she headed back the other direction.

"I'm no expert at construction, but this isn't an ideal job for a warm day, is it?"

Starting guiltily, he turned from the window. Bryce stood at the top of the stairs, a foam cup of juice in one hand and a couple of Colleen's muffins in the other. "A Carolina summer isn't ideal for anything besides lazing at the beach. But since the nearest beach is more than a few hours away and we *do* have to pay bills even in summer, we do what we have to." He stripped off his gloves, removed the long-sleeve shirt he'd pulled on over his T-shirt to protect his skin from the fiberglass and accepted the food. "It's nice of Colleen to insist on feeding us, but personal delivery isn't necessary."

"It gets me out of making beds and scrubbing toilets," Bryce said with a shrug. "Leah has this idea that I can fill in for Meg while she's on her honeymoon."

He'd always helped out with making beds, scrubbing toilets and anything else that needed doing, Beau knew from months working for the family. More likely, his reason for coming was personal—he had something to say to the man who had done Laurel wrong.

Bryce walked around the space. It was large enough for another room or two if expansion was ever needed. Right now the plans called for a rough finish, but any remodeling could be easily completed at a later date.

Finally he settled, leaning against one window sill. "It's been a hell of a summer for the Camerons. Matthew finished high school, Meg finished college and got married, Douglas got his big promotion, and Laurel came home. Now Leah and I are going to be grandparents."

All good news for them, Beau thought as the mower came into earshot, then slowly disappeared again. Not so good for him.

"Though I have to admit, we'd kind of hoped the prospective parent would be married before that day came."

Beau finished the banana nut muffin, downed half the juice, then peeled the paper back from the apple cinnamon muffin before tackling the subject head-on. "Look, I don't even want kids of my own." He said it with a certainty that he'd felt yesterday, the day before, the entire twenty-eight years before. The certainty that had suffered a few hairline cracks this morning while he'd been watching Laurel with Annie. "It takes a better man than me to raise another man's kid."

"Thank you," Bryce said wryly.

For a moment the comment puzzled Beau. Then he remembered that of the five Cameron children, only Annie was Bryce's, though they were as close as any birth family could be. "At least you were all family to start," he said with a scowl. "They were your cousin's kids."

"And you think that made it easier? Truthfully, I was no fonder of Terence Cameron than I imagine you are of Buddy Jenkins."

"But you didn't mind taking responsibility for his kids." Beau sounded skeptical. He felt skeptical. And curious.

And just the slightest bit hopeful.

"Other than the brown hair and eyes, they didn't have much in common with the man I disliked. He'd never had much time for them. They weren't the better part of himself. They were merely obligations that took too much of his time and his money."

The better part of himself. Kids could be that—should be that. But how did a man ensure it? By being the best father he knew how to be. And what did *he* know about being a good father? Nothing. Less than nothing.

No, that wasn't true. He knew that virtually everything his father had ever done was wrong. He knew not to scream at a kid, not to hit him and tell him how worthless he was. He knew not to blame a child for all of his own problems, not to disappear for days at a time from his life.

He knew a lot about things not to do. His old man was a textbook example.

But what did he know about things to do?

He knew Laurel could teach him.

So could Bryce and Leah and the baby himself.

And what if they taught him what he'd long suspected? That his fears were founded? That he was more like his father than he wanted to admit. That he wasn't cut out to be a father, that he didn't have what it took. Where would that leave them all?

In a place more miserable than either he or Laurel had ever been.

This wasn't a simple matter such as whether a man could make it in a business of his own or whether he had what it took to make a marriage succeed. It wasn't something that could be handled with on-the-job training, something that allowed for learning by trial and error. This was *important.* A child was at stake. He'd damn well better know that he could do it—and do it well—before he got involved.

But he was already involved.

He shifted his attention back to Bryce. "How did you know you would be a good father?"

"I didn't know until I tried."

The answer left Beau feeling vaguely unsatisfied. "But that's not fair to the kids. What if you'd been lousy at it?"

"Then I would have learned to be better." Bryce shrugged and offered the words Beau had been reminding himself of a lot lately. "Life isn't fair. It doesn't come with guarantees. There's no carved-in-stone law that says I'll be a good father and you won't. There's no test you can take, no training that can prepare you."

"I've never even held a baby," Beau said flatly. He'd never had the desire, had never thought there was any reason. His hands were meant for power tools and trucks, not comforting or cradling something so small and defenseless.

"Neither had I until Annie was born." Bryce grinned. "It's like nothing else you'll ever experience. You feel such awe and wonder...and such fear."

He'd felt enough fear in his life. Maybe it was time for a little awe and wonder.

Maybe it would never be time.

As the mower cut another path across the near end of the yard, Bryce stood up. "I guess I'd better get back to the house. As long as Leah's filling in as maid, I get to handle all the office work. I'll see you around."

Beau didn't respond. He had plenty of other things on his mind. Like responsibilities and risks. Lessons and failures. Awe and wonder and fear.

Like living alone and miserable or taking a chance on something better.

Taking a chance on himself.

On Laurel.

On love.

By the time the weekend arrived, Laurel was ready for a break. She'd worked hard the whole week, spending mornings and late afternoons outside and the hotter midday hours in the house with the overdue gardening books and sketch pages filled with plans for the new garden. She'd helped Matthew wait tables at lunch and dinner and volunteered for kitchen cleanup in the evenings.

And she'd spent her nights moping. Tossing and turning. Dreaming hopeless dreams.

Today she had the day off, Leah's car and her blessing—her fervent request—to go someplace else and do something or, better yet, nothing.

Problem was, there was no place she wanted to go.

At least, no place where she was wanted.

She parked on a side street one block off Main and wavered indecisively on the sidewalk. Another kill'em-all-and-let-God-sort-'em-out movie was playing at the theater. Her pocketbook was healthier since she'd gotten paid for her work, but her budget outlook was still bleak and prohibited any reckless spending. Soon enough she'd be buying maternity clothes and other necessities, but there was no reason why she couldn't windowshop. At least that would occupy a little of her time.

She drifted in and out of shops, seeing tons of things she would like to give her baby but buying nothing. Leah had taken her to the attic one evening and shown her Annie's crib, her high chair, a sturdy rocker and the boxes of baby clothes and baby toys. She was welcome to any and all of it, her mother had generously offered, and Laurel had spent that evening and the next looking at tiny clothes, miniature quilts, bonnets and booties and bibs.

Both nights the baby things had made her cry, because she was so happy and so sad, because she'd made so many mistakes, because she couldn't give her baby much of anything at all. Not even a father.

But she had all the love any child could ever want.

She found herself in the antique-cum-junk store of the type she loved to shop and wandered through an endless maze of treasures and trash before stopping in front of a short, squat chest. It was nothing fancy—oak, old, though not enough to qualify as an antique, with a finish that had seen better days. She liked it, though. The crib in the attic was oak, also, and the pieces shared the same comforting sense of solidity, as if they had done their job all these many years and would continue to do so for many more.

She was reaching for the price tag that dangled from a tarnished brass drawer pull when two men approached. "Sorry," one said with a nod as they picked up the chest and walked away.

With faint regret, Laurel continued her meandering path. She examined items so ugly it was impossible to imagine that anyone had ever parted with money for them and items so old that she couldn't begin to figure out their purpose. She looked at pottery of the sort she loved, at quilts that were little more than rags, at furniture that truly was antique and of some value. And when she'd explored every last nook and cranny, she walked outside and stopped on the sidewalk with a heavy sigh.

She truly was pathetic. So she'd spent some part of her first three Saturdays home with Beau. That was no reason to feel so lost without him. She didn't need him to entertain or amuse her.

No, but she needed him to love her.

With another big sigh, she looked down the street in one direction, then the other. She didn't want to do any more shopping, didn't want to waste her time seeking a distraction that didn't exist. She should just go home, shut herself in her room and not come out until…oh, December sounded about right.

Intending to do just that—at least, the going-home-and-to-her-room part—she turned toward her mother's car in the middle of the block. At first her gaze skimmed over the man waiting beside the car, but the instant it hit the deep purple truck on the other side, it jerked back to him.

He looked so handsome and so unsure that her heart ached. The poor guy couldn't win for losing when it came to her. All he wanted was a simple relationship with her, nothing more.

All he got was complications. Major ones.

She hadn't seen him since their conversation Tuesday morning and assumed he'd taken her request—*please stay away from me*—to heart. But then, she hadn't looked for him. She'd developed the most amazing case of restricted vision, able to do any and all of her chores without seeing anything more than the few feet directly in front of her. He could have driven or walked past her a dozen times, and she wouldn't have noticed. Wouldn't have let herself notice.

She considered not noticing now—walking in the opposite direction, pretending that her window-shopping wasn't done, that she had other places to go and better things to do than deal with him. But when she began moving, it was toward the car. Toward him.

She stopped a few feet away and rested her hand lightly on the hood of his truck, feeling the heat quickly transfer from metal to skin. "Good morning."

He nodded warily.

Heavens, they hadn't been this awkward with each other since the rainy morning he'd offered her a ride from the MountainAire Lodge to the inn. It saddened her that they could share so much and remain so distant.

She gestured toward the back of his truck, where a blanket-wrapped object filled the front third of the bed. "Finally buying some furniture?"

"I've picked up a few things. I—I finished the upstairs room—got it painted and everything. Would you like to see it?"

The part of her that harbored even the tiniest hope wanted to say sure. The part that was hungry for even a minute of his company wanted to say yes, of course.

The part that was trying to learn to get by without him made her smile faintly and shake her head. "I don't think—"

"Please." He looked so serious, as if they were discussing a subject of tremendous significance, not the paint and trim job he'd done on a room that he intended to leave unused.

Because she wanted to see the room and wanted to spend even just a few minutes with him, because she'd been foolish to ask him to stay away and because he so rarely said please, finally she nodded. "All right. I'll follow you—"

"Why don't you take your mother's car home? I'll pick you up there."

Her first inclination was to refuse. Her second, and stronger, was to extend the few minutes together in any way possible. With nothing more than a nod, she eased past him, got in and, once he was in the truck, drove away.

Back at the inn, she parked in Leah's usual spot and entered the house through the back door while Beau turned around and parked at the edge of the yard. Leah was in the office, working on the next week's menus.

"What are you doing back so soon?"

Laurel handed over the keys, then dropped into the chair in front of the desk. "I ran into Beau."

Leah waited without response.

"He wants me to see the work he's done on his house. He's waiting outside."

"He's finished already?" Her mother sounded surprised. "If he's outside, why are you inside?"

"I really shouldn't go. Being with him even for a little while makes it harder to be without him."

"Do you want to spend this morning with him?"

"Yes, but—"

"No buts," Leah interrupted. "It's a simple question, yes or no. Do you want to be with him this morning?"

"Yes."

"Then go. Enjoy it. You'll spend enough time alone in this life. Treasure the time you spend with him."

Laurel wanted to protest, but couldn't make an argument. Her mother was right. Time alone abounded. Time with Beau didn't.

"I'll be back soon," she said as she stood up.

"This is your official day off, remember? Don't hurry back on our account."

She retraced her path through the house, closed the screen door quietly behind her and crossed the lawn to the truck.

Treasure the time, her mother had advised, but there was nothing precious about the long minutes it took to drive to his house. He seemed edgy. She felt sad. They didn't talk at all.

She should have stayed home, should have told him that nothing he'd done to the upstairs bedroom was worth prolonging the heartache. It couldn't resolve their problems, couldn't ease the pain or narrow the gulf that separated them. Her mother hadn't been right at all, but very, very wrong. Time with Beau *was* limited, but time spent with him like this—when they couldn't even find something meaningless to talk about—wasn't better than being alone. It was painful and sad.

He parked beside the house, and they walked silently to the door. After opening the door, he looked as if he wanted to say something, but the moment passed and instead he simply gestured for her to enter.

The house was cool, quiet, still. Merely walking through the door eased a bit of the tension that tightened her muscles. It was a coming-home sort of feeling, a safe-and-protected feeling that seeped into her bones and made her want to give a great, relieved sigh, a luxuriating *ahhhhhh*.

But she didn't. She climbed the stairs, walked past the drywall and lumber stacked in the hallway and turned at the door to the first room. And stopped. And stared.

He'd finished it, he'd said, paint and everything, and that was exactly what he'd meant. *Everything.* Furniture, carpet, cushions on the window seats, books on the shelves.

The ceiling was white, the walls yellow—not the pale shade she'd imagined but a bolder, brighter, sunny hue that made the room warm and welcoming. The trim was white, but the rocker between the windows was oak, old and worn and vaguely familiar. The cushion on the chair, the shades at the windows and the pads on the window seats—white with lots of yellows and greens, with bunnies, bears and balloons—matched the sheets on the crib that stood against the opposite wall.

The crib. Annie's crib.

A lump blocking her throat, she took a few steps into the room. The forest-green carpet was thick underfoot, muffling sound and inviting a person to stretch out and read— or a child to sit and play. And propped up on the window seat was the perfect playmate. With his threadbare fur, the bear should have looked out of place, surrounded by the shiny and the new, but he didn't. He looked, in fact, as if he'd found the perfect place to belong.

She turned in a slow circle, unable to take it all in, then ended facing Beau in the doorway. He looked more nervous, more unsure, than any man she'd ever seen. Swallowing, she forced the lump away enough to speak. "But you don't want children."

"That's what I always thought. But the question never actually came up, so I never had to figure out exactly what it was I didn't want."

"And now you have."

Nodding, he came a few steps closer. "I didn't want to do to any child what my father did to me. I didn't want to hurt any child, to teach him that he's worthless, to do any harm that might stay with him forever. It wasn't that I didn't want to be a father. I didn't want to be a *bad* father. But the fact that *my* father was a bad father doesn't mean

I will be, too. I haven't done anything else the way he has. I don't drink. I work. I don't mistreat people. I accept responsibility. I don't hate everyone I meet. I don't blame my problems on the rest of the world.'' His grin was nervous, wavered, then disappeared. ''All in all, I'm a pretty decent guy, and considering the role model I had, I think that's pretty amazing.''

Her own smile quavered. ''I think you're pretty amazing, too.''

His next few steps brought him within touching distance, but he didn't reach out. ''I don't know if I have what it takes to be a good father. There are no guarantees, no tests to take, no training to prepare you. But I know that whatever I'm lacking, I can learn from you and your father. I can learn from my father's mistakes. I can learn from my own mistakes. If you'll just give me the chance...''

She wanted to throw her arms around his neck, hug him tight and cry yes, yes, of course. Instead she carefully sat down in the rocker, perched on the edge of the seat so it wouldn't rock, and asked, ''What about Buddy?''

Pulling a low stool from against the wall, he sat down in front of her and finally touched her, claiming her hands. ''Do I wish you'd never met Buddy Jenkins? Yes. Do I wish you'd never left me for him? Hell, yes.'' Though it seemed impossible, his expression grew even more serious. ''This baby will be *our* baby. Buddy might have helped create him, but *I'll* be his father. *I'll* be the one to raise him and teach him and love him.''

''Can you?'' she whispered, her heart aching. ''Can you love Buddy's child?''

''If our worthiness to be loved was determined solely by who our fathers were, you never would have fallen in love with me. My father was about as worthless as they come, even more so than Buddy. If you can love me, I can certainly love this baby.'' He paused, swallowed hard, then said, ''I love you, Laurel, and I know I can be a good husband to you and a good father to your baby—to our babies—if you'll give me the chance. Please... Will you marry me?''

Because she wanted to spend the rest of her life with him, because she loved him dearly, and because he so rarely said please, she nodded. Tears seeped into her eyes as her fingers tightened around his. ''Yes, Beau,'' she whispered.

He pulled her from the chair, lifted her into his lap and into his arms and sealed her answer with the sweetest of kisses. And, like the raggedy bear on the window seat, Laurel knew in her heart that she had finally found what she wanted most in life.

A place to belong.

And a family to belong to.

Epilogue

Epilogue

The faint cry drifted through the night. More asleep than awake, Beau turned onto his side and checked the clock on the night table. Three minutes after midnight. Right on schedule. He listened for a follow-up and heard only the soft even breathing of his wife at his side.

They'd started getting ready for bed as soon as they'd returned from Laurel's parents' house a few hours ago, but it had been a lengthy process. The baby had required feeding and changing and cuddling, then he and Laurel had done a little cuddling of their own. *Only* cuddling for three more weeks. It seemed an interminably long time.

Finally the second cry sounded, this one stronger than a whimper but not yet up to the full-fledged wail. He slid out from beneath the covers, pulled on the sweat pants he kept beside the bed and went upstairs, making his way easily through the dark.

The nursery was dimly illuminated by a night light that cast a pale glow over the walls, more so by the moonlight shining through the windows. It was a bright night, only a day or two from a full moon, and the snow that covered the ground and the rooftop reflected much of the light back into the sky.

He moved the blanket aside, rolled the baby onto her back, freed her lower half from the sleeper and quickly changed her wet diaper for a dry one. Throwaway diapers were easy. He'd mastered those the first time or two. Getting wiggling, kicking feet back into the snap-up legs of the sleeper had taken him a little longer to manage, but that was no problem now, either.

In fact, he thought as he scooped her into his arms, tucked a blanket around her and walked to the rocker, there wasn't much about this parenting business that wasn't a breeze. Diapers, bathing, feeding, burping—that was all pretty logical. Comforting, cradling—that came naturally.

So did the loving.

He settled in the rocker where moonlight, filtered softly through white, yellow and green curtains, gently touched the baby's face. She was named after Laurel's grandmother—Martha Eleanor—and called Elly, and she was the light of everyone's life, especially her daddy's. Sometimes, when he thought of how close he'd come to losing both her and her mother last summer, he got a seriously sick feeling down inside. In losing them, he would have lost himself, because they were his life.

"It's Christmas morning, sweetheart," he murmured as they rocked. "You're a little too young for the Santa Claus game this year, but next year he'll be coming about now to bring you more gifts than a child of one year and three weeks will know what to do with. The year after that you'll be old enough to appreciate the whole myth, and the year after *that*... Maybe that year we'll give ourselves a baby brother or sister for Christmas."

Elly gazed up at him, her big brown eyes—exactly like her mother's—opened wide. Her hair was brown, too, like her mother's. In fact, she looked exactly like Laurel's baby pictures, though a few people in town—who didn't count on their fingers, who neither knew nor cared where he was when Elly was conceived—had assured him that she took after him, too.

The idea, impossible as it was, pleased him enormously.

"Of course, you got a pretty good haul last night at your grandparents' house. I guess that comes with being the first grandchild. Everyone spoils you until the next one comes along. But you'll always be first with your mama and me. You'll always be special."

She yawned, and her entire face wrinkled. She was a delicate little thing, so tiny and perfectly formed. When he'd watched the nurse lay her in Laurel's arms a snowy night three weeks ago, he'd thought she was too impossibly small for him to safely handle. What if he dropped her? What if he hurt her?

And then Laurel had laid her in his arms, and she had fitted so perfectly. It was amazing. Nothing less than a miracle.

"I woke up alone and figured you'd sneaked off to be with your other sweetie." Tying her robe belt around her waist, Laurel crossed the room, pulled the footstool close and sat down. "Was she crying?"

"Just the usual reminders that she was up here."

"I think she gets lonely for you. You're off at work all day. She likes to know you're here all night." Laurel picked up Elly's hand, and the baby tightened her tiny fingers around Laurel's thumb.

"You know I'd be home more if I could." In fact, in a perfect world, he would have a setup like his father-in-law's, where work and home were one and the same. Where he could take frequent breaks to spend time with his daughter and, when she was napping, other breaks to spend time with her mother.

But life wasn't *totally* perfect.

Just almost so.

"She's going to sleep," Laurel whispered.

It wasn't hard to miss. For a tiny, delicate little creature, Elly managed a world-class snore. Sometimes it seemed to vibrate through her entire body, and a few times he'd seen her wake herself, always with a wide-eyed, startled look that said, "Was that *me?*"

For a time he continued to rock, then, as the weariness seeped deeper into his bones, he carefully stood up and returned Elly to her crib. He eased her onto the mattress, rolled her onto her stomach and turned her head to the side. She whimpered once, twice, then settled into the rhythm of her snoring again.

Laurel took a heavier blanket from the oak chest with the tarnished brass drawer pulls and spread it over their daughter. She leaned over the side to give her a kiss, and Beau did the same before following his wife from the room.

At the bottom of the stairs, instead of turning into their bedroom, she stopped in the center of the steps leading into the living room. The furniture she'd chosen after the wedding last summer made the house much more a home than he had ever thought it might be.

Rather, *she* made it a home.

In front of the French doors that led to the snow-covered deck, the first Christmas tree he'd ever had stretched eight feet toward the ceiling. The hundreds of colored lights that covered it were unplugged now, leaving it a tall, conical shape stacked underneath with gifts.

He wrapped his arms around Laurel from behind, and she curved her fingers around his wrists. "It's been a remarkable year," he murmured. "My first real home. My first wife."

"Your *only* wife."

Only. Absolutely and for always. "My first child, with more to come."

"One or two more." She sounded amused.

"At least three. Maybe four." The words brought no argument from his first and only wife, perhaps because he followed them with a kiss that made her shiver. "My first Christmas tree and my first real Christmas. I'm a lucky man."

"Blessed," she agreed.

He turned her to face him. "I love you, Laurel."

With an oh-so-satisfied sigh, she twined her arms around his neck. "I love you, too, Beau. Merry Christmas."

Just as he bent his head to kiss her, a soft, testing-the-waters cry came from upstairs. When nothing but silence followed, he gave her a slow, sweet kiss, then murmured, "Merry Christmas, darlin'."

And a happy new life for them all.

* * * * *

*Watch for Marilyn Pappano's
next book,* Murphy's Law, *coming in January 1999
from Silhouette Intimate Moments.*

Silhouette Books is delighted to alert you
to a brand-new MacGregor story from
Nora Roberts, coming in October 1998,
from Silhouette Special Edition. Look for

THE WINNING HAND

and find out how a small-town
librarian wins the heart of elusive,
wealthy and darkly handsome
Robert ''Mac'' Blade.

Here's a sneak preview of

THE WINNING HAND....

The Winning Hand

There was something wonderfully smooth under her cheek. Silk, satin, Darcy thought dimly. She'd always loved the feel of silk. Once she'd spent nearly her entire paycheck on a silk blouse, creamy white with gold, heart shaped buttons. She'd had to skip lunch for two weeks, but it had been worth it every time she slipped that silk over her skin.

She sighed, remembering it.

"Come on, all the way out."

"What?" She blinked her eyes open, focused on a slant of light from a jeweled lamp.

"Here, try this." Mac slipped a hand under her head, lifted it, and put a glass of water to her lips.

"What?"

"You're repeating yourself. Drink some water."

"Okay." She sipped obediently, studying the tanned, long-fingered hand that held the glass. She was on a bed, she realized now, a huge bed with a silky cover. There was a mirrored ceiling over her head. "Oh my." Warily, she shifted her gaze until she saw his face.

He set the glass aside, then sat on the edge of the bed, noting with amusement that she scooted over slightly to keep more distance between them. "Mac Blade. I run this place."

"Darcy. I'm Darcy Wallace. Why am I here?"

"It seemed better than leaving you sprawled on the floor of the casino. You fainted."

"I did?" Mortified, she closed her eyes again. "Yes, I guess I did. I'm sorry."

"It's not an atypical reaction to winning close to two million dollars."

Her eyes popped open, her hand grabbed at her throat. "I'm sorry. I'm still a little confused. Did you say I won almost two million dollars?"

"You put the money in, you pulled the lever, you hit." There wasn't an ounce of color in her cheeks, he noted, and thought she looked like a bruised fairy. "Do you want to see a doctor?"

"No, I'm just...I'm okay. I can't think. My head's spinning."

"Take your time." Instinctively, he plumped up the pillows behind her and eased her back.

"I had nine dollars and thirty-seven cents when I got here."

"Well, now you have $1 800 088.37."

"Oh. Oh." Shattered, she put her hands over her face and burst into tears.

There were too many women in his life for Mac to be uncomfortable with female tears. He sat where he was and let her sob it out.

"I'm sorry." She wiped her hands at her somehow charmingly dirty face. "I'm not like this. Really. I can't take it in." She accepted the handkerchief he offered and blew her nose. "I don't know what to do."

"Let's start with the basics. Why don't you take a hot bath, try to relax, get your bearings. There's a robe in the closet."

She cleared her throat. However kind he was being, she was still alone with him, a perfect stranger, in a very opulent and sensual bedroom. "I appreciate it. But I should get a room. If I could have a small advance on the money, I can find a hotel."

"Something wrong with this one?"

"This what?"

"This hotel," he said. "This room."

"No, nothing. It's beautiful."

"Then make yourself comfortable. Your room's been comped for the duration of your stay—"

"What? Excuse me?" She sat up a little straighter. "I can have this room? I can just…stay here?"

"It's the usual procedure for high rollers." He smiled again, making her heart bump. "You qualify."

"I get all this for free because I won money from you?"

His grin was quick, and just a little wolfish. "I want the chance to win some of it back."

Lord, he was beautiful. Like the hero of a novel. That thought rolled around in her jumbled brain. "That seems only fair. Thank you so much, Mr. Blade."

"Welcome to Las Vegas, Ms. Wallace," he said and turned toward a sweep of open stairs that led to the living area.

She watched him cross an ocean of Oriental carpet. "Mr. Blade?"

"Yes?" He turned and glanced up.

"What will I do with all that money?"

He flashed that grin again. "You'll think of something."

When the doors closed behind him, Darcy gave into her buckling knees and sat on the floor. She hugged herself hard, rocking back and forth. If this was some dream, some hallucination brought on by stress or sunstroke, she hoped it never cleared away.

She hadn't just escaped her life, she realized. She'd been liberated.

MORE MacGREGORS ARE COMING!

In November 1998, *New York Times* bestselling author

NORA ROBERTS

Brings you...

THE MacGREGOR GROOMS

Daniel MacGregor will stop at nothing to see his three determinedly single grandsons married—he'll tempt them all the way to the altar.

Coming soon in Silhouette Special Edition:

March 1999:
THE PERFECT NEIGHBOR
(SE#1232)

Also, watch for the MacGregor stories where it all began!

December 1998: THE MacGREGORS: Serena—Caine
February 1999: THE MacGREGORS: Alan—Grant
April 1999: THE MacGREGORS: Daniel—Ian

Available at your favorite retail outlet, only from

Silhouette ®

Take 2 bestselling love stories FREE

Plus get a FREE surprise gift!

Special Limited-Time Offer

Mail to Silhouette Reader Service™

3010 Walden Avenue
P.O. Box 1867
Buffalo, N.Y. 14240-1867

YES! Please send me 2 free Silhouette Special Edition® novels and my free surprise gift. Then send me 6 brand-new novels every month, which I will receive months before they appear in bookstores. Bill me at the low price of $3.57 each plus 25¢ delivery and applicable sales tax, if any.* That's the complete price, and a saving of over 10% off the cover prices—quite a bargain! I understand that accepting the books and gift places me under no obligation ever to buy any books. I can always return a shipment and cancel at any time. Even if I never buy another book from Silhouette, the 2 free books and the surprise gift are mine to keep forever.

235 SEN CH7W

Name	(PLEASE PRINT)
Address	Apt. No.
City	State	Zip

This offer is limited to one order per household and not valid to present Silhouette Special Edition® subscribers. *Terms and prices are subject to change without notice. Sales tax applicable in N.Y.

USPED-98

©1990 Harlequin Enterprises Limited

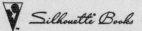

Christine Flynn
Susan Mallery
Christine Rimmer

prescribe a massive dose of heart-stopping romance in their scintillating new series, **PRESCRIPTION: MARRIAGE**. Three nurses are determined *not* to wed doctors— only to discover the men of their dreams come with a medical degree!

Look for this unforgettable series in fall 1998:

October 1998: **FROM HOUSE CALLS TO HUSBAND** by Christine Flynn

November 1998: **PRINCE CHARMING, M.D.** by Susan Mallery

December 1998: **DR. DEVASTATING** by Christine Rimmer

Only from

Silhouette ®SPECIAL EDITION®

Available at your favorite retail outlet.

Silhouette®

SPECIAL ▼ EDITION®

TM

COMING NEXT MONTH

#1201 FATHER-TO-BE—Laurie Paige
That's My Baby!
When Celia Campbell informed honorable Hunter McLean she was carrying
his child, he was stunned! He couldn't recall their impulsive night of passion,
much less envision playing daddy the second time around. He knew that
getting married was the right thing to do, but could he open his heart to love?

#1202 THE WINNING HAND—Nora Roberts
MacGregor Series
Sweet, unsophisticated Darcy Wallace was feeling very fortunate! After
winning the jackpot, she caught dashing and dangerous millionaire
Robert MacGregor Blade's eye. But she would need more than luck to
convince this confirmed bachelor of her dreams to gamble on a future—
with her....

#1203 FROM HOUSE CALLS TO HUSBAND—Christine Flynn
Prescription: Marriage
Heart surgeon Mike Brennan had a gentle touch, a soothing voice—and, boy,
did he look sexy in his scrubs! But nurse Katie Sheppard had vowed *never* to
marry a doctor—particularly one who was her best friend...and best-kept
secret crush.

#1204 THE RANCHER AND THE AMNESIAC BRIDE—Joan Elliott Pickart
Follow That Baby!
Josie Wentworth of the oil-rich Oklahoma Wentworths didn't know the
first thing about working ranches—or grumpy, gorgeous cowboys. But a case
of amnesia had the socialite princess riding the range—and yearning for a
lifetime of lovin' with the man least likely to say I do!

#1205 PARTNERS IN MARRIAGE—Allison Hayes
A housing shortage in Turtle Creek? Whatever was Shelley Matthews
to do? First, the schoolteacher moved in with devastatingly handsome
Blue Larson. Then, despite her misgivings, she offered to be the Lakota
Indian's partner in marriage. Dare she trust in happily ever after again?

#1206 THE BODYGUARD'S BRIDE—Jean Brashear
Women To Watch
In the name of justice, Jillian Marshall vowed to avenge her sister's murder.
Nothing stood in her way—except for dangerously attractive bodyguard
Drake Cullinane, who had an agenda of his own. Only he could soothe the
pain paralyzing her heart, but how much would she sacrifice for love?